LAMENT FOR A MAKER

Michael Innes

"'Lament for a Maker' is such an original piece of grisly fascination as we may seek, perhaps, only from an inventive scholarly, witty and poetic mind; Michael Innes . . . has that sort of mind; and he has done his most dramatic work here."

—*New York Times*

"Magnificently written."

—*Times* [London] *Literary Supplement*

"Mr. Innes, already a ranking baffler, achieves the surprising stunt of outdoing himself in this one."

—*Books*

Also available in Perennial Library by Michael Innes:

APPLEBY ON ARARAT

APPLEBY'S END

THE CRABTREE AFFAIR

DEATH BY WATER

DEATH ON A QUIET DAY

HARE SITTING UP

THE CASE OF THE JOURNEYING BOY

THE LONG FAREWELL

THE MAN FROM THE SEA

ONE MAN SHOW

THE SECRET VANGUARD

THE WEIGHT OF THE EVIDENCE

LAMENT FOR A MAKER

MICHAEL INNES

PERENNIAL LIBRARY
Harper & Row, Publishers
New York, Cambridge, Philadelphia, San Francisco
London, Mexico City, São Paulo, Singapore, Sydney

A hardcover edition of this book is published by Dodd, Mead, & Company, Inc. It is here reprinted by arrangement.

First PERENNIAL LIBRARY edition published 1984.

Library of Congress Cataloging in Publication Data

Innes, Michael, 1906–
Lament for a maker.

Reprint. Originally published: New York : Dodd, Mead, 1938.
"P/729"--
I. Title
PR6037.T466L3 1984 823'.912 84-47667
ISBN 0-06-080729-6

---

84 85 86 87 88 10 9 8 7 6 5 4 3 2 1

CONTENTS

NOTE

Every character in this book is entirely fictitious
and no reference whatever is intended
to any living person.

I

THE NARRATIVE OF EWAN BELL

1

It will appear full plain in this narrative that Mr. Wedderburn, the writer from Edinburgh, is as guileful as he's gentle—and that he has need of all the guile that Eve passed on from the Serpent may be supposed, him with his living to make among the lawyers. Shrewd he is. And as a first proof here is Ewan Bell, the shoemaker of Kinkeig, taking pen in hand to begin fashioning a book—and all because of the way he has with him, Mr. Wedderburn. It was like this.

We two were sitting in his private room at the Arms, with a glass of toddy against the weather; and, faith, in those last days I had been through more than snow and a fierce December wind, so that time had been when I scarce thought to see toddy and a brave fire again. We sat chewing over the whole strange affair—such, certain, had never been known in these parts—and syne Mr. Wedderburn looked up from his glass and "Mr. Bell," he said, "more than anything else it has been like a novel."

"Indeed, Mr. Wedderburn," I replied, "that's true; for it's been nothing but plain work of the Devil from start to finish."

He smiled at this in a canny way he has: often you think Mr. Wedderburn must be seeing some joke other folk don't see. Then he looked at me right gravely and said: "I believe you could make an uncommonly good story of it yourself, Mr. Bell. Why not try your hand?"

I was fair stammagasted at this: strange days, I thought, when a civil-spoken lawyer should say such a thing to an elder of the Kirk in Kinkeig. Power of invention is ever an evil lure, unless it be used for the godly purpose of conceived prayer. Yet here was Mr. Wedderburn insinuating I was a romancer born, and presently urging me to write an account of the whole adventure—not to any moral end but because it had the makings of a bit tale! There is ever something whimsical in Mr. Wedderburn, dour as he can be at need, and this plan was sure the daftest ever. I said I had no fitness for such employment, being but a cobbler growing old at his last.

"Why, Mr. Bell," he said, "it's well known that after the minister and the dominie the sutor's[1] the man of learning in the parish."

"He's said to be the atheist too," I replied right dryly, "and there are exceptions, maybe, to each rule." But I own I was pleased at what he said. Partly because I like the old words; long after Will Saunders had changed his bit board from *Flesher* to *Family Butcher* (which is a daft way of speaking, surely) I had bided Kinkeig's sutor still. And partly I was well-pleased because I felt the saying true of our parish at this day: true and a bit more. For though we have a right learned minister in Dr. Jervie never a dominie have we at all, the time of such being over and they replaced by unreliable young women: you can hear the scraich of the Kinkeig schoolmistress above the noise of the whole school scattering, and what man would want that by his lug in the morning? And though Miss Strachan—which is her name—has her letters from Edinburgh University she has nothing the learning of the old dominie; I mind having a bit crack with her once and she thought Plutarch had written his books in the Latin tongue: I was fell put out to change the subject. And yet pleased with herself she is: at Edinburgh she wrote a bit paper—thesis, she calls it—on *The Cinema as an Aid in Visual Education,* and her as proud as if she'd written Bain's *Logic* or the *Rhetoric* of Dr. Hugh Blair. I mind Rob Yule asking once: "And what is Visual Education?" and before the woman could reply Will Saunders cutting in sharp: "It's what Susannah afforded the elders." A daft speak and

[1] Cobbler.

black affronted the schoolmistress: he's but a coarse chiel, Will.

But it looks ill for my writing if I am to ramble like this.

I knew fine that if anyone in the parish was to tell the tale it must be myself, for none could expect it from Dr. Jervie, who has learning for more important things. And, truth to tell, I am not an unread man, it being forty years since I followed Sir John Lubbock through the *Hundred Best Books*—and I doubt if the bit lassies at the colleges do that. Nevertheless I said to Mr. Wedderburn now: "*Ne sutor ultra crepidam*"—that being, strange enough, the way the Romans told a man to mind his own affairs. And I won't say that the fetching so neat a reply out of my head didn't put me better-humoured still. Anyway, I was right content feeling those awful days were over.

But Mr. Wedderburn gave no more than a nod to my bit Latin and went on. "Do you but begin, Mr. Bell, and we'll get others to take up the tale and tell of their own part in it."

"Including yourself, Mr. Wedderburn?" I said this sharp, thinking to bring home the senselessness of the plan to him so.

"To be sure," said he—and what did he do on that but order in more toddy!

I was fair stammagasted again. "Well," I said, doubtful, "I suppose there was Sir Walter."

"To be sure there was, Mr. Bell. And we can be as anonymous as he was. You'll remember Lockhart tells what a mystery the Great Enchanter was."

I was pleased at his taking it for granted I'd read Lockhart's *Life of Sir Walter Scott*. But even so, I believe I would have held out if my vanity hadn't betrayed me. For I was just going to say *No* outright when—faith!—another appropriate bit Latin came into my head. "Mr. Wedderburn," I said, "I'll take it to *avizandum*"—which is what his friends the judges at Edinburgh say when they're afraid to give an opinion without sleeping on it. And at that he laughed and we left it until he was going back south next day.

And then, when he was waiting for the car that must get him through the snow to the junction, I learnt a bit more of what was in his mind. He had a young friend, he said, a feckless chiel, who had written daft tales, mysteries, about folk the like of whom he'd never met, and of events quite beyond nature. Mr. Wedderburn was concerned to call him back to what he thought reality. And as the Guthrie business had been real enough—though half beyond nature itself—and the folk such folk as this writer-lad might have some understanding of, Mr. Wedderburn thought it would be fine if we could let the chiel have all the materials, in a series of narratives, to work over as he cared; either just editing, or writing over the whole. And certain it would be he would so contrive it—what would be indeed necessary—that our names and the like were changed, and Kinkeig and all in it get no more notoriety than they had already had.

Well, it seemed a benevolent scheme, and a chance of fetching a little good out of much ill. To make a long story short, I gave Mr. Wedderburn my promise. In the following pages I begin a record of the events that brought about the death of Ranald Guthrie. I shall start—as the poet Horace advises—*in medias res* and then hark back to earlier matters. If Mr. Wedderburn's young friend in Edinburgh distrusts Horace he can e'en change about.

2

WHEN the tale came down Glen Erchany that Ranald Guthrie had taken his own ungodly life there was little grieving in Kinkeig. A coarse man he was known to be for all his years and gentry, who had lived nigh solitary like a crow as long as most could remember: a recluse, the last minister called him. And there was a story how the minister, years back, had made away up the glen to call on Guthrie and beg a subscription to a work of charity. Some said Guthrie, thinking the minister had come to chide him over the aye-empty great pew in the kirk, fired off a rusty gun at him. And some said he had but let loose the dogs—and some said the rats, for the Erchany rats were more famous in that land than all the rats of Hamlin town. And whether gun or dogs or rats all Kinkeig laughed, for the minister—him that was before Dr. Jervie—was ill liked. But if folk disliked the minister they fair hated Ranald Guthrie. And that was strange at a first thinking, for while the minister was ever about folk's houses, crying out "Is any of you indoors?" and next moment stepping over the door-sill with his havering and expecting a dram forbye Guthrie was far enough away and himself plagued none. But folk hated his very name, he was that near-going.

Guthrie was the nearest-going man in all the lands about, and there were some that were near-going enough. Rob Yule, who farmed the fine parks down the Drochet and had more silver than most, would walk behind the cart that brought his meal home from the mill, crying to the lad to go warily; and he had a bit grocer's shovel and when a handful of meal dripped from the cart he'd be down with his shovel and scraping it up from the dirt. And Fairbairn—him at Glenlippet whose wife was crippled with rheumatism, and such a church-worker that she made him keep a motor so she could be sure always to get to the Dorcas and such—Fairbairn took out the motor licence by the quarter—her being by ten years the older, and him being ever in hope. But neither Rob Yule nor Fairbairn could hold a candle in meanness to Ranald Guthrie—Guthrie who was as well set-up among the gentry as Rob was among the tenant-folk, and who had been a great scholar too, men said, in his day. Of all the dwellers in the glens about it was only of Ranald Guthrie you could honestly say he was as mean as an Englishman. Most in Kinkeig had suffered through him, for he owned the lands far round and his factor, the creature Hardcastle, took kindly to the pinching and screwing he was employed in. When the word got round Kinkeig that

Guthrie had done himself a fatal mischief there were many that were right glad and a few that were sorry. The many were glad, hoping surely for a better laird. But the few with a spark of imagination were sorry, for to them the pity came that Guthrie had not thought to take the coarse creature Hardcastle with him, to do his pinching and screwing for him when he was set-up—as syne he'd be sure to be—among the propertied souls in hell. But Hardcastle's neck was as sound as the day his mother first scraiched at the ill sight of him; and there was that look in his eye—Laurie the policeman said—you could tell he expected to come fair comfortable and well-feathered out of the tragedy. When folk heard there had been a strangeness in Guthrie's end and that the sheriff himself was coming to Kinkeig to get the truth of it there were tongues enough to prophesy that Hardcastle would soon be gaoled; and when the strangeness grew with the daft gossip of what had befallen the corpse, so that the hanging of young Neil Lindsay was on the lips of every gawpus and bap-faced old body in the parish, there were plenty that would still have Hardcastle involved as well. Old Speirs the stationmaster, him they called the Thoughtful Citizen because he was ever blethering out of the English newspapers, went about saying that for certain Hardcastle was an accessory before the fact and would be held on suspicion as sure as sure. Full of criminal law was old Speirs ever since he started stocking Edgar Wallace for Dr. Jervie's loons, and would air his views every night at the Arms, with a pack of bothie billies listening to his foolishness as if it were the wisdom of Solomon. But there—I'm losing my thread again.

3

IT was a hard winter. Armistice morn saw the clouds gathering leaden behind Ben Cailie, the snowy summit standing brilliant still against them in a bleak early sun. Then the sky darkened and at eleven, while the minister was holding his service by the memorial, the first flakes fell: you could tell at once it was going to lie, the way it lay on the minister's robes. Some thought he would interrupt the service, but he went on unheeding; and a few folk put up umbrellas and the rest gathered shawls about them—widow-bodies mostly, their thoughts twenty years back and more—and sang the hundred and twenty-first psalm.

Unto the hills around do I lift up
My longing eyes. . . .

Sweet and strange it was, no hills could be seen, neither Ben Cailie nor the braes about, the words like a queer parable of faith in things invisible. And then the flakes came thicker, not dancing but in a steady fall, and took the psalm from folk's lips and muted it, so that the singing might have come from far away. There is ever something piercing the mind in an open-air service in Scotland, so piercing they are but seldom held: we had our stomach full of that in the days of the Solemn League and Covenant.

This eleventh of November, I say, was the beginning of a bitter season. For the snow that began that day in flakes so broad folk said it would be gone the morning's morn lay for a fortnight in a still, cold air: you could see the boughs quivering at the tips with the weight on them. And that snow went out with a quick thaw and a great storm, a hurricane fit to bring down in ruin another Tay Bridge, that went howling up the glen to rip great sheets of lead from the crazy battlements of Castle Erchany. And hard on that, with the stubble lands still steaming, came a black frost.

The snow was falling again in mid-December and the bairns were right pleased with the white Christmas they were like to have. But as it fell fine and unceasing day by day the canny in Kinkeig began to look to their provisions and outlying crofters made sore haste to get an extra load of corn to the mill. The Thoughtful Citizen said the winter would be a record, sure, and a grand season for the curlers. And that was fine comfort for those who were thinking of their bit cows. There's this to be said for making your stock of Edgar Wallace and Annie S. Swan: they need no cake and no mucking.

By the time that snow stopped we knew there had to come but another fall and a bit drift to snow the place up entirely, for though the country has snow-ploughs enough these days it would be long before they'd think to let drive at a remote place like Kinkeig. So we sat down in next to idleness, the old men with a bit whetstone maybe sharpening a scythe against the spring and the farmer billies toasting their big bellies before a gey fire and nodding their heads over a catalogue of tractors from Henry Ford. And the silence the snow brings thickened about us: never a sound in all the glens except the peewits, that went crying their own strangeness still to the strange and blanketed earth, with whiles a bit stir in a cornyard as some wife went out to meat the hens. There's ever a sense of expecting something in a white Christmas season, and has been belike since A.D. I. And sure there were plenty to say afterwards that they had felt an Expectation; they hadn't known of What, it was just a Feeling, awful, they never minded the like. And one old wife said that when the minister was preaching on the Herald Angels and she was trying, decent-like, to conjure up a bit picture of them in her mind like what they put on Christmas cards, she had a vision of the daftie Tammas, coming louping through the snow from Erchany and yammering murder; it would be just a week before he did that same certain enough, but she hadn't let on at the time, thinking it a right unchristian fancy. Mistress McLaren the smith's wife, that was; she must be said to have a talent for what the stationmaster calls publicity.

If a strange silence had fallen upon nature with the snow those weeks there were plenty of human tongues in Kinkeig to make good the deficiency. The less work always the more gossip, and there must have been even more claiking than usual about the big house. Castle Erchany is far enough from Kinkeig, but it's the laird's house and forbye the nearest gentry house barring the manse by many a mile, so it's a natural centre for idle talk. It would be that were it owned by the driest and quietest folk in Scotland—which it's not. The Guthries have ever had a way with them that catches the eye and sets folk either crying out or whispering: their valour of the shining kind, their treasons showing lurid in the discovery, their births at a strange term, a rape or a romance keeking out from behind their canny wivings, violence or madness or some unlikely ecstasy casting flare or shadow over their end. Many old families have as much colour to their stories as the Guthries, but few have as much colour that have contrived too to hold what they have through the centuries. The Guthries have been at Erchany since long before the Reformation—and, Reader, I warn you that back beyond the Reformation with them you and I must presently go. But for the moment my best course seems by way of Ranald Guthrie and the bogles. It was with this that the chief gossip of those weeks began.

Ranald Guthrie was near-going: how near-going few in Kinkeig knew. For though all knew about the bogles—it was the fashion he treated the Gamleys and not the bogle business itself set folk talking—that was far from giving the measure of his meanness. I had long known myself that his meanness was next to madness—ever since the time his American cousins had tried to prove it on him. Since my mind is on it we'll take that affair first.

It was a couple of years back that two English creatures, very shifty-eyed folk under their little bowlers, came inquiring round Kinkeig about Guthrie, getting the billies to talk over a dram at the Arms and wheedling the women—who needed little encouragement to haver anyway—by giving pennies to the bairns. And one of them came in on me bold as brass and asked could I remember anything peculiar about any dealings I'd had with Guthrie? and I believe the chiel would have crackled a pound note at me had I not looked at him right stern. Fine I knew Guthrie to be peculiar: only the week before he'd sent a pair boots to sutor—with the laces all frayed and knotted so that I'd put new laces in and thrust the old inside when the boots went back to him. And the next day down came the daftie Tammas with the old laces in one hand and the silver to pay my bill in the other—less one half-penny for second-hand laces returned: had I not written *Net Cash* right large he'd have had discount as well. But knowing Guthrie peculiar was one thing and conspiring with a bit London informer another, and, faith, I sent the creature away with a flea in his lug. But that was not the end of it. For the next week a pack of doctors came.

That was sensation enough for Kinkeig: a motor full of medicals in black coats and stovepipe hats, as if they were holding themselves ever ready to attend their patients' funerals; three from Moray Place in Edinburgh and a fourth, a full-fleshed gawpus, from Harley Street in London. They took up Dr. Jervie—right unwilling he was, but his brother was a colleague of one of the Moray Place lot and that gave them a handle—and away they went up the glen to Erchany. What happened there most folk had from Gamley, who happened to have come up for orders from the home farm. The doctors got into the house and bided about half an hour—the time, no doubt, it took Guthrie to discover what they were nosing after. Then there was hell let loose—with Cerberus well to the fore, for this time certain it was the dogs Guthrie unleased. And syne out of the house and across the moat came the medicals, scraiching and roaring, the London one holding himself behind where the fiercest dog—a tink mongrel enough—had taken a great collop out of his behind. Into the cars they got and were driven to the manse, the fat one crying as if he were no more than a bairn sore spanked by his nurse. And later in the day—standing by Dr. Jervie's sideboard, poor chiel—he wrote a long report for the American cousins. Ranald Guthrie, he said, had had a warm and affectionate nature fatally warped during the trauma of birth. And it was a great pity he had never been given a bit plasticine—or even a good patch of dirt for mud pies—

during his early and formative years, for that might have made all the difference. As it was, he had a right unpleasant way with him and was subject to severe nervous disturbance, but he was no more certifiable than the folk who had fee'd the doctors. And as for prognosis, he gave it as his considered opinion that Mr. Ranald Guthrie might very well grow worse, and the American cousins have some hope yet. On the other hand he might very well grow better, or for that matter he might very well remain the same. And there the Harley Street medical left off, adding a bill at a guinea a mile from London, and a claim for damages to a like amount—though the tink mongrel had taken only what hc could well spare, gross fatty that he was, and who would grudge a Guthrie dog a bold bid for a square meal? Anyway, that was the end for the time being of the American cousins trying to get control of the Guthrie affairs. Guthrie had served them a very queer turn, it appeared, and it was this had put the attempt in their heads.

This and a bit more I had from Dr. Jervie, us running the kirk session together and so having a bit talk at times over the graver affairs of the parish. More than once our thoughts had turned to the folk at Erchany, for the minister was right anxious about the young girl, Christine Mathers. But that will come: it's the bogles I'm on the now—a bogle, you must know, being no more than what the English call a scarecrow.

Well, all Kinkeig knew how Guthrie was fair haunted by the bogles in the fields round about; fair haunted, that is, by the thought some feckless chiel might have left a bittock silver in the pooches when breeching and jacketing the sticks. An unco sight it was to see the laird striding his own parks from bogle to bogle, groping ghoul-like among the old clouts for those unlikely halfpennies. About he'd go and back again, visiting the same bogle three times, maybe, in the same day; so that folk said it was plain daft. But the Harley Street fatty said No, that was just neurosis, *folie de doute*, and no sign of madness, any more than getting up in the night to bar the door when you were full certain you'd barred it already. No doubt he was right from what you'd call a strictly medical point of view.

What Guthrie did on his own land he did on the tenants' land too, and there were some made jokes about poaching and pooching and others said the pooching rights should go with the shooting rights in the leases. The strange thing was that Guthrie had as much respect for other people's property as for his own, and you could see he knew it an unco thing, prowling his tenants' land to such an end. For on the home farm he'd stride to it as if it were as natural a part of a landowner's tasks as giving a look to the dykes and fences. But off his own ground he'd stand canny in a lane ten minutes maybe, giving a look here and a look there with his great eyes, the eyes folk said had a glint of gold in them, and then he'd loup warily over the dyke and be up to the bogle as quick and quiet as a ferret. Uncanny it was, this strait need to do so daft a thing: you'll realize the uncanniness of it the better if you remember he was not the first Guthrie to wear boots; dirt as he was in most folk's speaking there was yet gentry plain in the presence of him. When the bairns mocked at him, as whiles they did the few times he came near a dwelling, never a sign of seeing them would he show—let alone give a bit swipe at them or curse as a common billy would do—but kept all his glowering looks as he strode past for some invisible devil of the middle air. So there was the more talk when he turned out the Gamleys.

The site of Erchany had been chosen long since for the strength of it, the land about right tough and stony, the home farm no more than a splatter of oats and turnips amid the larch woods. Rob Gamley was called grieve, he and his two grown sons tended the land together and had the farmhouse and a wage for their labour. Gamley had a young wife, his second, and by her two bairns, the children of his old age that he fair doated on. Twins they were, a bonny boy and girl, spoilt maybe and wild enough for certain: and it was over no more than an impudent prank of theirs that the trouble came. For one day late in October they were playing together some way from the house when they saw the laird making across the next field and giving a bit poke here and there with his stick, rational enough. But fine the bairns knew what he was after, for straight in front was a brave new bogle their father had set up but the day before. And wee Geordie Gamley, a fair rascal for sure, slipped through the hedge and up to the bogle and hid behind it with his hands in the pooches of the jacket of the thing. Along came the laird and out came Geordie's fists from the pooches as it might have been the very arms of the bogle, and he waved them before the laird and cried out the old rhyme:

Nickety-nickety, nick-nack,
Which hand will ye tak'?

Alice in the back of the hedge laughed out blithe and wild, Geordie ran back to her laughing and fleering and away the two of them skedaddled as fast as their legs would carry them, for you may be sure they were right scared of Guthrie and his evil eye for all the bold trick they'd played him. But Guthrie went straight to the big house and got a bit silver and syne went over to the farm; there he put the silver on the table in front of Gamley, called the twins bastards and their mother by a worse name and gave them all twenty-four hours to get off any land of his. Gamley being but a fee'd man had no choice but to go and go he did—with never a word spoken, his wife said, only strode about the house packing, himself as pale as a sheep's skull found bleached in the heather. He didn't even think to strap the twins, and that made his wife fear the thing had sent him fair demented. No doubt it was to Guthrie he would fain have taken the strap.

The Gamleys went right away to a foreign part, beyond Ben Cailie and ten miles down the loch; there they got a short lease on a bit clay, poor stuff it showed itself at the turn of the season, with a cot folk said that scarce kept wind and rain from them; for though Gamley had something put by he could get no better at the time. A right mean trick it was thought Guthrie had played them and more than ever his name was dirt in Kinkeig. The old folk gave a bit polish up to their dark tales of the mad Guthries and the bloody Guthries of times past, and stopped telling tales of the gay Guthries and the good Guthries altogether, though they had store of those as well. And someone revived the daft speak of Ranald Guthrie's having the evil eye, which is no more than a coarse superstition current among Catholics and highlanders. It was fine for Mistress McLaren, her that was to have the vision of the daftie Tammas: all over again the whole of Kinkeig had to suffer the yarn about her pigs.

4

THERE have been Guthries before this that have been held magicians. Alexander Guthrie, a loyal chiel in James II's time, is said to have put so strong a spell upon John Lord Ballwaine, procurator to the Douglas, that he compelled him against his own lord's command to appear before the king. And another Alexander, left to fatten on seagulls' eggs on the Isle of May for couching with the daughter of one Cochrine, an upstart at the court of James III, lapped his cloak around him and ran to the sea's edge and in one loup landed on the Bass Rock and in another on North Berwick Law and before the sun was down was bedded again with his leman safe in France. If Ranald Guthrie of Erchany had no such picturesque jiggery-pokery to his credit he had at least the tradition behind him, and was known to be learned in strange sciences forbye, whiles digging pits amid the fortifications of the Romans, the coarse heathen, and whiles giving out he was collecting and studying runes—and that runes were anything different from the like things the witches boil up in cauldrons only the minister and myself perhaps clearly knew in Kinkeig parish. And, certain, Ranald Guthrie had an eye, and though it was but the eye of all the Guthries—their menfolk being as alike generation by generation as the Hapsburgs or the Stewarts in the old pictures—it was enough to set weak-witted bodies like Mistress McLaren dreaming of deadly curses and fearing for their pigs and kine.

You may mind that McLaren was the smith. A while after the medicals had been—and the business of the medicals set some foolish folk's minds chewing again on the laird's magic—McLaren had fallen into a fair hot dispute with Guthrie over the shoeing of the broken old cuddy they kept at Erchany for Christine Mathers. Most of Guthrie's contacts with the Kinkeig folk—and they weren't many—were by way of dispute, and this was a bad one. For McLaren, fair furious over some sixpence or shilling withheld, had called Christine the laird's daughter to his face and though Guthrie knew well enough how to crush impertinence by ignoring it he was right angry, McLaren said, and Mistress McLaren was sure he nursed a hatred for them from that day. I don't think myself that Guthrie remembered or heeded such things: if you'd held the book of human nature long open before you you could see he was the kind that is driven and tormented by some deep and single thing—and that to the point of a large oblivion of much that went on around him. But Mistress McLaren was sure that if he could he would put the evil eye on her pigs. For she saw Guthrie as the evilest thing between the Firths of Forth and Moray and her dirty brutes as the importantest and it seemed natural to her silly soul that the one should attempt to bring destruction on the other. Dr. Jervie and the ministers at Mervie and Dunwinnie, she said, should arrange it that one or another was ever up and waking; her grannie had told her that was the sure way to keep the evil eye from out a district.

Well, the pigs had been set by Rob Yule's boar, the old body was fair daft about the creatures and would lean over their sties snuffing up the smell like a tourist taking the Ozone at Nairn in an advertisement, from the fret she took she might have been waiting the birth of a Prince of Wales. One day she had boiled them up an awful grand brose—

every sow, she said, had to eat for twenty, after all—and she had just taken it out to the court to cool a bit when who should she see striding down the lane by the Drochet but the laird himself. Mistress McLaren was fair frantic; she was sure that if Guthrie but cast eye on the sows never a litter would there be. So she poured the brose right quickly into the troughs at the back of the sties, drove the pigs through—and they needed no urging when they smelt the grand brose—and shut the bit doors to, so that Guthrie would have to be right curious if he were to get a keek at the brutes. But Guthrie for all his learning had the instincts of a farmer; he winded the pigs, said a civil word to the McLaren wife, and was presently peering into the sties and running his eye over the dirty backsides of the creatures as they sloshed and slavered over their brose. The next morning all Mistress McLaren's pigs were dead. And though some tried to talk sense to the old runt, asking what did you expect if you fed breeding sows a great piping hot brose, nothing would persuade her but that it was the laird's doing, him that never came to the kirk and was plain familiar with the Devil. This, I say, was the story we all had to hear again after the Gamleys were put out; and indeed the opinion grew from that time in Kinkeig that Lucifer himself was enthroned at Castle Erchany.

It seemed to be Lucifer's wish to bide as lone as might be on that bad eminence. A week went by and folk were wondering whom he'd put in at the farm in the stead of Gamley, and when nothing happened they wondered if maybe he could get none to endure the thought of such a fee, for the Gamleys had laboured right hard tearing up that tough land and all to put the silver in Guthrie's pocket. But there was no news of the laird's speiring round for a grieve; that made folk right curious and then one day Will Saunders went to market at Dunwinnie and came back with the speak that Guthrie's bit kye had been trucked there two-three days after the Gamleys left. It seemed clear there was to be no more tillage at Erchany; Will said that with the spring a shepherd would be fee'd and yet another bit land go back to the sheep. Soon, he said, there would be nothing left of old Scotland; only a pack of highland gillies to lick the dowps of a feckless grouse-raising gentry, that and a few million coarse Irish creatures starving on the Clyde.

Whatever was in Guthrie's mind—and there were stories enough going around—the closing of the home farm made Erchany a strangely isolated place. For it had been ever a Gamley that brought down the gossip from the glen-head, and now there was none there on claiking terms with Kinkeig except wee Isa Murdoch. And presently Isa came away too; had she stayed much longer at the big house, she said, a fit mate she'd soon have been for Tammas himself. The old wives welcomed the maid, that day she came down from the castle with her bit tin box on her head, much as the faithful angels might have welcomed Abdiel, filling her up with tea until she looked five months bairned, and hanging on her words as if she were the first to bring news of a second Livingstone out of Africa. And, faith, her tale was like a keek at some remote and savage place.

It's time I said a word about the household at Castle Erchany; unco it was in a dwelling that had once counted its retainers by the score. Ever since the Guthries came near to ruin through the Darien scheme the castle has been half desolate: in the eighteenth century the family scarce had silver to breech themselves, for their pride was as high as their debts and they would part with no acre of land. And when they rebuilded their fortunes in the early years of the Old Queen they were right slow to repoint their walls or replenish their gear—there being something of Ranald's temper hereditary, maybe, to the stock. But always until Ranald came home from Australia and inherited the lairds had lived in fair style, with steward and footmen and maids enough indoors, and whiles a chaplain forbye for the dinging a bit Latin into the heir and a bit Divinity into those that must be got decent within the kirk. Ranald was the first that was fair miserly: on his coming he turned out the servants much as he was to turn out the Gamleys; most of the rooms he locked the door on, and where lock was wanting he drove in nails rather than send to Dunwinnie for the locksmith; no penny would he spend and no soul would he see, but lived lone and low like a mouse in a cathedral.

All that is old history, for it was in the year 1894 that Ranald Guthrie became laird of Erchany. But now at the time I'm writing of things weren't much different. Mistress Menzies, her that had bred up Christine, had gone to her grave, poor gentle soul; in the family, if such you could call it, were but Christine and Guthrie; the Hardcastles, man and wife, had a wing of the house to themselves, Mistress Hardcastle doing any bittock work she couldn't ring out of Isa Murdoch, the one servant; and sleeping in a barn and doing the very mucky work was the daftie Tammas. It was no place for Isa, the great shabby, shadowy, echoing house deep in the shadow of the larch woods, her that was but seventeen and liking fine the Saturday bus to Dunwinnie, or a romp with the loons about the Kinkeig cots in the gloaming. Folk wondered she hadn't given her notice long since, some said it was because she was right fond of Christine and loath to leave her in so coarse a place, and some said it was the grown Gamley lads, that they had all the soft and fragrant carpeting of Erchany Forest for their sporting with the maid and didn't fail to take advantage of it. But whether it was Christine or the Gamleys that kept Isa at the big house, none doubted her story that it was Guthrie himself that drove her away at last.

Most times it was little that Isa saw of the laird. Nigh all day he'd bide in his study high in the great tower and when he went out to dander through the woods or whiles fish the Drochet it would be down the long tower staircase that dropped past his own private rooms and out by a little postern door remote from the rest of the house, a door of which the key was ever in his pocket. Isa would see no more of him than a keek at meals, and that was maybe enough. Only once a week she was allowed up to his bedroom for the thoroughing of it and then she would hear him pacing the study above, murmuring verses, another's or his own. For you must know that Guthrie was poet as well as scholar. Years ago he put out a book of poems, a slender thing in black and yellow covers that fair scunnered those who thought a Scottish laird's poems would naturally take after Rabbie Burns. I was a younger man myself then, unwilling to admit that a sutor will do well if he but knows a few classics, and once a week I used to read what they were writing of the new books, over in the Dunwinnie Institute—ten miles there and ten back, and long before the Saturday bus. And there bides in my memory a review in one of the London papers that ended: *Mr. Guthrie cultivates the abyss.* I thoughts *cultivates* an unjust word: the reviewer creature had confounded Guthrie with the many poets of that day who were but playing at damnation. Guthrie—I must have believed these many years back—was damned in good earnest. I was romantic, maybe.

But to return to Isa Murdoch. A glimpse at meals was all she saw of her master, and the murmur of his chanted verses was all she heard, until a bit after the Gamleys left. Then one day when she was sweeping the corridor outside Christine's room—the schoolroom, they still called it—she turned round and saw Guthrie standing over her and glowering. It almost sent her clean skite at once, she said, she'd never met in with him about the house before and never before had his awful gowking eye fallen on her—Guthrie, as I've told, going ever about with his gaze fixed on the middle air. She saw the glint of gold in his eye, she said, there in the dusky, dusty corridor, and when his lips parted—Guthrie who had uttered devil a bit of a syllable to her in all her Erchany days—she expected to hear a spell that would undo her surely.

Guthrie said quietly: "Open the house."

5

A STRANGE day they had of it, Christine Mathers and Isa and the Hardcastle wife, opening up Castle Erchany. They forced back the lofty shutters on their rusted hinges and set the slant autumn sunlight feeling through the dirt and destruction of forty years, blight, mildew and rot, and cobwebs as big as in the transformation scene at a pantomime. Isa turned the key in a pair of doors she had never glimpsed before and found herself in a billiard room, the great swathed table looming like some monster in his shroud, or like a stretcher in a giants' morgue. She went up and touched it, wondering and a bit feared, never the like had she seen before. And at her touch on the corner of the thing a mouldering pocket gave way and down fell a couple of balls with a crash to the floor and rolled into the darkness. Isa said she felt a real clutch of fear at her throat then; it was as if the great muffled mysterious thing had stirred to life as she put her hand to it. She ran out, crying for Miss Christine, and the next thing she knew she had nearly spitted herself on a sword; it was the laird had taken down a rusty claymore from the wall and was doitering about with it like mad Hamlet looking for King Claudius of Denmark. But this time Guthrie looked straight over Isa's head as usual and muttered something about having such airs that folk might know you kept a sword upstairs—and at that upstairs he went, sword and all, and wasn't seen again that forenoon.

But at lunch time came another shock, for the laird must needs be served in the great chamber, a dark grand place that spoke of the pride of the Guthries in times gone by. Chill and echoing, the echo half muted by the chill damp air, it was choke-full of lumber at one end and had a regular minstrel chorus of rats in the gallery at the other. Before a carven fireplace, that big you could have stalled two-three Shetland ponies in it, was a long Flemish table, sore eaten by the worm, and down this Guthrie and his ward Christine Mathers faced each other—with wee Isa Murdoch, right feared now by the whole strange adventure, bringing them their bit stewed rabbit not on some old cracked plate but on a half-polished silver dish. Syne Guthrie ordered up wine from the cellar and when the dusty bottles were before him he gowked at them as if they held some strange elixir new-sent him from another planet, as well he might seeing that nothing but water and milk was ever drunk at Erchany. Mistress Hardcastle had sent in a corkscrew, Guthrie's hand hovered on it as if he would open a bottle and see, then he started up and called to them to get on with their work and that they hadn't yet opened the gallery.

Going upstairs Isa asked Christine did she know what the laird was about, and after all these years was he going to hold in with the gentry? But Christine seemed to know nothing, her thoughts were far away as ever, it was but a dreaming life she had led at Erchany, though with passion maybe behind every dream. So Isa was none the wiser, and presently they were at the stairhead and facing the gallery door.

The Erchany gallery was the work of some late seventeenth century laird, building before the lust for distant commerce nigh beggared Scotland and the Guthries. He had been among the English and liked fine the way they builded their great houses in Tudor times; at Erchany he knocked all the topmost rooms together and made a long low gallery. Three turns it had to it and would have been a right roundabout but for the tower—for he couldn't drive his fancy through the nine foot walls of that. 'Tis said that after building it the Guthrie was fair out of patience on all but smoring wet days: then he would dander round his gallery getting exercise, as blithe as a lark. For a Guthrie 'twas an innocent pleasure enough.

None had ever been in the gallery in Ranald's time and when Christine and Isa took a keek at the door they must have felt none would ever enter it again. There was but the one door, massive and iron-bound, and it was here that Guthrie, closing nigh all Erchany forty years since, had cheated the locksmith of his labour. Christine turned pale, Isa said, as she glimpsed the fury that had gone to the closing of that door. Great nails had been driven slantwise through the boards deep into the jamb, the blows with the strength and skill to them of a man who had handled axe and hammer in the Australian bush. It was to save his silver that Guthrie, near-going that he was, had put shutter and key to Erchany, but here surely was some other passion, forty years past or forty years hidden, that had yet left record of itself like a sculptor's passion, deep bitten into the dark oak.

Up to this the laird, save for an order here and an order there, had taken small part in the confloption he was causing; almost, Isa said, he seemed misdoubting of what he was about. But now he came upstairs and saw the two women standing helpless before the gallery door, and sudden he fell into a fair stamash. It was seldom Guthrie raged, cold and proud he was and with a strange cruel curtesy, and it sore frighted poor Isa anew to see him fair rampage before that door, as it might have been Satan raging before the portals warded by Sin and Death. Syne he strode to the landing window and called out, hoarse and high, to Tammas pottering in the court below to bring him his axe and see that it was right keen. For turned seventy though he was Guthrie ever felled his own timber, and could have given points at it to the coarse creature Gladstone, him that fooled the Midlothian folk in 'eighty. Up came Tammas then with the axe, him with his great gomeril mouth open and slavering, it with a subtle curve to its long handle that was unlike the common woodmen's axes here about. Guthrie threw off his jacket and standing spare and straight in his sark cried "Stand back!" in such a voice that Tammas tripped over his own mucky feet and fell head over heels downstairs. Isa scraiched and Christine ran down to see if he had mischieved himself, but devil the glance did the laird give to anything but the great oak door of the gallery. In a moment he was hacking at it as a man might try to hack his way out of a burning cottage—only he was fair skilly, the blows came light and fast and where any slummock of a chiel would have bedded the axe like Excalibur in that tough wood Guthrie took chip and chip just where he wanted, the axe leaping back free every time. At the first blow there was a great scampering behind the door, the gallery rats fair frantic at the shattering of generations of repose. And at the second blow the Erchany dogs in the court gave tongue and Tammas down the stair recovered sufficient breath to set up a yowling like a soul in the eternal bonfire. Down in the kitchens the Hardcastle wife heard the rumption and, half blind and half dottled that she was, she ran out to the court and tolled the great cracked rusty bell that had meant fire or foray centuries past. Almost, there had been no such uproar in a Scottish keep since they found King Duncan with his bloody sheets about him.

But Guthrie worked on unheeding, driving deep furrows here and there about the door. After an hour, the sweat pouring from him, he called for water, washed out his mouth and spat; then he drove at the living wood again; pale he was, Isa said, and with a burning spot to his cheeks, but his wrists were like steel still and his legs without a tremor. Four o'clock came, and five; a last sunbeam, thick with dancing dust, was climbing up the worn stone stair and in the court the lengthening shadows of the battlements were closing like black and jagged teeth upon the eastern wall; at six half the gallery door fell inward with a crash. And at that Guthrie came down, changed his clothes and called for his supper, the same as if he had been about some common task enough that day. Only he broached a bottle of wine, the same that had been brought up for luncheon, and offered some to Christine—that grave and formal, Isa said, he might have been entertaining a stranger, douce and decent, to the fit honours of Erchany.

These were the events of the day before Isa Murdoch left the big house. But the events of the night—which was when things went clean over the maid—are yet to come. And then I'll be telling you something of Christine Mathers, and something of how I came myself to have part in what befell at Erchany.

6

EITHER the sore clout he gave his head on the stairs or the unco conduct of the laird fair upset the daftie Tammas. At the best of times he was an unchancy chiel, whiles almost sensible-like and whiles clean crazy; whiles right sweet and gentle so that you were real sorry for him, not all there that he was, and whiles girning and glowering as malicious as the foul fiend. Always though he had kept from troubling the maids, he seemed to know nothing of the purpose of them any more than some neuter thing. Isa had never been feared of him, ever she gave him out his meals at the back-kitchen door with no more thought than if she had been meating the hens. But maybe the fall he had gave the daftie's system a jolt the Harley Street slummock could put a learned name to, for that night the way of nature came to him and he decided to make try for Isa. Late in the night a rustling that was more than the capers of the Erchany rats awoke the maid, she opened her eyes in a full moonlight and saw Tammas just louping in at the window. One keek at the face of him was enough for her, she was out of bed and through the door while her legs had still strength to carry her. Tammas gave a sort of slavering yammer horrid to hear and was across the room in pursuit.

Isa's first thought was to run to Christine, but even the two of them might be helpless against the frenzy of the creature and anyway it seemed not right to lead him that way. She wavered a minute at the corridor's end, where she might get either through to the wing the Hardcastles had or, turning the other way, reach the tower and seek the laird. And right feared as she was of Guthrie she knew that he was more to trust in this than the factor Hardcastle, who had ever a lurking lechery in his look and was a craven, it might be, forbye. So she kilted her bit shift about her and made for the tower, she was half-way before it came to her like a clutch at the heart that the laird double-locked himself in his fastness of a night and there would be no getting into the tower and up to him. She stopped at that, the daftie still not far behind her, and looked round despairing-like for a place to hide. Then her glance went out through one of the great windows that look on the court and across the court, high up, she spied a moving light. Guthrie was not shut away in his tower but up in his new-opened gallery. And at that Isa made up the main staircase, never listening now to hear if the demented Tammas was following still, but taking the uneven stone treads as if she was running for a prize at the Sabbath School picnic.

Not until she was more than half-way up did she think to cry out and then she had no breath for it, devil the thing but a bit sob and gasp would come from her throat. So she stumbled to the top and through the broken door and then a real cry broke from her, for there was Guthrie in a kilt, awful pale, and with a great battle axe in his hand. Then she saw it was nothing but a likeness, an old painted thing gleaming from its tarnished frame in the moonlight, and but one of a row of paintings down the gallery. Guthrie himself was to seek, he would be somewhere round a corner—the gallery, you remember, having three turns to it in all.

She ran down the long dim-lit room and sudden she heard a breathing sound close behind her. It must be the daftie, she thought, and still no sign of the laird, and at that she jumped into a bit alcove, nigh ready to cast herself from a window. And certain a window was there, one that looked not to the court but out behind the castle. The glass was half gone and sudden she heard a bit song drifting up in the stillness, it was *The craw kill't the pussy-oh,* Tammas's song:

The craw kill't the pussy-oh,
The craw kill't the pussy-oh,
The muckle cat
Sat doon and grat
At the back o' Meggie's hoosie-oh. . . .

Fair thrilling and gracious the daft old words floated up to Isa, she herself near mad for joy. Looking out, she saw Tammas in the moonlight making for his own cot and singing full blithe to the moon, the moon might have waned of a sudden and taken his madness clean from him, he looked up at the moon and Isa saw his face calm and gentle as he made for his bed.

And then Isa heard the breathing sound behind her again. She knew at once it was the laird; as she turned in at the gallery she must have turned away from him and now he was coming up behind her. When she realized that she was alone with Guthrie in this uncanny long-deserted place she was nearer ready to die of fright than ever. For the danger of being couched and maybe bairned by Tammas was a horror she knew the measure of, many a tale of the sort she'd heard that she shouldn't, but the dark power of Guthrie was a thing unguessed, its outlines overran the boundaries of the maid's knowledge. A danger is ever the worst that has no shape to it, and there's a straight difference between instinctive and imaginative terror.

So Isa held her whisht and cowered down in her bit hidy-hole; when Guthrie went by she would slip to the door and away back to her room, where she could bar door and window against another fit of the draftie's. And now Guthrie was coming close up, the queer breathing of him was nearer and she was right certain his awful eye must light on her. But she was well hid behind two great magical contraptions she could make nothing of: big terrestrial and celestial globes they turned out to be. The gallery had been a library place at one time with all the gear of a gentleman's library about it, only Guthrie had caused the most of the books to be carted to the tower before he shut down on it, great scholar that he was. Little remained on the shelves but tall and mouldering folios, and squat quartos in their heavy continental gilding, Protestant theology for the most part brought from Geneva, the metropolis of orthodoxy in the olden time. Perished entirely they were, the musty smell of perished leather heavy in the place, for of such godly matter Guthrie—God help him—had little thought.

All this was nothing to Isa. She minded only that the laird was up and past her and that now maybe she might slip unseen to the door. But half a keek showed her she was fast prisoner still; Guthrie was standing not five feet away, wrapped in an old torn dressing-gown and in his hand his bedroom candle that made a warmer wavering circle of light amid the chill moonbeams. It was cold in the gallery; Isa shivered—maybe at the bite of it, crouching in her shift as she was, and maybe at the look of the laird. Guthrie, she said, might have been the Guthrie carven in stone on the great tomb in the kirk. Right pale he was, transfixed it might have been in some deep and murky thought; and on his high lined brow, there in the nip of a November night, there glistened beads of sweat. Like a statue he stood, only his breath coming fast and deep and a glint to his eye more lowering than the common told of some inner tale that had grip of him.

It might have been half an hour, Isa said, he stood there unmoving, and if one remembers the strain on the nerves of the maid one may think perhaps that he stood three minutes so, or four. And then he strode straight towards her.

Isa said she gave a little cry at that and Guthrie's hand came out to drag her, as she thought, from hiding. At that she shut her eyes and tried to think of a bit prayer. But no prayer came—nor yet the touch she had expected on the shoulder. Instead, the great globe she was crouching by stirred at her side, its cold smooth surface brushed eerily over her naked arm, she took another keek and saw that the laird was like in a trance still, refusing to see the maid that cowered right under his nose. Idly, and now murmuring some unintelligible words, he was turning on its rusted axis the dust-encrusted miniature world that lay beneath his hand. It creaked and grated, the wee world with its faded sprawl of oceans and continents, much as the moon might do if made to quicken on its poles again. Then above the little strident noise of the turning world, hoarse and piercing came Guthrie's voice, his words now clear to Isa, all in a blur of fear though she was.

"He will! It's in the blood, and by the great God he will!"

The worst fright Isa got that night was from the way Guthrie's words were spoken, for it was right fearsome to think there was something the laird himself was feared of.

When she told her tale in Kinkeig there were smart folk said the maid had read her own feelings into Guthrie, and the stationmaster—him they called the Thoughtful Citizen—said sure it was a case of transferred emotion. But Isa stuck to her story the laird was sore feared of something; and before many weeks passed folk were to say, Well, he had good reason and Isa was a sharp maid to have probed to it; the stationmaster said he had ever thought her a perspicacious young person.

Guthrie had no sooner spoken than he turned about and fell to pacing the gallery, but ever between Isa and the door or thereabout so that she was fast prisoner still. Whiles he went silent and whiles he chanted his verses, verses, Isa said, with a queer run of Scottish names to them and then ever a bit of gibberish—it might be coarse foreign stuff—at the end. Isa made nothing of them, nor ever had of his chanting; devil the loss, she thought, was that. Half it came to her to come out and brave the laird, but she had bided over long watching him at his daftness and he would be very angry surely, did she discover herself. So she pulled her bed-gown about her—a bit flimsy geegaw rubbish, no doubt, and not the good flannel her mother had sent her to the big house with—and resigned herself to endure the cold until Guthrie's going. At least he couldn't lock her in, the door in smithereens as it was. And soon she was feeling in a queer way that the laird was company, up there in the lonely gallery; she was half sorry when he moved off a bit, hoping though she was that he would turn a corner and give her a free run from the room. Once she gave a bit cry—the second time she had cried out to him—it was when she felt a tug low down on her gown, a great grey rat it was, as bold as brass and with eyes, the fancy took her, grown wicked like the eyes in all the Guthrie faces dim round the gallery. But again the laird heard nothing; he was wrapped strangely in his own inner darkness, ever chanting the same strange run of verses, as intensely as a Catholic creature might go over and over some set of words in a shipwreck. Syne he would stop and gowk fixedly Isa couldn't make out at what, the candle held headhigh and at arm's length. And once he broke off in his chanting, there was a long silence in which Isa heard the tapping of the ivy outby and the whisper of the night wind in the larches, then he cried out in the Scots he whiles knew fine how to use: "What for would it not work, man?" And then, right awful to hear, he whispered: "What for would it not work?"

There was another bit silence. Isa was that strung-up she could feel the moonbeams tickling her back and when Guthrie syne gave a high crackling laugh, the like as if something were breaking in him, she fainted.

7

WHEN Isa came to it was to find Guthrie gone and the rats nibbling her fingers. Right painfully she got to her knees and then to her feet, hardly would the stocky legs of the maid carry her, and groped her way from that awful gallery and to her room. There she wasted no time but cast a splatter of cold water, shivering as she was, over her face, and got from that the strength to pack her box and the clear-headedness to pen a bittock note for Christine. Syne she crept to the kitchen and got herself a piece, fair famished she felt after her vigil, and at keek of dawn was out of the castle, her box on her head like it had been a basket of clouts, and keeping a wary eye for Tammas in his barn. Right glad she was when she had rounded the loch and the dark larches closed upon the grey house, gruesome it seemed to her now, and she was away and down the tail of Erchany brae and on the long glen road to Kinkeig. At full dawn the snow began to fall and toilsome and bitter though it made the road she was the blither for it; it seemed to cast a white carpet of oblivion between her and the murk of that night.

You may be sure that Isa's story wasn't long in getting round Kinkeig—the old wives, as I've said, making a great thing of it in that idle winter weather. And like all tales that run around a Scottish village it lost nothing in the telling; it got about that wee Isa had been forced to hide behind the dowps of two great idols and that syne Guthrie had come and prayed before them stark naked—idols he'd dug up from the camps of the coarse Romans, no doubt, and prayers that he'd had of his study of heathen runes. Or if it wasn't Guthrie was naked it was Tammas—Isa's story, though unco surely, being not quite scandalous enough to please some. It must be said that Isa herself behaved douce and decent considering the fuss was made over her; she told her tale readily enough, but without, as you might expect, a bit fresh embroidery each time. There were but two additions she made that might have been fact or fancy. She minded, she said, like as if she had heard it in a dream, Guthrie calling out something about America and Newfoundland, and that was mixed in her head with two names: Walter Kennedy and Robert Henderson—devil the idea she had of who they were, nor Kinkeig either except Will Saunders said he minded there had once been a Walter Kennedy, a crofter, away down the loch, but long since departed he was, and like enough to America or Newfoundland. And the other thing she thought she minded in some half-conscious moment after her swoon was Guthrie crouched down over a table and poring over something, book or paper belike, she had no memory of what. That was the sum of Isa's tale. Kinkeig chewed on it a whole week, and I won't say I didn't chew on it myself; it's a catching thing gossip and little comes in to sutor when there's snow on the ground.

Isa's leaving the big house was almost the end of news from up the glen. Two-three times in the thaw that followed the first snows the creature Hardcastle came down about his business, and once he went on to the junction and shut himself up in the wee telephone box there. The news of that fair affronted the postmistress, Mistress Johnstone, it was as much as to say anything he put through from her bit office she'd sure go claiking round with, her sworn to secrecy by the king as she was. Right aggravating she felt it, for didn't folk ever think they had a right to a bit news from the postmistress over their cup tea and blame her unreasonably for an uncompanionable body when there was none to give? Howsoever, Jock Yule, the station lad, who had never a thing to do all day but sweep out what he called the waiting-room and whiles help truck a few sheep, got a keek at Hardcastle in the box; he was reading from a pack papers into the mouth of the thing, and that meant, certain, he was sending telegrams direct through the Dunwinnie exchange. The larks might be in fear of the skies falling, folk said, if those at the big house were taking to spend their silver like that.

The next thing was that when the week's freight came in Jock found he had half a lorry-load of cases to get up to the castle, hampers and the like from Mackie's and Gibson's and two-three other great shops in Edinburgh. It seemed right clear that Guthrie, who sent down once a year to Kinkeig, folk said, for a pound of tea and a packet of kitchen salt, had taken final leave of his senses at last. Jock himself was that scunnered he wouldn't have been surprised had the laird tipped him half a crown on delivery and offered him a dram forbye. But all the laird did, after Jock had had an unco time getting his lorry up the glen in the thaw, was himself to check the cases into the house against an invoice and then haggle a bit over the cartage; not so daft, in fact, after all. And Jock said that, unthanked as his task had been, he felt half sorry for the man: sleepless he looked and old—and forbye bewildered, like a man in two minds.

Well, it was as good as a Christmas box to many in Kinkeig to hear that Guthrie was in a right fash; if the laird was fretting folk were real content to hear it, whether they could plumb to the reason of it or no. But plenty tried their hand at an explanation and plenty more at controverting them that did the explaining. The stationmaster got a good deal of respect by saying he could distinguish alternative hypotheses: it's wonderful how a couple incomprehensible words will impress folk little acquaint with letters.

One bit speak I can mind at the Arms, if but by the unco happening that put an end to it.

Once in a while, you must know, I take a look over to the private bar—most of the better-thought-of folk of the parish think it a decent enough place for a bit crack of an evening. Will Saunders was there, and Rob Yule, and whiles in came the stationmaster, still with a hypothesis, so to speak, in each pocket—for it was ever his way to seem holding back a bit inner knowledge: to hear him talk on politics you would think he held in with the editors of the *Scotsman* and the *Times* themselves. And behind the bar was Mistress Roberts, banging the pots about to show she was real unfriendly to the liquor and had never thought to come to the serving of it; a sore trial she was to Roberts but not undeserved, folk said, for all the time of their courting had she not been slipping him wee tracts about the poisonous action of alcohol on the blood-stream, and might a publican not have taken warning from that? Mistress Roberts said never a word until in came wee Carfrae, the greengrocer. Carfrae never touches, only he comes into the private for a gossip and Mistress Roberts keeps him a special ginger beer; at one time she put a row of the stuff behind the bar with a notice: *Sparkling, Refreshing and Non-Injurious,* but at that Roberts put his foot down, everything had its place, he said, and the place for a notice like that was in the sweetie-shops. As I say, wee Carfrae came in for this dry drink of his, and it was him restarted the speak about Guthrie.

"Mistress," he said, giving a sad look over at Yule and Saunders and myself, "I'm thinking there's a power of evil idle talk in this parish."

"There is that for certain, Mr. Carfrae, and has been ever since the failure of the Local Option." And Mistress Roberts made a great rattle with a pile empty bottles of stout.

"No doubt we've some control of our tongues here in the private," said Carfrae with another ill look at us in the corner, "but out there in the public are two-three ignorant billies claiking away fair scandalous about the laird."

"Poor soul!" cried Mistress Roberts, "he has much to endure, I'm sure"—and she cast her eyes up to heaven like a hen after a bit drink. "It's right disgusting what they find to say about him and that strange maid Christine."

"Shameful," said Carfrae, licking his lips as if the ginger had been extra tasty; "and the more shameful to speak of since it seems like enough to be true. Bred up to it from a wean, poor lass, the same as you might breed up a sow."

It's the kind of speak makes me times doubt the blessings of Reformation and agree with those that say the muck-rake came to Scotland along with presbytery. But Dr. Jervie—and I think he's in the right of it—says, No, that's a false thought: it's the tough land and the short leases, the long-grey storm and the chill raw air seeping to the heart, that robs us of half our right sensuous life and sends us to warm and stir ourselves before the fires of evil speaking and whispered lust. I've learnt long since to hold my whisht when folk unbridle their tongues so, and I held my whisht now. But Rob Yule, for all that his silver has long lain cold in his cellars, has a warm heart and a quick temper, and forbye he had ever liked Christine. So he rose now to the creature Carfrae's bait. "Is the old lie about the maid," he said, "wearing that thin that there's a new one needed?"

You must know that Christine was Guthrie's ward and bore his mother's name. She had come to the big house as an infant—the child, it was explained, of Guthrie's mother's brother, who had been killed with his young wife in a right terrible railway accident abroad. I can remember well enough that none doubted the story until just such a white idle winter as this I'm writing of; it was then that the wee speak grew that what had been given out was no true part of Christine Mathers' story and that Ranald Guthrie was more to her than uncle. But it was only the secretiveness and the ill name of the laird, the few sensible bodies in Kinkeig ever thought, that gave gradual colour to the claiking: when the maid was never sent to school folk said it was because Guthrie was ashamed of his natural daughter. That was what Rob

Yule was calling the old lie—and now here was the wee man Carfrae, sure enough, with another. Fine, he said, you could understand Guthrie turning away Neil Lindsay: wasn't he jealous of his young mistress, the dirty old stock that he was?

The Roberts wife rinsed a glass. "You mean she's not his daughter at all?"

Carfrae hesitated and looked warily over at us. "It's just the talk," he said. And then he gave a bit snicker into his Sabbath School cordial.

Mistress Roberts made a shocked-like click with her tongue and poured herself out a cup of tea: she ever has a great teapot at her elbow in the private and anyone comes in she'll like enough offer a cup to, gratis; it makes Roberts fair wild. The Thoughtful Citizen said Faith, these were terrible lax times for sure and it was a real pity they'd stopped the papers publishing the full revelations of the Divorce Courts; there was nothing kept people more moral than reading those awful-like examples of fast life among the English. And as for Guthrie, it was just awful to think he might have brought up the maid not out of duty as his natural daughter but to make a mistress of her.

Carfrae snickered again at this, and hummed and hahed and hinted and at last the stationmaster saw what he was driving at, and however much he'd read of fast life among the English I think he was decent enough to be honestly shocked. He looked quite stern at Carfrae and "Are you suggesting," he said, "that these are not mutually exclusive propositions?"

I doubt if the wee greengrocer man understood this—but certain he understood Rob Yule. For Rob walked over to him and took the glass of ginger beer from his hand and emptied it, careful-like, in Mistress Roberts' nearest aspidistra. "Carfrae," he said, "the Non-Injurious is wasted on you, man. It's over late for such precautions: you're nought but a poison-pup already."

It wasn't what you could call an ugly situation, for the greengrocer was far from the sort would put up a fight against

Rob Yule, there was just no dander to rouse in him. But it was right uncomfortable; Carfrae was looking between yellow and green, like one of his own stale cabbages, the stationmaster was havering something about its being technically an assault, and Mistress Roberts had taken up her teaspoon and was stirring furious at the teapot—which was what she ever does when sore affronted. And then Will Saunders, who had been holding his whisht the same as myself, thought to cut in with a bit diversion. "Faith," cried Will, "and look at the aspidistra!"

I don't believe the plant had really suffered harm from the Non-Injurious, but the way Will spoke and his pointing to the poor unhealthy thing in its pot fair gave the impression it had wilted that moment. I mind I gave a laugh over hearty to be decent maybe in a man of my years and an elder of the kirk forbye. Rob gave a great laugh too and then we saw that this time Mistress Roberts was real black affronted, she rattled her teapot like mad, herself making a noise like bubblyjock with the gripes. After all, the Non-Injurious was some sort of symbol to the wife of her struggle against Roberts and the massed power of darkness that was the liquor trade she'd married into. And it was to placate and distract the old body, no doubt, that Will thought to cry out: "Mistress Roberts, could we have a look at your grand atlas and see Newfoundland?"

Both the Roberts loons are at sea, and their mother right proud of the great atlas they gave her to follow their wanderings in. So, ill-thoughted though she is against those that are helping keep the roof over her by drinking a decent pint of beer, she couldn't resist that invitation; away she went and was presently back with the atlas, and a fresh pot tea forbye.

So we all—except the greengrocer Carfrae, who was still chewing over the insult to him—had a keek at the map, and Will asked, Would Newfoundland be in America? I said it was as much in America as Canada was and no more; you could say it was in the Americas maybe. And then Will wondered, Where was it Guthrie's American cousins lived, the creatures that syne tried to have him proved mad?

Mistress Roberts was that delighted she forgot Will's tink joke on her aspidistra and offered tea all round; even when Rob Yule said, No, he'd have another pint thanks and pay for it she drew it without as much as a sour look. She thought Will had found for certain what was troubling the laird and why he had cried out to Isa's hearing about Newfoundland and America. Myself, I wasn't that impressed.

But Will said that was why Guthrie was opening Erchany; the cousins had near got him in the asylum on the strength of his meanness and solitariness, and now he had heard they were plotting at him again and it was driving him to make some show of sane liberality: no doubt he'd bring Christine to witness he was in the habit of cracking a bottle of wine for her. And if we knew the name of the cousins, which we didn't, certain enough it would be Kennedy or Henderson, the same that Isa minded him calling out in his gallery. At this the stationmaster said there was a great fascination, sure, in amateur detection, and Rob Yule said that might be, but there was more sense in a bit solid knowledge; if Will didn't know the name of the American cousins he did, and it was nothing but plain Guthrie. He had been but a wean when the younger Guthrie lads went out to Australia but he minded well his father saying they'd near gone to America instead, their father's brother's sons were there, and that they didn't go was said to be because there was bad blood between the families.

"There," cried Will, "blood!" The greengrocer gave a start, as if it was his blood was being called for, and Mistress Roberts paused with her teapot in the air, bewildered. But Will was thinking he'd fitted a bit more into his picture. "Wasn't Guthrie havering to himself that night about something being in the blood? And wouldn't it be the malice of the American Guthries he was thinking on, those that have tried to dispossess him and are maybe at it again?"

The stationmaster said it was highly colourable. And wee Carfrae, who had been glowering in his corner but just couldn't resist joining in the speak again, said, Maybe—but there had been others besides the American creatures at feud with the Guthries of Erchany. Wasn't there Neil Lindsay, now, that dark chiel with his mind buried in the dim past and believing for certain that he and his were enemies to the Guthrie for ever? And at that the stationmaster said he didn't see Guthrie fashing himself over a mad Nationalist loon; still, it was right to explore every avenue.

"I'd like fine," I said, "to explore Guthrie's gallery."

They all stared; I've always found that the less one says the more it's attended to. "And forbye," I said, "I'd like to know what were the verses the man was chanting that night."

They stared more at that and the stationmaster said he didn't see how Guthrie's bit poetry could be a relevant factor.

"Maybe you don't," I said, speaking in the cryptic-like way the stationmaster himself likes to employ.

Rob Yule gave a bit laugh at that and said perhaps I could tell them what was in Guthrie's mind: was Will right in thinking he had opened up Erchany for fear of the Americans?

"I think it very unlikely that the American cousins are fretting any more about Guthrie, or he about them." And at that I knocked out my pipe and prepared to dander home.

Reader, there's ever a judgment waits on arrogance. I had got to the door of the private when it opened that briskly I had to jump back from it and in came a strange young lady in motoring clothes. "Am I interrupting?" she asked, and seemed right certain she wasn't, marching straight to the bar and speaking crisp-like but friendly to Mistress Roberts. "The postmistress can't be found and I've just no time to look for her. Would you very much mind telephoning this? I'll have a sherry." And out of her pocket she pulled a paper and a bit silver.

I don't doubt we all gowked at the girl as if she had been a two-headed calf. But she never minded us but just stood, a slip of a young creature and yet with something extra-purposeful to her, drinking her sherry while the Roberts wife went through and telephoned her telegram to Dunwinnie. Syne she turned round and had a look at us, brief and concentrated, as if we were something with a couple of asterisks against us on a Cook's tour. Then when Mistress Roberts came back she took her change, said a word of thanks and was out of the Arms in a winking. Half a minute later came the sound of her car making off up the road as if it didn't think to stop this side of Inverness.

There was silence for a bit. We were all thinking it unco that just as we had been talking of America and Newfoundland in should step an American lassie—for that she was that no one who had ever been to the Dunwinnie picture palace could doubt. Mistress Roberts stood polishing glasses behind the bar, and there was a gleam in her eye that didn't come just from the effect of scouring the mortal sin of beer from them. She had the news now and she knew it.

Presently Rob had a try at her. "It would be a telegram, Mistress Roberts, the young lady was sending?"

"It was that," said Mistress Roberts, and gave the rest of her whistle to breathing hard on a pint pot.

"To book her a room for the night up the road, maybe?"

"Maybe ay and maybe no, and it's nobody's business but her own," said the Roberts wife, virtuous-like. She hadn't yet forgiven Rob for the way he'd treated Carfrae's Non-Injurious. But it was plain she was fair bursting all the same; for two-three minutes she polished her glasses as if she were trying to take the black from the face of the Devil. Then "Faith," she said, "I was right stammagasted!"

This time Carfrae tried, and we knew he was much liker to get round her. "There was something unco in the message, mistress?"

"Maybe ay and maybe no again. If you must know it was to someone in London and it just said, *Hope to have important news soon.*"

Will Saunders got up and joined me by the door. "I don't know," he said, "that there's much occasion for what Carfrae calls evil idle talk in that."

"Maybe no and maybe ay. But I'll tell you this. Mr. Bell there ought to be real interested in the signature." And at that she banged down the last of her glasses and turned to give a bit stir to her teapot.

"The signature?" I said, puzzled.

"Just that, Mr. Bell. The lassie's signature was Guthrie."

8

AND now there's only what the author lad in Edinburgh will call the Testimony of Miss Strachan and I'll be coming to Christine—Christine who you may think will be the heroine of his book. You'll remember Miss Strachan is the schoolmistress, her that wrote a paper on Visual Education. Maybe it was no bad subject for her; she's a peering body by nature, hungry in other people's affairs, and joins a sharp eye to a long nose. And no doubt it was the inquisitiveness of her that took her the long way round to visit her auntie at Kildoon.

Every week-end Miss Strachan cycles over to visit her auntie, an old body with a sum of silver put by that a niece would naturally be very attentive to. Most times she holds down the highroad to Dunwinnie and turns off short at Thompson's Mains, Kildoon being but a rickle of houses two-three miles over the moor from there. But whiles in summer, being given to what she calls the lure of the wanderer, she makes away up the glen past Erchany and then bumps and rattles her machine over the braes until she strikes a bit shepherd's track that takes her down to the bridle-path through Glen Mervie. Toilsome it must be and none so chancy at the best of times; the schoolmistress tells you she's near mad on the Athletic Ideal, and none can say she's not right tough and stringy. But that it was just the lure of the wanderer that should take her up Glen Erchany in a quick thaw after a first winter snow was a thing right hard to believe, forbye it being just the time all the speak was going round about the affairs at the great house. Some said it was the lure of Tammas was working on her and that for one with small chance of a lad in his right senses the news of how the daftie had briskened uplike must be very attractive. But there's no need to enquire into the woman's motives; it's enough that in the last week-end of November up the glen she went.

The Drochet was green and leaping with the snows from Ben Cailie and the fir trees were still and dripping in the thaw, only whiles a whisper of wind stirring them would send a scatter of drops across the path of the schoolmistress as she pedal-pedalled her bit boneshaker through the slush and up the brae. It was only when she was near the glen head, which is to say on the tail of the Ben itself, that she saw the storm coming from over the loch, east away, the beginning of the great storm that came with that thaw. Dark and sullen and secret the loch would be in its frame of dark snow-weighted trees, then far to the east the surface would break and stir, the whole surface would tremble, would leap to points of foam, over the working foam-flecked surface great shadows scurrying and sweeping in sudden washes of stormy light and shade, syne the gale, sweeping up the braes from the long funnel of the loch, would catch at the drooping branches of the trees and toss them, showering now their icy drips, up the darkening sky where the storm clouds would be massing in sudden tremendous triumph round Ben Cailie.

It must have been a daunting sight to the schoolmistress did she think to make Kildoon by her mountain paths that night. But if her eye was on Erchany the storm came very convenient; within miles and miles around was no human dwelling save the great house and the deserted home farm hidden among the larches away below. So when the full blast came down, fit to blow the bit things from off her as she rode, she held on past her usual track and was presently dropping down to the cots of Erchany farm.

More than half-way she'd got and could see through the blur of the storm the shuttered windows and silent cattle court, right desolate in that savage desolate place, when over a dip and towards her, white and hurrying like it had been an uneasy ghost, came the slim figure of a maid. Next minute the schoolmistress saw it was Christine herself—indeed it couldn't well be another in that remote spot—and she thought Christine must have seen her from down by the farm and was hurrying to meet her, friendly-like, in the storm. So she gave a wave, and a bit call that was straight snatched from her lips by the wind, and hurried down the path as fast as the machine she was wheeling would let her. But syne it came with a bit shock to the schoolmistress that Christine hadn't seen her after all; the maid was holding up the brae slantwise away now, climbing fast with the long loon's limbs of her and with nothing against the blast but some light woollen thing that was soaked already and clinging as she strode. Real alarmed for her, Miss Strachan said she was; maybe she was a bit alarmed for herself too, for with the storm coming down she was in sore need of welcome at Erchany and now the Gamleys were gone only Christine Mathers was certain not to shut the door on her. Anyway, she dropped her bicycle by the side of the path and half walked, half ran to intercept Christine as she climbed. And presently she came full in front of her and called out: "Miss Mathers, Miss Mathers, isn't it awful weather to be out?"

This time the schoolmistress could hardly believe that the maid had failed to hear her—but hearing or not she strode straight on unheeding. The schoolmistress stopped in her tracks, right taken aback and not knowing whether to be affronted or alarmed, she wondered was Christine sleepwalking or was she gone clean crazy with the awfulness of Erchany and the laird. And at that her heart near louped into her mouth, for at the thought of Guthrie she saw—and it was as if a flash of lightning had split the driving stormclouds above her—the Guthrie in Christine. That was what had ever stammagasted the gossips—that the maid showed nothing of the Guthrie stamp on her—and now here she was striding out as if she would scale Ben Cailie, looking neither to right not left but gowking at the middle air, her cheeks whitened to real pallor and with flaming spots of colour to them, her lips moving as if it were in some prayer or chant. Just so, like a creature possessed, would Guthrie himself go by, you might speak to him if you dared but devil the answer would you get.

Miss Strachan's revelation, the judicious reader will think, would count for little in a court of law, being but the fancy, in a dramatic moment, of a body whose head was choke-full of scandal and prejudice. But certain she was that struck with the thing had come to her she made never the effort to stop Christine again, but stook and watched her in her uncouthy course until she was fair lost in the drive of the storm. And fair lost the schoolmistress must have felt herself, for the wind was rising and rising, the fall of night wouldn't be long, and sleet was coming down enough to sore damp the Athletic Ideal of a whole Olympic Games. The home farm, where once she got a cup of tea from Mistress Gamley, was she well knew deserted; and with Christine gone off on her mad rampage there would be none at the great house but Guthrie and Tammas and the creature Hardcastle with his doddered old wife. And attractive as the mystery of the dark ancient place may have seemed from the snug security of the Kinkeig schoolhouse, it was something she found she had little stomach for now: we may take leave to think the silly body stood there in the sleet and cursed the lure of the wanderer roundly. But that didn't help her to as much as the side of a dyke or a bit dry straw. As the stationmaster might have said, she could distinguish three alternatives: she could stay where she was, or she could go on and break her neck as Christine was surely like to do, or she could struggle down to Erchany and the doubtful hospitality of Ranald Guthrie. And it came to her then, poor soul, what a right awful place the great house was and how ill the douce woman Isa Murdoch had fared there, so that almost she decided to struggle on and try to find Glen Mervie. Then from somewhere came a rush of good sense to her head, she went back for her bit machine and syne faced the old wives' horrors of Guthrie and his eye and swords and gallery.

That resolution lasted her till she was up with the home farm; then she minded what a grand loft the Gamleys had had, Geordie and Alice had used to sleep there and awful fun they'd known, the two rascals, on the outside stair that climbed to it in the side of the cattle court. Like enough, she thought, the Gamleys had left behind the pallets the weans had slept on; could she get up there she'd be snug enough till morning, her having two-three cakes of chocolate with her such as wanderers and them that go in quest of Scotland and such stite always carry. So she made into the court and pushed her mucky bicycle into a byre and mounted the long stone outside stair, slushy and unchancy as it was. She tried the latch of the door, sure enough nobody had thought to lock it, and sure enough there were the pallets, right cozy seeming after the bitter wind and the roaring storm. She'd be better here on her lone, she thought, than seeking the company of the uncanny folk at Erchany.

She was soaked to the skin despite the fine mackintosh she had, and going to the far end of the dim-lit loft she started to get out of her clothes. She was near stripped, she says—and you'll notice there must always be a bit nakedness in Kinkeig gossip—she was near stripped when suddenly it darkened in the loft. The door must have blown right to, she thought, and she turned to keek at it and what did she see but the figure of a man in horrid silhouette against the waning daylight. More, she recognized that spare figure. It was Ranald Guthrie himself.

So you see the schoolmistress had got herself into a situation not unlike wee Isa Murdoch's: I don't know but what the author lad will scent some danger of monotony here. But certain Miss Strachan was far from feeling the position monotonous; she gave a yelp that would have startled the laird as much as he had startled her if he hadn't at that moment banged to the door and thrust home a great bolt on the outside. For devil the thing had he seen of the dripping

Bethsabe at the far end of the loft, nor maybe would his reactions have been much like King David's if he had; he was only concerned to make the place fast against the storm, and a minute later the schoolmistress heard his feet going slush-slush down the stair again.

Syne when she'd recovered a bit from her start she saw the position wasn't so bad if only Guthrie would go away. She wasn't hopelessly a prisoner; there was a trapdoor down from the loft to the house, only never used and with no loft ladder to it, forbye she had her clothes and the pallets and she could still maybe swarm down an improvised rope-ladder like she had used to do at the training college when they were dinging the Athletic Ideal into her. And once down she could surely get out by one window or another when she wanted to. Meantime she huddled on her wet clothes again, there seemed nothing else to do with a man about the place.

And certain enough Guthrie was still about; she could hear him through the thin flooring of the loft pacing about the one-storey house much as he must have paced about his gallery. She wondered what the laird was doing out from the castle in the storm, almost it seemed he must be waiting for someone, and that thought was no sooner in her head than as if in answer to it Guthrie cried out in a loud voice: "Come in!"

There was silence on that, as if he had cried out to the air or as if the words had startled him they were spoken to into a momentary stillness. Then again came the laird's voice, and Miss Strachan swore there was something mocking to it.

"Come in, man!"

Again there was a pause, and then the sound of a door thrown open with a strong thrust that might have been a reply to that mockery in Guthrie's voice. Then another pause and Guthrie's voice again, so quiet and different this time that it scarce came up through the old cracked flooring.

"So it's you."

The schoolmistress, whether because of the wringing clouts on her or because of something in the way the words were spoken, shivered in her soggy shoes. But you may be sure her long nose was twitching by now, and her sharp eye searching in the gloom for a good crack to lay her ugly lug to. And syne came the voice of Guthrie's unknown visitor, young and strong and defiant, a voice that the schoolmistress couldn't put a name to.

"Where's Christine?"

"It's not Christine you're seeing to-day, Neil Lindsay. Nor any day henceforth, now I've found you out, the two of you."

So that was who. Neil Lindsay was little more than a name to Miss Strachan, half English from Edinburgh as she was, but she knew enough of the lands about to understand there would be fur flying if a Lindsay had been thinking to court Christine Mathers. It was like to be flying now in the long farm kitchen below her.

"Where is she, Guthrie?"

Defiant the repeated question and the calling Guthrie so, Lindsay but a crofter chiel as he was; fine he knew, though, he had history to licence him, as you'll hear. And now the schoolmistress heard Guthrie answer, right dry and quiet: "I chanced to follow Christine and found her finding your message. I sent her back to the house and waited here myself. Was I wrong? Do you complain?"

"She's her own mistress."

"Not if you're seeking to make her yours."

The schoolmistress liked this fine; she strained her ears and heard what might have been Lindsay taking a swift step towards the laird. Then he seemed to check himself and his voice came, carefully controlled, desperately earnest. "I want to marry her, Guthrie."

The laird said: "It can't be."

"She wants to marry me."

"It can't be."

"We're marrying, Guthrie, and it's not you can stop us."

"That I can, Neil Lindsay."

"For how?"

"Christine is under age, and you know it."

"That will mend. And there's another question."

"Indeed?"

"What is Christine to you?"

They were wasting no words, the two of them, in hammering out what lay between them. And the schoolmistress was in an ecstasy; snug and unsuspected in her loft, she was hearing what would make Isa Murdoch's story pale round every teapot in Kinkeig. So she reached for a bittock chocolate and only wished she could risk lighting a cigarette: a right coarse habit in a woman. Then she put her lug to the floor again to hear what Guthrie should find to reply.

But she was reckoning without the winter ways of Glen Erchany. The storm, that had been but spitting and girning till now, burst all in a moment into its full fury, the wind howling—a thing it does less often in nature than in books—and the sleet, now turned to rain, dashed in gusts against the slates like bursts of machine-gun fire. Guthrie and young Lindsay might be singing *Auld Lang Syne* together for all she could hear, or—what was more like—they might be fair murdering each other. She was right anxious, she said, for both of them: real solicitous-like is Miss Strachan.

Faith, though, her fears were justified. For in two-three minutes came a bit lull in the elements and she heard Lindsay's voice harsh with anger. "Say that again—"

And Guthrie said: "Married or unmarried, I say, and if it's not too late, she'll never be bairned by you."

And at that there was the sound of an open-handed blow, and then Lindsay, low and shocked. "Christ forgive me—you that might be my grandfather! I'm sorry, Guthrie; not all the bad blood that is between our folk—"

Guthrie said: "You'll pay."

And these words, as melodramatic as an old play in a barn, were the last the schoolmistress heard. For at that moment the first blast after the lull blew open some door in the cots and she, that must have been more scared than she'd allow, took it for a pistol shot and started up in the loft scraiching murder.

A fair scunner it must have been for them below, Lindsay took himself off straightways and Guthrie turned at once, cool enough, to deal with the surprise. Straight out and up the outside stair he must have gone, for before the schoolmistress had so much time as to fall into a tremble at the fool she'd made of herself he was through the loft door and gowking at her. "Madam," he said, "am I to understand you are in some distress?"

It didn't comfort Miss Strachan any to find she had to deal with the English-travelled Guthrie, him that was all black irony and politeness; she'd sooner have had the Guthrie Lindsay had been dealing with, the laird who affected more of the Scots than the gentry have allowed themselves this century past. She gave a bit snivel—we may suppose—as she replied: "Oh, Mr. Guthrie, sir, I'm the schoolmistress at Kinkeig and I was riding by when the storm came and—"

"I am very glad," said Guthrie—and standing outlined in the doorway he gave, she could see, a bit bow—"I am very glad the farm has given you shelter. But I think you cried out? You have been alarmed? Our hospitality has been at fault?"

She could feel his louring eye, black shadow though he was, and the awful edge to his smooth words fair unnerved her quite. "It was a rat, Mr. Guthrie," she cried; "I was sore frightened for a minute by a rat."

"Ah, yes," said Guthrie. "The rats are troublesome round here. As it happens, I have just been dealing with one myself."

At that horrid speak the schoolmistress fair felt her blood go chill in her veins; she was that miserable that had she dared she would just have sat down and wept. And some further snivel she must have given, for the next words she reported of the laird were: "You are overwrought; let me take you to a less disturbed asylum." The word "asylum" really suggested to her muddled head for a moment that she was to be handed over to the daftie, she would have dashed past him if she could and out into the storm and the night.

But the laird advanced with his heavy courtesy, like Sir Charles Grandison in Richardson's fine novel, and fair handed her out of the loft as if it had been a ballroom. In the open she got another turn, for darkling as it was she could see his face as pale as Pepper's Ghost and across it the great weal of a blow from an open hand. All the way round the arm of the loch and to the big house, where the laird wheeled her bicycle with one hand and armed her with the other like she had been the Duchess of Buccleuch, she could hear dinning in her lug his last words to the Lindsay chiel: "You'll pay." And then at the great house he suddenly tired of his play and summoned the Hardcastle wife and said: "Provide for this young woman for the night." With that he gave her a cold bow and went his own gait, and the schoolmistress was probably as mortified by her sudden drop from "madam" to "young woman" as by anything had happened to her that awful day—though for that matter "young" was a word of charity she might be grateful for: you must remember Guthrie hadn't seen her in a full light.

Nor did Miss Strachan see anything more of Guthrie save for a glimpse of him in the morning. She was up at keek of dawn, the rats had given her devil the wink of sleep all night and the supper she'd been offered was that meagre that long before she could decently get up she'd nibbled as much of the rest of her chocolate as the vermin hadn't snatched from her bedside. Right eager to get away she was, the storm had abated, and her best plan, she thought, was to trudge back to Kinkeig wheeling her machine—there would be no riding it, certain, with the track the way it was. So she wheedled a bit bread and treacle out of the old witch of a wife Hardcastle, said ta-ta to her right willingly, and away down the path she went. You must know that the path goes hard by the neck of the loch that comes close up to Castle Erchany, the same that they used to fill the moat from in the olden time. And there was Guthrie staring down Loch Cailie at the watery angry sunrise, intent as if he expected a message dropped for him from the chariot of the sun. And sudden as the schoolmistress looked he raised both arms and held them, hands outspread, against the lift like as if he were trying to see the blood coursing through the transparence of them. Uncanny it was and the schoolmistress minded the daft speak of how he would whiles pray to the idols of the coarse old heathen; she fair louped it round the first twist among the larches and I doubt she didn't stop once, any more than wee Isa had done, on the first of the miles that took her clear of Castle Erchany. But at least she bore her spoils with her: never had such fuel for claiking been brought down the glen before.

And that was the last anyone but myself in Kinkeig heard of Ranald Guthrie before the tragedy. It was the night of the twenty-eighth November Miss Strachan spent at the great house. It was on the tenth December, just before the great snows all but closed the glens entirely, that Christine Mathers came to me with her story.

9

It was seldom Christine came down to Kinkeig. After all, beer at the Arms and gossip in the kitchens and maybe a bit sprunting[1] about exhaust the attractions of the place except on the Sabbath. And Guthrie would never let Christine sit under Dr. Jervie; he had small use for the kirk and less for our minister. For a bit after his coming, when he'd got to know the affairs of his parish right well, the minister walked up to Erchany and got a bit talk with the laird and hinted it was a pity to breed up so fine a maid as Christine so lonely as he did and so much the mark for idle talk. Perhaps it was because Dr. Jervie was a scholar and he respected that—scholar himself that he was—that Guthrie didn't set the dogs on him as he did on the last minister—who was but an empty

[1] *Sprunting.* Running among the stacks after the girls at night. *Ed.*

pulpit-thumping billy enough with neither matter nor doctrine to him, 'tis true. But he listened coldly and coldly bowed Dr. Jervie out at the end, and ever after if they met in a lane the laird would walk unheeding by. He had never, sure, been seen in the kirk, nor Christine nor the Hardcastles either—and as for Tammas I doubt if the poor daftie had ever heard there is such a thing as the Shorter Catechism.

Christine, I say, came seldom to Kinkeig, and when she did it was to visit Ewan Bell the sutor. She and I had been long acquaint, for the first nurse that Guthrie ever got for her was my own sister's child. There was a pony-carriage at the great house then and the laird, who had some mellower years during the childhood of the maid, let them drive about much as they pleased, and often they came down to visit Uncle Ewan, for I was that to the bairn as well as to my right niece. A childless and unmarried man, I grew right fond of little Christine Mathers. And when she grew and Guthrie got Mistress Menzies to the house, the weak-minded gentle fine-bred lady he kept to give Christine her strange and lonely breeding, whiles she would still come to see me, bringing maybe her troubles at Erchany and maybe just her questions about the world. Then as she grew again and her maidenhood came to her and she saw the strangeness of her life, a Miranda islanded with a black-thoughted Prospero, she became a secret maid, and with a growing sorrowfulnes, too, deep at the heart of her. Whiles she still came to see me, but her contacts now all mute: curled on a table, she would give herself to the scent and the texture of my bit leathers, as if she drew from them the strength one can draw from raw strong things. And now her comings had been rarer, she would look at me as if she might open her heart, but in the end nothing would she speak of but idle matter of the day. Dreaming she would sit, toying with a bit leather, all opening into womanhood as simply and resistlessly as the flower of the heather on the braes. Fine I knew what had happened long ere the schoolmistress brought the unlucky name of the lad to Kinkeig.

You must know something of the Guthries and the Lind-
ays—a little more, maybe, than you'll find in Pitscottie's
hronicles. It won't keep you long from meeting Christine—
's not a treatise on Scottish feudalism I'm writing—and I
arned you fairly, Reader, back beyond the Reformation we
ust presently go.

You'll know that while in the highlands the organization
f folk was ever by clans, branch upon branch each under its
hieftain ramifying out from the stock of the chief, in the
owland parts was no such thing, the unit being ever the
amily. And great and spreading as a family might be it had
eldom the cohesion of the clan, so that the strait binding
ogether of families, and alliance betwixt this family and that,
nade ever the labour of the lowland landowners. That district
vas secure and strong in which the lairds were well bound
ogether by band and covenant.

Now while the Guthries were yet but bonnet-lairds at
Erchany the Lindsays of Mervie were great folk, barons that
held in chief from the crown, and whose land ran nigh to the
nneses', the coarse Fleming creatures, between Moray and
Spey. And in the boyhood of James III, when Scotland was a
ight lawless and faithless place, the Guthries entered into
bond of manrent with the Lindsays. The bond is yet preserved
n which a Ranald Guthrie swore to Andrew Lindsay "to be
or him and with him, his kin and friends and their quarrels,
n council, help, supply, maintenance and defence, as far as
good conscience and reason will, in the straitest form of band
of kindness against and before all living men except his
allegiance to our Sovereign Lord the King alone." Whatever
nducement the Lindsays in their wealth gave, or whatever
persuasion in their power they exerted, the bond was a most
nviolable oath for the five years' space it was to hold. But
the word about the king was but a pious and empty speak:
ever in a bond of manrent was some thought of union against
the power of the crown.

And against the crown in time it was invoked. For the
Lindsays stood in a like bond of fealty to the Earl of Huntly,

and to Andrew Lindsay came the day when the Earl wrot that his cousin the laird of Gight had been summoned t underlie the law in Edinburgh, and that the safety of his lif required the instant presence of Lindsay and his carles at St Johnston, thence to ride with the Earl to Edinburgh. S Lindsay summoned Ranald Guthrie and his men to Mervie and Lindsays and Guthries together rode to St. Johnston— which is Perth—and there joining the Earl all held forwar for Edinburgh, there to overawe the king's justices on th laird of Gight's behalf. Only Andrew Lindsay, feigning matte of business, tarried a day behind, and riding fast and hard t Erchany there lay with Ranald Guthrie's wife.

For a year and a day Ranald Guthrie held himself quiet then he gathered such power as he might and made a fora upon Mervie and took up Andrew Lindsay, all unprepare from amid his carles, and carried him away. The Guthrie carried Lindsay to their own lands and there they hacked th lecherous fingers from him, and they sent him home with a hour-glass round his neck to mind the Lindsays they ha bided that year-and-a-day only that the bond of manren might be expired and the Guthrie faith unbroken. An Andrew Lindsay died.

That was the beginning of the feud betwixt Lindsays and Guthries, and all the mischieving that was betwixt them would be but a drear tale to tell. But as the generations passed the power of the Guthries grew and that of the Lindsays ever declined and in the Killing Time they were broken entirely, there were no Lindsays of Mervie known any longer among the gentle Lindsays of Scotland, and the burgher folk from Dunwinnie came and quarried all the New Wynd and half the Cowgate from the ruins of Mervie Tower. And the Guthries, that had long memories and unforgiving hearts, would give a bit laugh as they whiles went hunting down Mervie glen.

But there were Lindsays enough in these lands still, crofter folk with no history, that might think themselves the heirs of the old gentle Lindsays if they would. So still there was the old enmity, Lindsays thinking always of the Guthries as the worse dirt of gentry and Guthries showing no more favour to Lindsays than they need: a strange uncharitable smouldering feeling that ever and again in the imaginative ones would flame into hatred and some vicious deed. It was ever a disgrace in a Lindsay to consent to serve kin of the Guthries of Erchany, and if young Neil Lindsay was more bitter than most against Ranald Guthrie before he met in with Christine it was for the shame of his father having syne worked for the laird's sister Alison. You must hear of Alison, for she was surely the strangest of the Guthries: Tammas, the claiks said, was her bairn by God knew whom.

There were four Guthries of Ranald's generation. John, the eldest, saw two fine sons drown before his eyes far out on Loch Cailie, and lived on, childless and melancholy, till Ranald inherited. Ian, the second son, and Ranald, the third, were they that to avoid the Kirk went among the coarse Australians; as daft as daft folk thought it and impious forbye, so that few in Kinkeig were surprised or sorry when the speak came of Ian's horrid death, killed and cooked by these same coarse Australians in their billycans. Alison, the daughter, was full twenty years younger than Ranald, the child of her father's old age and her mother's unlikely years. She was all a Guthrie, dark and driven, and her passion was for the creatures of the air. And uncannily the birds flocked to her: they flew about her head by day and were her dreams by night, she roved Scotland for the lore and the society of them, and made a book of birds and lived finally in a Highland shielan, a lone rude cot white within and without with the droppings of the birds and in the end, folk said, she said she understood the voices of the birds, and some said she said their talk was all of heavenly places, and some said she said their talk was all of hell. And a certain Wat Lindsay, this Neil Lindsay's father, because his brothers were enough to tend the croft, and because he too had skill with birds and they were a lure to him, so far forgot the old bad feeling of the feud as to serve Alison for a time, and he swam out across

Loch-an-Eilan for her and photographed the last nest of the osprey found in Scotland for many a long day. And that was Alison, who died unmarried in her shielan on the fair side of middle age; and that was why young Neil bore a fierce and troubled mind to the laird: it was the shame that his dead father had done such service for a Guthrie.

It was little I knew of Neil Lindsay before Christine came to me, for he lived with his brothers on a croft remote in Mervie, the same where his ancestors, as he imagined them, had their tower. He had fought his father and his mother and his brothers, folk said, for knowledge, the English knowledge out of books that would appear but dirt to the Lindsays, small crofters as they were sunk in the hard heartbreaking losing battle of all remaining crofter folk against the very march of time. A hundred years ago, or fifty, he might have found the right Dominie to prepare him and syne carried his sack of meal on his back to the College in Aberdeen and got his letters there. But what the stationmaster calls the Progress of Education has made things harder now for lads like him, the path of learning being encumbered with the getting of wee bit certificates in trifling lores at every turn, Neil Lindsay's knowledge was fragmentary and fitful and imaginative, the knowledge of a keen and right impatient mind ever conscious of opportunities denied, for he was the kind that would have gone far with the free and careless schooling of the gentry, but that was too independent to go scraping from standard to standard in the Board schools. It's of his sort that rebels are made and, sure as sure, Neil had taken up, 'twas said, with a hantle of folk, Nationalists, who thought Scotland should be free and independent once more. But Will Saunders said he saw nothing in a plan that was all Scotland for the Irish—meaning the Nationalists would hand us over to the coarse teeming folk on the Clyde—but that he was all for a just redistribution of colonies and it was good time England was given back to the Scots, faith it was. This, though, is all aside from my story. What comes next is Christine's tale of how she met in with Neil.

On Midsummer Day it was she had taken a piece, the lonely maid, and gone over the glen-head and far down Glen Mervie on a brave morning, the clouds were fleecy and sailing above her, away to the left by the hidden loch the snipe were but new-fallen silent and whiles a wild goose would soar its way across the lift, flying surely to the distant sea. The long day, a day with almost no night to it, was before her and sudden she thought to go where she had never been, to the yet snow-flecked summit of Ben Cailie before her. So she went half down the glen, past the Lindsays' croft that she scarce knew the name of, and up through a plantation where the last autumn's sycamore leaves lay blended in their skeletal tracery with the springy carpet of larch needles. Syne she was through to the pine woods and syne through a spleiter of mountain ash, and then the bare shoulder of Ben Cailie was before her, to the left she could see the long silver splash of the loch, and far away over the rolling braes behind her the blue peat smoke was going up from Kinkeig. Whiles came the tinkle of a burn, fine hidden threads of snow-water falling down and down the Ben from the topmost snows: whiles came the warm-sounding trembling bleat of the ewes in the pastures below; and ever there was the crying of the peewits that Christine used to feel was her own cry. Far and lonely the climb over heather and rock and scree, a great camp of mountains rising on the one hand and on the other a broadening glimpse of the parks beyond Dunwinnie, that went rolling with their bright burden of green corn towards the invisible sea.

So all that morning nearly Christine climbed to the great brow of Ben Cailie, every foot taking her, all unknowing, to the destiny of her. Devil the soul did she expect to see until the gloaming brought her home again and she wondered for a minute what would happen if she had an accident up there, for none knew she was climbing Ben Cailie and it might be long before they thought to look that high. But she wasn't frightened; she'd been up all but the final pinnacle before and there was small danger to one with a foot half as sure as

Christine's, Christine thought. She was thinking this as she made across a rocky ledge with a seven-eight foot drop maybe to soft heather below, and it was at the moment of her thinking that she saw the man.

He was standing beyond and below her by a great outcrop of rock, a young man in a blue shirt and old grey trousers, gentle or common he might have been and beautiful he was, standing absorbed and still. So still he stood he might have been a figure in the granite he was studying, until his hand moved—sensitively, Christine knew with a knowledge that strangely moved her—over the weathered surface. With just such a touch must the old Pictish men that held these lands long syne have felt for the stone that was the end and the beginning of their craft.

It was but few lads that Christine in her solitary growing-up had known, and if I spoke of her a while back as Miranda I was thinking of a Ferdinand, maybe, in this Neil Lindsay. For a long minute Christine gazed at him and then she made to slip by unseen. But Nature, that moves in us by strange courses enough if need be, caught at the sure foot the maid had been congratulating herself on and sent her tumbling down that unchancy seven-eight feet to the heather, for all the world as if she fair wanted to hurl herself at the stranger's head.

In a moment Neil Lindsay was up with her; he must have turned at the sound of her trouble and louped across like a panther. Christine was all dazed, she felt the earth spin and the heather heave under her, once it heaved and again, and the second time was the lad raising her in his arms. She opened her eyes and he was looking into them with a kind of amazement and he said, "Are you hurt, lass?" as sorry and as anxious as if she were his own sister. She said she was fine and he made her move all her limbs right gently to make sure, and then he said quietly, "Well, don't do it again; it's not what Ben Cailie's for this fine morning." Christine laughed at that, but he seemed straight to have forgotten he'd tried to make a bit joke, he was looking again into her eyes and as a lover looks.

So that was their meeting. Neil took her to the summit of Ben Cailie and she rubbed her face with snow that Midsummer Day, and all tingling from the snow and the long climb she grew bold to ask him what he was doing up on the Ben? He tossed his head at that and flushed slow and dark; it turned out he had a bit book with him, the *Geology of the Grampians*, and was far advanced in the lore of it, though lone and secret his studying had been. And Christine, that had been gently bred and yet in a manner so strange and lonely that she felt all her own knowledge had been a struggle too, listened to the talk of him near all that day, never wondering that a strange crofter chiel, with the silence of his kind written on his face, should be talking to her and talking so, eager and wary, as if he would turn that sensitive and exploring touch he had from the hard granite to the very contours of her mind. It was only when they were far down the Ben again and Mervie in sight that he grew shy, and then perplexed as if a thought had come to him that might have come before. He was Neil Lindsay, he said, and who was she? And when she told him and he realized it was her that lived with Guthrie of Erchany and was his daughter said to be he gave her a look she had no understanding of, for though she knew well of the old daft feeling between Lindsays and Guthries she had never thought it a thing her generation could take any heed of, evil old folly that it was. But the blood had come to the lad's face when she named herself, then it drained away to leave a pallor under the tan of him, then he uttered a curse that startled her, and then he took her in his arms.

From that moment it was all over with Christine. Through all the varying moods of their later meetings, secret always, and though sometimes she said it and sometimes she didn't, she knew she was his for ever. And Neil, many-mooded too though he proved to be, was as fixed as the great rock they'd met in the shadow of; wedded to him and bedded she would be and the two of them would away to Canada, where he had a cousin, a scholar grown, would set him in the way of the work he wanted.

This, then, was the story Christine told me at last, and that it came out after a world of hesitation and false starts was no more than partly because of the natural sham-fastness of the maid. Partly it was because of the strain she was being put to at Erchany; the way the laird was going on she was grown nervous and doubting there could be any confidence in the world except the one confidence between Neil and her. Guthrie was absolute against the lad; ever since the day he had met in with him at the home farm he had fair been like a demon, silent, but with rage or a like passion burning in him. No more was Neil easy, he was right passionate against Guthrie in his turn and he churned the thing up in his brooding mind with all the ancient wrongs of the Lindsays in a way Christine had little patience with. It was a Highland temper he had of his mother came out in Neil in those months of waiting and brooding; Christine misliked the seeing it gaining on him, and it wasn't long after the home-farm affair that she knew the time for acting had come. Neil was for storming Erchany like young Lochinvar and carrying her to some place they could be married in secret: he had just the money put by to carry the two of them to Canada, but devil the penny more. Christine was loth to go in secret, her instinct was against it, she felt Guthrie had some power over her she could break only by fighting him in the open: she knew, though, that did Neil but say it in a particular way away she'd go, that that was how she was to be to him. For it was the power in the thing she most felt. When I asked her—perhaps in foolish words enough—"And you really want to marry him, Christine?" she looked at me almost mockingly for a moment and just said "I'm driven."

So Christine wasn't to argue with in her choosing; all I could aim at was help as I might be able. And the first thing she asked me was: "Mr. Bell, is there a lawyer in Dunwinnie?"

I told her there had been old Mr. Dunbar and that now there was a young lad, Stewart his name, that had been in his office and had the business after him. Though I wondered a little at her question I thought better not to ask what was in her mind; syne she got up from the corner of the bench she'd been sitting on and crossed over to my bit shop-window and stared out absently at Kinkeig in its returning blanket of snow. "There must be papers," she said quietly and without turning round, "certificates."

I said indeed there must be papers—things were far wrong if there weren't—but if she was Guthrie's right ward and a minor, and if he was that eccentric he would say or show nothing, it was hard for me to tell whether she had a right to see them or no. She might send her Neil to see Stewart, the lawyer lad in Dunwinnie, if she wanted, but it was an old man's advice to bide her time: when the laird got accustomed to the way things had fallen out he'd see that both Guthries and Lindsays should have more sense than to be playing Montagues and Capulets. And she would do well, I said, to din the same thing into her Neil; after all, when a crofter loon with nothing but remote hopes in Canada came courting the ward of a rich laird he must expect a rebuff or two before he got his way.

But Christine shook her head. "It's all very different from that." And she picked up a bit leather and fell to tracing little waves on it with her finger, like as if she was copying the furrows that had gathered on her pretty brow. "Have you seen my uncle lately?" she asked.

I shook my head. "I haven't seen him, my dear, this year past."

"But you'll have heard talk?"

"I haven't lost my hearing yet, Christine."

She smiled at this. "Yes, there's always talk in Kinkeig, I'm sure." She hesitated. "But you may have heard that—that he's gone mad?"

She was that anxious-looking that I left my last and gave her a bit hug—a thing I hadn't done for many a long year.

"Don't fash yourself over that," I said; "they were saying no less of him before you were born. It's what Kinkeig would say of any laird that didn't talk grouse and oats and pretend to be right kirk-greedy on Sundays. And the Guthries have had the name of it since the days of Malcolm Canmore."

She gave a bit laugh, and fine I thought I'd comforted her until my old ear caught the note of it. Then I walked to the window and had a look out myself.

Behind me Christine said in a new hard way: "He's mad."

10

CHRISTINE had a loyalty to the laird, and she was the kind that would strive to keep her loyalty while enduring much, or even right through a strait fight. So it was a scunner to hear her say that of Guthrie—and to hear the unco paradox she backed her speak with forbye. For what made her right sure that the man was truly crazy at last was that he was spending a bit silver like a rational being. "He's violating himself," Christine said.

It was only one had lived long at Erchany, I thought, could estimate the force of her evidence. The first thing was the putting away of the Gamleys: some sort of quarterly or yearly agreement Gamley had from the laird in writing, and to get them away he had paid out a little bit of gold—real gold that Christine had seen him taking from his bureau, and that was the only ready coin at Erchany might serve in an emergency. Right strange it was, Christine said, for the gold was her uncle's plaything.

I opened my eyes at that. Well I knew Guthrie's near-going ways, his sad dealings with the bogles and all, but I had never thought of him somehow as the simple picturesque miser you might meet with in a book. "You mean," I cried, "he sits thumbing the stuff over?"

"Yes. He calls it numismatics, and he's even taught me a little. Have you ever seen a Spanish gold *quadruple* of Phillip V, Mr. Bell—or a *genovine* twenty-three carats fine, or a bonnet piece of James V, or the coinage of the Great Mogul? I think I could be a miser myself easy as easy when I look at them. But uncle likes to be thumbing little piles of guineas and sovereigns as well, the same that he must have paid Gamley with. And doesn't that show?"

It showed, I thought, that the laird had been unco eager to rid himself of those at the home farm, for if he had the disease of gold as bad as that it must have been a fair violation, like Christine said, to hand a pile to his grieve. And for a minute I had a picture in my mind, almost as vivid maybe as the vision of Mistress McLaren I've told you about, of Guthrie sitting in his dark tower, with no more than the bit candle that was another right miser's touch to him, thumbing and thumbing at the gold, a symbol no doubt of something we could have no knowledge of, and whiles calling on the maid to watch and admire numismatic-like, that he might have some feeling of a rational basis to the irrational lust was driving him. And little as I knew of Neil Lindsay I was glad Christine had found him; the glint of that gold, like the glint of gold some folk thought to see in Guthrie's eye, had somehow made the whole picture of the man and his castle darker for me.

"Doesn't that show?" Christine repeated. And then she added: "But he doesn't play with the gold so much now; he's got the puzzles instead."

I looked at her fair startled—not by the words, which I didn't understand, but by the tone of them and the growing strain on her face. It was plain there was an atmosphere about events at Erchany that was working on the maid and that she found it hard to express the force of. "Puzzles?" I said, fair puzzled myself.

"Uncle has been ordering all sorts of things from Edinburgh—that's another strange spending. There have been provisions as if we were going to be besieged at Erchany, expensive things some of them I've never seen or heard of! And a big crate of books."

"Surely the laird has ever been a great reader, Christine."

"Yes—but he doesn't *buy* books! And these are a kind he's never heeded before: medical books. Up there in the tower he's poring over them night after night."

I thought for a minute I saw a right horrible light here. Was Guthrie really going mad—as Christine thought and as the Harley Street simp had said might happen—and, feeling it come on him, was he reading desperately to get light on himself and cure? "Christine," I asked gently, "would they be books about the mind?"

Fine she understood me as she shook her head. "The ones I've seen are not. There's one by a man Osler on General Medicine, and one by Flinders on Radiology, and one by Richards on Cardiac Disease—" She broke off with a frown, and her noting and remembering the hard words brought home to me right vividly the effort she had been making to plumb things at the great house.

Myself, I could make nothing of this fancy of Guthrie's, so I harked back to something else. "What of the puzzles, Christine?"

"Jigsaw puzzles they're called—you know them? I think he got them cheap from a catalogue. Spirited war scenes, Mr. Bell. You're awfully puzzled for a time about the German soldier's head, and then you find it's been blown right from his body and fits snug in the top left-hand corner. The whole thing will be called the Battle of the Marne, maybe—and Uncle likes me to help him. There's little I have to learn about tanks and hand-grenades and the sinking of the *Lusitania*. Perhaps it's Uncle's idea of a finishing school for me."

There was a spark of fun in Christine's voice; nevertheless, she'd spoken the first bitter words I'd ever heard from her. I said, Well, it seemed a foolish ploy enough but with no vice in it, so need she worry?

Christine gave a half-impatient, half-despairing toss to the lovely hair of her. "It's taken the place of the gold!" she said. "So don't you *see?*"

For a minute I must have stared at her like an owl. And then, uncertainly enough, I did see. For had I not been saying to myself that the gold was a symbol that answered to something deep in the man?

But Christine's mind had turned another way. "Mr. Bell," she said, "why did little Isa Murdoch leave us? Has there been a story going round about that?"

It was a question I'd been fearing, this. Christine had enough to fash over these days without a bit more worry about the daftie Tammas, and yet if she didn't know of the unchancy way he'd turned on Isa it seemed but right to warn her. But syne she settled this by saying: "Was it just Tammas?"

"Partly that. But partly it was she was driven to hide in your uncle's gallery and heard him murmuring his verses and talking strangely to the air. She was easily frighted. But Christine, did you ever hear of your uncle holding in with any folk called Walter Kennedy and Robert Henderson?"

At that it was her turn to stare like an owl—but only for a moment. Then she laughed as clear as clear: right sweet it was to hear her. "Oh, Uncle Ewan Bell," she cried, "did you ever hold in with Geoffrey Chaucer?" And at that her spirits suddenly came on her wildly; she jumped up as if the worry were gone from her entirely and fell to pacing up and down my bit shop, her hands clasped behind her and her eye on the middle air like as if it was Ranald Guthrie himself. And then she chanted:

> "He has done petuously devour,
> The noble Chaucer, of makaris flouir,
> The Monk of Bery, and Gower, all thre;
> *Timor Mortis conturbat me.*
>
> "In Dumfermelyne he has tane Broun
> With Maister Robert Henrisoun;
> Schir Iohne the Ros enbrast hes he;
> *Timor Mortis conturbat me.*"

Christine turned at this and laughed again. Then she went

on in her own right voice, grave and sweet:

> "Gud Maister Walter Kennedy,
> In poynt of dede lyis veraly,
> Gret reuth it were that so suld be;
> *Timor Mortis conturbat me. . . .*"

I laid down my awl. "So that was who!" I said. "Folk in a poem."

Chris.ine nodded. "Quoth Dunbar when he was sick. And quoth my uncle in his gallery—also sick, maybe." And syne she chanted another verse:

> "Sen he has all my brether tane,
> He will naught lat me lif alane,
> On forse I man his nyxt pray be;
> *Timor Mortis conturbat me.*"

And at that she came and sat down beside me, sudden as heavy-thoughted as before. "Dunbar's *Lament for the Makers,* that he made when he knew another poet, and that himself, was going to die. Uncle often chants it now, and no doubt Isa heard him."

I remembered then Isa had said Guthrie's verses seemed to have a run of Scottish names to them and then a bit of foreign foolishness forbye. So Dunbar's poem it must have been, and the names Kennedy and Henderson she'd thought to hear through her swoon were no more than echoes from the poem again. And fine I could have solved the mystery myself and without Christine joking at me about Chaucer had I only had the wit to think, for Dunbar's poems have been familiar to me long enough, and stand on my shelf indeed in the right learned and elegant edition of Dr. Small.

And that was the end of my talk with Christine that day, for syne she looked at the clock and picked up her bonnet and was away through the snow that briskly that I guessed Neil Lindsay was somewhere at the end of her journey. Rambling and inconclusive the talk had been; I had an uncanny feeling at the last of having been left groping for I didn't know what in the shadowy rooms and crumbling corridors of Castle Erchany. That evening I sat by my bench long into the gloaming, never thinking to put up the shutters and take a dander to the Arms; the thing was working on me and I wanted solitude.

Strange that young Neil Lindsay, looking to break from the traditions of his folk and make a new life in a new land, should concern himself with the old bitterness of the Lindsays against the Guthries. And stranger that Guthrie, a scholar and once a poet, whose meditations must be of time and change and the nature of things, should have any thought for that past and narrow hate against the Lindsays. For if the latter-day Lindsays, common folk and poor, might maybe take Ranald Guthrie as a type of those that have all and in taking more have beggared the simple folk of Scotland, and but add to that real resentment the colour of a long-past history, what was that to Guthrie—a rich man in the security of his possessions, that should never heed or mind the common envy of the poor? Was the laird doing more than treat Neil Lindsay's suit as any man, proud of his lineage and his lands, would treat the suit of a crofter billy to one that lived as a daughter in his house?

But Christine thought her uncle was mad or maddened; and unco it was I should be right troubled by her thinking what near all Kinkeig had long thought. The thing was that Kinkeig was ever prepared to think and say any foolishness that had a spice to it, whereas Christine was a level lass and douce, and one that had learnt from Mistress Menzies and Guthrie to use words exactly. She meant what she said of the laird, and that her feeling was something she could scarce give convincing reason for didn't make it trouble my mind the less.

Sudden it came to me I hadn't asked her if she knew of any word lately from the American Guthries: might they not be worrying the laird after all—and the cool maid that had come that night to the Arms one of them? For it was clear that if Guthrie's conduct these past months was to be accounted for there was more required than the matter of Christine and her Neil Lindsay. The parting with the Gamleys, the orders from Edinburgh, all that Isa Murdoch had seen and heard at the opening up of the great house and in the gallery: these seemed to be happenings before Guthrie had learnt who it was would be courting Christine, or that any was courting her. And I thought of the medical books the laird was pouring over, and of how he had fallen to beguiling himself with wee puzzles carven out of wood. And I thought of him cleaving his way in a fury into his long-deserted gallery, and of how he had wandered there, and of his standing at Isa's last keek at him staring out over Loch Cailie. And ever Christine's voice came back to me, hard as if she were facing deadly danger, saying her uncle was mad. And then, searching for the pattern that must be in all this, I seemed to hear the voice of the laird himself, crying out in the Latin refrain of that old Scottish poet that he was harried by the fear of death . . . nay, of Death himself.

At that I went back and found the book and blew the dust from it and turned to the poem.

Lament for the Makaris
Quhen he was seik

I that in heill wes and glaidnes,
Am trublit now with gret seiknes,
And feblit with infirmitie;
Timor Mortis conturbat me. . . .

And I read through that hundred-line lament for the dead poets of Scotland to the end:

Sen for the deth remeid is non,
Best is that we for deth dispone
Eftir our deth that lif may we;
Timor Mortis conturbat me.

11

IT was a hard winter. Looking back on this prologue to what befell at Erchany I see the figures of it whiles driven helpless before the great storm that caught the schoolmistress, whiles sharp-etched on the memory in gestures as extravagant as the leafless star-hung trees showed in the long nights of black frost; and ever the fatal hurrying story of them punctuated by the falling and melting curtain of the snows. When the Thoughtful Citizen got his papers through the drifts—which he didn't always—he would come ploutering down to the Arms and tell us the Fleet Street chiels had said things were right hard in Scotland, there were tremendous snows, and the season was a record just as he'd said. It was the station-master himself was a record, Will Saunders put in—a right cracked one and would to God he'd run out of needles or break a spring.

The very day Christine visited me it was that the leaden skies opened above the ready snow-covered braes and the fine flakes fell and fell, the glen and all the rolling parks thicker and thicker mantled, as pure and silent and still as the marble floor of heaven before the Almighty thought to create the Angelic host. Often in those days, days that went flitting by towards Christmas as white and quiet as stainless ghosts, I would wonder what was happening up the glen. I scarcely expected news; none could get through that deepening barrier unless it might be Tammas, who took an unnatural strength to himself with the coming of the snow, folk said, like as if he were a creature in a fairy-tale. Many is the mile of deep snow I've struggled through myself as a lad, when every week, winter and summer, I'd tramp to my bit reading in the Dunwinnie Institute. But I doubted if I'd ever made such a journey as now lay between Kinkeig and Erchany, and I was right surprised when, in fact, Tammas did come through.

As dead beat he was as Satan after he'd fought his way

through Chaos—and, indeed, he was like a visitor from another world. There had been a car or two struggle through from Dunwinnie on the previous day—the twenty-second December—with news of great doings there at the tail of the Loch: curlers coming by the hundred, 'twas said, in special trains. But on the twenty-third nothing came and we doubted if anything more could come; Kinkeig was cut off from the world, and Erchany from Kinkeig again. All except for Tammas, hoasting and gasping on my doorstep, the breath steaming from the great slavering mouth of him like a dragon.

But a dragon would have had more sense than was left in the daftie after his trudge. What he said was a mere yammering there was nothing to be made of, he never heeded my invitation to come in but thrust a bit letter at me and was louping away down the road before I could speak again. I looked at the letter and it was from Christine: at that I never heeded more about the daftie but took it straight in and read it by the fire.

UNCLE EWAN BELL—I was a little fool with my fancies: will you forgive me? It is all right—I am *sure* it is all right, though strange—and I have only to wait till Christmas Day!

Uncle came in this morning; he seemed in a rare pleased mood; he stood in front of the little fire he had made Mrs. Hardcastle light for me, and he said, "I've finished the biggest of all the jigsaws." Then he must have seen my thoughts were far away, for suddenly he said softly, "Must you have him, Christine?" I said just "Yes," no more—for I've told him long ago how much it is *yes* and how I can't help myself. He said, "You shall go with him."

I don't know why, I trembled and couldn't speak, perhaps with my sick fancies lately I thought he was speaking meaninglessly from a distraught mind. But he repeated, "You shall go with him." And then he spoke harshly of the disgrace and that we must go, if we did go, once and for ever; that there was money for me that I should have and that Neil should come for me at Christmas and that we might away to Canada. But that he would have no wedding or word of a wedding in these parts, and that—but I needn't repeat words I want and shall soon have the chance to forget.

So this is Goodbye: I won't forget *you,* Uncle Ewan Bell. I am so happy, happy—and yet afraid. I'm fey, I almost think—but that is foolish! If there are things I don't understand—what does it matter when I'm going with Neil?

Tammas is being made to go down—I suppose for letters—though the snow is drifting deep now: I hope he'll come to no harm. He's my chance to send this—otherwise you mightn't hear from me till I was far away—and what oceans of Kinkeig gossip, in that case, you'd hear first! Good-bye and love, dear Ewan Bell.

CHRISTINE MATHERS.

I shall be safe with Neil, and he with me.

So it was good-bye to Christine—and at the thought she was going far from Kinkeig I felt heavier-hearted than for her sake I should have done. Over and over again that night I read her letter—and ever I was the heavier-hearted. At last I must have fallen asleep, old man that I am, over my dying fire, for I awoke chilled in the night and with Ranald Guthrie's voice again in my ears:

Timor Mortis conturbat me. . . .

It was right anxiously I spent the next three days.

12

THE evening of the day Tammas came—Monday the twenty-third it was—saw a bit stir in Kinkeig. For long after 'twas thought the roads were closed for that fall, when the gloaming was falling in shadows of grey and silver over the snows, there came a wee closed car ploughing and slithering into the village from none knew where: it had missed the North Road through Dunwinnie maybe and was seeking it again. Folk got no more than a keek at it through their windows, for everyone was indoors that weather—all except the bairn

Wattie McLaren, that had run out from his tea to have a look at a snow man he and the other bairns had been making that morning. The wee car stopped; it was a young wife was in it, Wattie said, and she called out to him, Was she right for the road south? And then maybe she misunderstood Wattie—which is likely enough—or the bairn told her a right mischievous falsehood he was frightened to own to later. Anyway, the wee car gave a snort and a shake, its back wheels slithered a minute before they got a bit bite in the snow, and then it turned right and held up the glen for Erchany.

Meanwhile Mistress McLaren—and you know enough of her to know she hasn't much sense—had missed Wattie from among her bairns—and she has enough of them, Will Saunders says, to be a right grand example to her own sows—and out she went to find him, just in time to see the red tail light of the wee car disappearing over the first brow of the hill. And at the same moment there came a great blast of a trumpet that put Mistress McLaren—who is fell religious in a gossiping way—in mind, she said, of the Herald Angels: a devout and seasonable thought, it can't be denied. But it was nothing but the horn of another car, one near as big as a house this time and with a solitary slip of a lad in it, and with chains to its wheels that put it in a better way than the other against the snow. No doubt it had gone astray through following the wee machine in front, and I know now that when the lad called out to the smith's wife it was to ask, Was he right for London? Mistress McLaren, you needn't be told, had about as much chance of picking that up aright as if the loon had asked her was he right for Monte Carlo; she took it into her head he was asking, Which way had the wee car gone?—always liking to think, Will said, that the loons are after the lasses. So she pointed, right pleased, up the darkening road to the glen and away went the great car with a roar for Castle Erchany. Most folk thought it unlikely the cars would get there, and equally unlikely they'd get back; the greengrocer Carfrae had a bit joke, you may be sure, about their helping keep each other's engines warm that night in the solitude of the glen.

. . .

After that nothing more that anyone knew of came through Kinkeig. A wind got up that night that swept the yet falling snow along as if it grudged the fine flakes of it their resting place on the mantled earth; all Christmas Eve it blew the fallen snow into great drifts all these lands about. On Christmas morning the wind fell but whiles the snow came softly down still; going early past the kirk I could scarcely hear the bell for the early service Dr. Jervie likes to hold, so muffled was the tolling of it in the fall.

It was when the few folk in Kinkeig that will admit Christmas a Feast of the Kirk were at service that Tammas came again, and clearer than the tolling bell I heard the great cry of him as he breasted the last rise, crying the awful death of his master Ranald Guthrie of Erchany.

And here, Reader, I lay down my wandering and unready pen and you'll be hearing, I think, what the English lad Noel Gylby, him that was in the great car, wrote to his maid in London. But you and I will meet in with one another again ere the story's told.

II

THE JOURNAL LETTER OF NOEL GYLBY

1

24th December

DIANA darling: Leaves—as Queen Victoria said—from the Journal of my Life in the Highlands. Or possibly of my Death in the Lowlands. For I don't at all know if I'm going to survive and I don't know—I'm kind of guessing, as my girl-friend here says—where I am. YES, I have a girl-friend, a most formidable and charming and rather mysterious American miss, and we are staying at a castle somewhere in Scotland and I have a feeling—kind of feel—that our throats may be feudally cut at any time by the seneschal, who—mark you!—bears the most appropriate name of Hardcastle, no doubt with underlings (though I haven't yet seen them) Dampcastle, Coldcastle and Crazycastle—a whole progeny of Crazycastles would be by no means out of the way. And we kind of feel—Miss Guthrie and I—that we are presently to be besieged, no doubt by the paynim knights Sansjoy, Sansfoy and Sansloy—and if you say, Diana, that the paynims are out of the Scottish picture I retort that I've had a quite awful night and a little inconsistency must be allowed.

Don't be furious, Diana, that I shan't be in town for Christmas after all; it's not my fault. Listen. I'll tell you about it. By way of apology, all about it. It is—and promises to be—amusing.

I got away from Kincrae and the horrors of my aunt's unseasonable sojourn there—do you know, positively, icicles were depending from the noses of those melancholy stags' heads in the hall?—I got away quite early yesterday morning, and though the roads were shocking I reckoned to get to Edinburgh last night (where there is a tolerable hotel) and to-night to strike off the north road to York, and then to make town in excellent time for our Christmas dinner—just as I wired.

But I'd got it wrong. The snows have been tremendous and even on the Highland road—where the snow-ploughs have been out—I was losing time on schedule badly. I had luncheon—a bit dinner you'd be wanting? the pothouse keeper said wonderingly—Lord knows where, and at the end of it my eye was already on my Edinburgh dinner. So I stepped on it—but still the going was bad. I had to catch the *William Nuir* at Queensferry; otherwise it meant round by Stirling and in late. Diana, you know what I did. I stopped and got out the map and saw it would be ever so much quicker *such* a way. Alas!

The route was all right, I think; it was the snow undid me. I was running along nicely on chains at about forty m.p.h. when the snout of the car went down and the tail went up, just like a launch dropping into the trough of a wave—only the feel wasn't that of water but of cotton wool. In about three yards I had come from that forty m.p.h. to a dead stop, and without a jolt or a tremble. That is how snow behaves in Scotland: its ballistic properties quite different, it seems to me, from the Swiss variety. But that's by the way. What had happened was I'd breasted one of those enormously humpy bridges (left about, I believe, by Julius Caesar) and there was a great drift on the farther side and down I'd sunk.

Luckily there was a group of North Britons in the centre foreground, bringing hay, they said, to the beasts; very kindly, they brought the beasts to me and yanked the car out backwards, and away I drove the way I'd come, the incident having put me back—as Miss G. says—two hours and ten shillings.

We approach Miss G. now—again at about forty m.p.h. and in the progressive municipality of Dunwinnie. I stopped there for petrol, Miss G. had stopped for gas—and we got it from the same pump, ladies first. You know, I always feel embarrassed when I'm out with the car in the society of smaller cars, and Miss G. has a fleeting appraising glance that said *puppy!* in a quite devastating sort of way. So I followed her modestly out of this Dunwinnie and—having heard her make competent enquiries about the south road—I followed her again all humbly second to the right. Unfortunately, Miss G. had tripped on it.

But she could drive. It was a narrow road—suspiciously narrow—and I didn't overtake her. We did about ten miles and then, turning into some nameless hamlet, I lost her: by this time it was nearly dark. I didn't like it a bit; for miles the road had been virgin snow and I was next to certain I was lost in the heart of Scotland. So I stopped to enquire: the village seemed deserted—like sweet Auburn—and I thought I'd have to go thumping on people's doors, when suddenly the figure of an old wife started up magically at my elbow. Of course I ought to have grabbed my map, said, "My good woman, what little place is this?", and then worked it out for myself. Instead, I asked her for the south road; I may even have asked her for London—habit, you know, creeping in with fatigue. Anyway, she seemed a most reliable old party, pointed at once and with immense decision to a turn among the cottages ahead—and away your devoted mut went.

About a mile on I picked up Miss G.'s tail light, and I was still humble enough to feel momentarily encouraged: my cousin Tim, who was Third Secretary or something at Washington, says they really are a most fearfully efficient race. Of course Tim himself is so nitwitted—But I wander.

Point is, I *was* wandering; a few miles on there could be no doubt of it. Miss G. had tripped and I was tripping after her—plunging and slithering rather through anything up to two feet of snow. I think I'd have turned back if there had been any turning, which there wasn't, the road being no road clearly, but the most miserable of tracks. Besides, the admired Miss G. was still ahead—I can't imagine how she kept going—and likely to be much worse landed than I was: if need be one could survive the night in my car. Gallant gentleman, you see, chugging chivalrously along behind. And presently I came upon her.

Came upon her is the word. I had done, I suppose, six

miles; I could just pick out her tracks with my headlights and I was following them rather than the occasional posts that marked the track, when very much the same thing happened as at the humpy bridge. Or began to happen. Down went my nose and up went my tail—and then there was the most appalling crash. In the stillness that followed, and as my wits were coming back to me, a female voice said gratefully: "Well, that's just sweet of you, stranger." Miss G.'s voice.

Sybil Guthrie—we may as well get a little more familiar—Sybil Guthrie had missed the track, gone over a bank, turned on her side, and crawled out. I had followed her over—a little higher up, for the Rolls had come down with a splintering concussion dead on top of her car. But I hadn't overturned and there I sat like a fool; I might have killed her. Anxious to do the right thing, I said solicitously: "Are you hurt?" She said: "Yes, really offended," and then she added more cheerfully: "Of course, if we're on fire there's plenty of snow. Does snow put out fires, though?"

But we weren't on fire. We sat each on a front wing of my car—the whole wreck seemed quite securely wedged—and warmed our hands on the radiator as we considered. Sybil—a nice girl—Sybil said she thought the village we'd gone finally wrong at was called Kinkeig; she'd been through it before and there was a pub if we could get back to it. Would that be best?

Quite proper instincts, you see, despite that appraising eye; out in the snow I was promoted from puppy to guardian St. Bernard at once. So I edged myself into the spot-light and looked uncommonly responsible and grave.

It had been snowing off and on all afternoon but at the moment—and apart from the fact that darkness had fallen—visibility was good. And as I edged myself I saw, far away but unmistakable, a single light. "I think," I said, "we'll make for the house straight ahead. Have you a small suitcase?"

It is unlikely—don't you think?—that Sybil was unimpressed; with just such brevity do the heroes speak. And, anyway, I thought I was saying the right thing; the village couldn't well be less than six miles, whereas the light—though lights can be enormously deceptive at night—could scarcely be more than two. Would you have dubitated or debated, Diana? Sybil just made a dive and yanked a suitcase—a small suitcase—out of the remains of her car. "Hieronimo," she said, " 'tis time for thee to trudge." A pleasant literary lady—as a Sybil should be.

The light must represent a dwelling and some sort of shelter; the danger was that we should lose it as we advanced. I left my spot-light on and directed it at a pretty prominent tree—which gave us a base we could probably get back to in an emergency—and then we set off. But not before the admirable Sybil had produced a healthy electric torch. Really, she might have come prepared for the whole affair.

What ensued was a sort of vest-pocket version of *The Worst Journey in the World*. It was dark, it was cold and there was, of course, snow. Indeed, "I'll say this is snow" was the only remark Sybil made *en route*. Sometimes we fell into it in all sorts of diverting ways, like people in the Christmas number of *Punch*. One would think it was a passive sort of stuff, snow. I assure you that time and again it positively surged up and buffeted us.

There were anxious periods while a hill or a line of trees was screening the light; there was a more anxious moment still when the light began to rise oddly in the air and I felt it might be twenty miles away after all and on top of a mountain range. Fifty yards further, however, and a blackness gathered round it more lustreless than the blackness of the sky. A vague bulk was defining itself; a few seconds more and we had succeeded in interpreting it. What was before us was a solitary light burning near the top of a high tower.

"Childe Rowland," I said, "to the dark tower came."

It was a trifle obvious—not at all up to Hieronimo—and I was quite glad that the words were drowned, somewhat alarmingly, by a sudden tremendous baying of hounds. But at that the obvious came to Sybil also. "Sir Leoline," she said, "the baron rich—"

"Hath a toothless mastiff bitch—"

"Which," Sybil said severely.

"I beg your pardon?"

"Which, not bitch."

"We'll look it up."

In the circumstances, you will say, a fantastic and foolish colloquy. And at this moment, as if to mark disapproval, the light went out. The hounds, however, carried on.

Rather nicely and chastely Sybil felt for my hand. "Mr. Gylby," she said—we had exchanged names—"I'm just a mite disheartened." So I gave a firm clasp—not the vulgar and suggestive thing you'd call a squeeze—and said in my brief way it was lucky the light hadn't gone out half an hour earlier. At that it appeared again for a moment, lower down and to the left. It vanished again and reappeared yet lower to the right. Someone was coming down a winding staircase.

I took a few steps forward and flashed the torch about the building; it gave sufficient light to show we had come upon something pretty sizeable. I was cheered by that; on such a night the gentry ought to do us proud; and I lowered the torch to see if we had been stumbling through a garden or along a carriage drive. What I saw made me give a little yelp: I was standing on the edge of an abyss. "Moat," said Sybil. She put a hand on the torch and flashed it to the left. "Drawbridge." I think she was rather thrilled; it was my turn to be a mite disheartened. I knew these castles: there would be icicles depending from the noses of the trophies in the hall—just as in the one I'd escaped from that morning. "Will you dreadfully mind," I asked, "sleeping in the haunted room?" To which she replied briskly: "I'm not psychic, Mr. Gylby," and added: "Look!"

Low down and over to the right there had appeared a crack of light. Cautious exploration along the edge of the moat revealed a second bridge—non-drawable—and over this a little postern door had been opened an inhospitable inch. We crossed, our feet crunching in the snow. At our nearer approach the hounds revved up, but still no more than an inch of candle-light showed through the door. So I knocked. Whereupon a plebeian voice said: "Is that the doctor?"

They'd got us wrong. "We are two people," I explained to the chink of candle-light, "that have had a motor accident." For it seemed fair enough to put it as strongly as that and I was all out to strike the note of pathos. But the information was not a success. The chink vanished. The door shut.

Sybil said: "I'll say!" I won't say what I said. But as I was saying it there came a development—nothing less than a great clanking of chains. Sybil said: "The Ghost!"

You will agree, Diana, that the days of keeping women in happy ignorance are over. I said: "The dogs."

But hard upon this agitating situation things ameliorated rapidly. A gentleman's voice made itself heard—presumably rebuking the churlish custodian—and then the door was flung open and the same voice said: "Please come in."

So in we went, each clutching a suitcase as if the place were a hotel. Our host had hold of Sybil's in a flash and said with the sort of heavy courtesy distinguished old persons can manage: "Welcome to Erchany. My name is Guthrie."

Said Sybil in her most fetching American: "How strange! My name is Guthrie too."

Mr. Guthrie of Erchany gave her a quick look with an eye that gleamed in the candle-light. "An additional occasion," he said, "for such hospitality as we can contrive. First, we must find you rooms and a fire."

All just as it should be and hardly worth so lengthily writing home about (darling, darling Diana!). All as it should be—and strange therefore that I received the immediate impression that this Mr. Guthrie is *mad*. I think he is mad, and what's more I thought he was mad before I had really viewed his Mad-as-a-Hatter's Castle.

It was something in his eye, I believe, as he first looked us over in that uncertain glimmer from his candle. Perhaps it is merely that he is a mathematician or a chess-player, for I had the oddest feeling as he looked at us that he was really plotting us on invisible graph or giving us our places on an invisible board. Perhaps, again, I was just feeling a bit of a pawn: one does after all that snow. But whatever the cause of my first impression, the feeling has grown on me since. And the dogs were the next thing that helped.

Of course one is careful to keep one's dogs in good condition through the winter and all that, but these dogs—the two that accompanied us in search of rooms and a fire—are starving: something quite out of the way in a country gentleman's house. I was devoutly thankful their less domesticated companions—still giving tongue in some court near by—hadn't been loosed off at us as first planned. And at that I glanced round for the retainer who had so unkindly received us. For a moment the laird of Erchany seemed to be quite alone, and then I became aware of a ruffian skulking in the shadows. This proved presently to be the Hardcastle I've mentioned; he looked ready and willing to brain us for our small change, and he was introduced with ceremony as the laird's factor. A factor, you know, means an agent, and his employment usually implies considerable estates. So it is odd that the laird's factor is undoubtedly a sort of butler and odd man as well—and odd that the laird himself appears to be in the deepest poverty.

Erchany is the strangest place. A wind had been rising during our walk, a really cold night wind that added considerably to the general discomfort. But when there is one wind outside there are about twenty winds in Erchany. One was blowing straight up the long corridor we were first led down, and on the floor a worn and tattered carpet was working like a sea, flowing towards us in little billows like some surface in a dream. A cross wind was blowing snowflakes through broken panes in a long line of windows, and these were caught by some further current and quite weirdly sucked up the staircase we presently ascended. It is a beautiful staircase, stone and with a great balustrade of fretted stone that must be the work of French mediaeval craftsmen, on each landing rampant monsters in stone with what I take to be the Guthrie motto: *Touch not the Tyger*. Not, Sybil whispered, homey—but impressive in a gloomy way. And that, incidentally, might describe our host, a tall, gaunt, aloof person, with strongly marked features and heavy—haunted, I was going to write—lines round the mouth and eyes; an intimidating old man even to a back view, which was all we had at the moment as he led us down a rather windier upper corridor, the cut-throat Hardcastle padding along with the suitcases behind. We met nobody—unless a scuttling rat or two be worth mentioning—until we came to a couple of facing doors: Miss Guthrie to the right, Mr. Gylby to the left. And on the threshold the laird of Erchany paused: was I, by chance, related to Horatio Gylby? It always pleases me to acknowledge great-uncle Horatio, that eminent *fin-de-siècle* professor of bad living and worse verse—so I said Yes, and that I had been his favourite great-nephew. Whereupon old Mr. Guthrie looked at me with a sort of absent interest, and murmured that once they had exchanged their compositions. So I suppose he is a poet. One wouldn't think of Erchany as a canary cage, or that the local owls have anything in the way of rivals as melodists. I now conclude that when the good laird gives me that peculiar chess-player's look he is simply searching for a rhyme for Gylby.

Sybil's room is rather nice; it seems to stand ready as a guest-room, which is somehow unexpected. A bed as broad as a battlefield, snowy sheets—not the right association for our comfort at the moment, this—and everything tolerably shipshape, with the only broken window pane neatly patched with brown paper. But in my quarters the establishment crashes badly: flutterings in the gloom of the ceiling; scamperings in the dirt of the floor; the bed undraped but not, alas, untenanted; the Erchany winds here playing unaccountably at slow motion and eddying in a stately saraband about the room. Guthrie, it must be said, did look round a little doubtfully. "Hardcastle," he called, "get your wife."

Diana, Mrs. Hardcastle; Mrs. Hardcastle, Miss Diana Sandys! Don't mind staring, Diana—I think the old lady's next to blind. And isn't she a beauty? No doubt Hardcastle, who can't be more than fifty, took her for the sake of her old-age pension—or perhaps she made a little fortune as the Bearded Lady in a circus. If these appear brutal remarks think of a fine gentlemanlike Renaissance poet having a good go at describing a witch; that will serve for the rest. Come to think of it, Laird Guthrie may very well be an enchanter and keep a witch or two on hand. I wouldn't put it beyond him indeed. But I suspect Mrs. Hardcastle has a kind heart: in a fumbling sort of way she made fires, brought really hot water, brought towels, even thought to bring soap—albeit of the kitchen variety—and a certain amount of bedding for my uninviting couch. And after that Guthrie said with a bow that we should meet for supper at nine.

We met—and at this point you meet Christine. I haven't at all got Christine yet, but in her way she is as striking as Guthrie, who seems to be her uncle. Striking perhaps in a temporary fashion—by which I mean that last night at our curious supper she was a pretty girl looking beautiful. And than that there is only one more absolutely beautiful thing: a plain girl looking beautiful. But don't worry, Diana, if you're out of the running for the absolute degree. You'll do. Indeed you will.

A pretty girl, as shy as a village girl and with a soft Scottish accent that chimes charmingly with Sybil's; a shy, smouldering girl with the manners—or manner—of an old-fashioned fine lady and seemingly quite without acquaintance with the world: this is Christine. A Scottish Miranda I thought as I watched her at that meal. And the notion grew on me—for she was Miranda in Miranda's first great scene, listening dutifully enough to the talk of Prospero, but the whole of her far away, straining out it might be over a stormy sea where she knew that fate was working for her. If this is rhapsodical or extravagant remember I am writing—at break of dawn—from an enchanter's castle.

In a lofty hall—like the staircase, it is on a scale that would make you think Erchany a much bigger place than it really is—the enchanter sat at one end of a tremendous great table and Christine at the other, Sybil and I islanded one on each side, and all of us in need of much more warmth than came from the small fire in the fireplace—a fireplace within which we might all have huddled round the embers and been a good deal more comfortable than we were. The villain Hardcastle had withdrawn—the Hardcastles, it seems, live in a separate part of the house—and the meal was served partly by his decrepit old wife and partly by Christine; so I was confirmed in my impression that the domestic resources of Erchany are limited. And indeed there are everywhere signs of either the most improbable poverty or a pathological parsimony. For instance, the whole of these proceedings were lit by a quite inadequate tallow candle-power; I think Guthrie may have looked the more sinister, Christine the more beautiful and Sybil the more enigmatic—did I tell you Sybil looks enigmatic?—as a result of being never out of a half shadow. I was just preparing to accept the theory that the land owners in these parts are unusually picturesque examples of the new poor when Mrs. Hardcastle tottered in with the first course. Diana dear, it was caviare, and served on silver plate.

This was what the North Britons appear to call a *scunner*—and the whole meal was equally surprising: it was much as if the Guthries, having prospered in the city, had returned to hold an expensive picnic amid the ruins of their former feudal greatness. I am afraid I looked from the tumble-down hall to the lavish canned eats, and from the eats to the emaciated dogs, and from the dogs to Mr. Guthrie of Erchany with ill-concealed bewilderment, for I noticed Christine regarding me with the same sort of absent interest her uncle had displayed in Horatio Gylby's kinsman—absent interest tinged with amusement. She was speculating, I imagine, on just how well or ill the polite young Englishman would carry off the peculiar situation in which he found himself.

For it was not, you will apprehend, a very comfortable meal. Guthrie occasionally uttered a courteous remark or enquiry: what was the state of our cars; had we friends near, and would they know we had come up the Erchany road? But in the main he was silent, either staring over our heads in some profound abstraction, or occasionally dropping and narrowing that chess-player's eye on us in a way I found myself liking less and less. I believe Sybil was aware of it; as you know she has an eye of her own, and I had a feeling she was beginning to pay him back in his own coin—anyway, she was studying him thoughtfully enough. It was Christine who chiefly bore the social burden: very nicely in her shy way. But she too had an eye, Miranda's eye, dilated in search of things to come. It was her eye, no doubt, directed my ear to the clock.

It is a big grandfather clock, nearly old enough to be in keeping with the hall, and with a loud and—as you would think—peculiarly slow tick. You know how competent actors can build up an illusion of overwhelming suspense, of mere, sheer waiting? I suddenly found the clock doing all that for me. In other words I found myself projecting upon an elderly and impersonal scientific instrument a mounting and urgent sense of impending catastrophe. A trick of fatigue and insufficient nourishment, I told myself—and turned conscientiously to tinned plum pudding and a generous brandy sauce. But the clock still ticked in the same menacing way. By the time Christine had taken Sybil out of the hall I was next to hypnotized by it: had it suddenly gesticulated with both its hands and cried out, *Sleep no more, Macbeth does murder sleep!* I should have been scared indeed but not surprised. And though suggestible, you know, I'm not wantonly goofy. It was Erchany was all strung up and waiting, and I was just getting the vibrations.

But presently I had what you may think a lucid interval—a simple and rational explanation of the tension in the air. Somewhere in the house there must be someone pretty seriously ill. Had not Hardcastle, when he opened his little door so cautiously, called out to ask if we were the doctor?

What they were waiting for was medical aid through these appalling snows, and our arrival must be a disappointment which had been politely masked. There seemed only two objections to this: first, the grudging and almost conspiratorial way in which Hardcastle had opened that inch of door (but that might be just his nature); second, if the emergency were sufficient to cause marked strain, it would have been natural to enquire whether Sybil or I was by any chance surgically given (but perhaps we look rather young). This idea lasted me about five minutes, and was shattered by Guthrie himself. "Mr. Gylby," he said as we rose from the table, "the snow may detain you some time and you must excuse our very simple way of living. Apart from a lad out in the offices, my niece and myself with the two Hardcastles form our entire household."

I made suitable noises about the trouble to which Miss Mathers—Christine, that is—was being put. Whereupon Guthrie foraged an unbroken box of cigars, held open a door and said with gravity: "I am glad you found your way here."

I am not sure whether the inner jolt I felt at that moment was mysteriously occasioned by these innocent words, or whether it was the result of the simultaneous appearance of the unspeakable Hardcastle, who seemed to have been hovering on the other side of the door, and who now came shambling forward much like one of the less pleasing devils of Hieronymus van Bosch. He appeared to be on the spot by arrangement; perhaps he comes every night at this hour for orders—certainly Guthrie wasted no time in giving him an order now. "Hardcastle," he said peremptorily, "if the lad Lindsay comes—though I don't think he can get up in the snow—you must let him in. I'll see him once again."

Hardcastle slowly drew a hand from behind his slouching back—I rather expected an open razor—and gave a dubious rub at an unshaven chin. Then he said—with what I took to be an effort at the surly fidelity characteristic of retainers in the best Scottish fiction—"If you'll believe me, laird, the lad's black dangerous."

"What's that, man?" The laird had stopped and was glaring

at his factor with what looked, in the dusky corridor, downright malignity.

"I say Neil Lindsay means mischief."

The solicitous vassal turn or whatever it was cut, it seemed, very little ice with the laird. "Lindsay," he said dryly, "can come up to the tower. Mr. Gylby, the ladies."

And on we went. My responses were becoming sluggish; we were half-way down the corridor before it occurred to me to doubt whether Guthrie had been quite as unmoved by the curious soothsayer-business as he had appeared. I think it may have been that I was not unmoved myself: the incident gave me something I had been searching for. I had dubbed the Erchany atmosphere *suspense;* I now suspected I might equally well have dubbed it *fear.* But who was afraid—and of what?

I had got to this point in my meditations—you will say I was badly in need of bed and sleep—when I nearly jumped out of my skin. Guthrie had said aloud: "Fear." Or rather he had said it in Latin: "Timor . . ." Softly but distinctly he had murmured: "*Timor Mortis conturbat me.*"

A glance at him showed he had forgotten my existence—at that I remembered I believed him mad. And striding down the corridor with his eye fixed somewhere near the ceiling he continued to recite.

> "Clerk of Tranent eik he has tane,
> That maid the anteris of Gawane;
> Schir Gilbert Hay endit has he;
> *Timor Mortis conturbat me.*
>
> "He has Blind Hary, et Sandy Traill
> Slaine with his schour of mortall haill,
> Quhilk Patrik Iohnestoun myght nought fle;
> *Timor Mortis conturbat me. . . .*"

Diana, you have never assisted at anything half so weird as the spectacle of this uncanny Scottish gentleman walking wrapt down his windy crumbling corridor, chanting that tremendous dirge of Dunbar's!

"He hes tane Roull of Aberdene,
And gentill Roull of Corstorphine;
Two bettir fallowis did no man se;
Timor Mortis conturbat me. . . ."

We turned a corner and the wind blew the words away from me, so that they became only a murmuring. At the same moment the candle spurted and I had momentarily a better view of his face than I have yet had in this murky house. And I swear the fear of Death was really stark on him.

The second corridor seemed interminable. At length we halted before a door, and I guessed that Sybil and Christine were on the other side. Guthrie was immobile, the rhythm of his murmuring had changed, he was looking at or through the door with an expression that now, I thought, held something of exultation. And then he cried out—but softly—

"Oh, my America, my new-found land!"

Once more, it was a *scunner*. And so was the succeeding moment. His hand fell to the latch of the door, and instantly his mind flicked back to me. He gave me a polite smile and said: "I usually spend half an hour here with my niece." I believe he can have had no recollection whatever of that chanting progress down the corridor. In other words, he seems almost a case of dissociated personality: two distinct Guthries, you know, playing hide and seek like twins in a stage farce. I was developing this picturesque thought—the miserly Guthrie *A* who starved his dogs and wouldn't repair his windows, the lavish Guthrie *B* who stuffed tinned caviare—I was developing this for some time after we had joined Christine and Sybil in what is called the schoolroom. It suggested another possible explanation of Hardcastle's calling out about the doctor: the laird was having a bout of this mild madness and the household was waiting quietly to smuggle in a leech. Not perhaps a brilliant idea—but that phrase of the indescribable Hardcastle's was beginning to worry me. *Is that the doctor?* I have decided that if Erchany holds a secret the key to it is in the explanation of that question.

Diana, if this rambling recital is interesting no doubt you will want to interrupt here and say: "Guthrie expects the dangerous Neil Lindsay; Hardcastle expects the mysterious doctor: surely they are likely to be one and the same person—Dr. Neil Lindsay, who is not necessarily expected in a professional way? What about his being, say, an undesirable suitor of your romantic Christine?"

On this nice point I can give you no reasonable satisfaction. That Christine has a lover—that she is in the state of having nothing but a lover on her whole horizon—I readily agree. And the lover may be Neil Lindsay—or he may be Hardcastle's "doctor." But that these two are one I somehow don't believe: something in the abominable Hardcastle's voice in speaking of them forbids it. Time may show.

It is time perhaps to say a word on time. It is now eight o'clock on the morning of Tuesday, 24th December; these dedicated pages, dear Diana, have occupied me for just three and a half hours—including pauses to relight the candle. For the wind has been rising steadily and this room is a very hall of Aeolus: giant winds bumping about on the ceiling, baby winds gambolling like cinquecento *putti* and trying out their tender voices beneath the bed. My last night's fire is a remote memory; it is quite fiendishly cold; I am sitting by the window—that being no colder than anywhere else—in a sort of igloo made of feather mattress, hoping for some sort of present summons to breakfast. Outside, the still falling snow is being drifted quite terrifically and I see hardly a chance of getting away for days. There was some talk last night, though, of the miraculous prowess as a snow traveller of Erchany's odd lad. So, if I am stuck, there is just a chance of getting a wire away to you by him. It must be long past dawn now, but visibility still poor, the sky is so leaden. From this window I see just dim, whirling whiteness. Only left-centre is there a break, a dark gleam that has been puzzling me for the last twenty minutes. It is as if the snow were melting away from a surface of hot dark steel: I believe it must be water—the frozen arm of a loch that curls right up to the castle—and this howling gale driving the ice clear of snow.

No sign of life or breakfast—so I add a few further notes on last night. The schoolroom where Christine had her learning—she has seldom if ever been away from Erchany, I gather—is now a pleasant, rather bare, species of den—Miranda's corner of the cave, furnished with a few elegant mementoes of Milan: in this case a really beautiful Flemish cabinet and some Indian bird-paintings that deserve a better light than the couple of candles that seem the standard illumination in public rooms in Erchany. When Guthrie and I entered we found Christine and Sybil sitting side by side on a low stool before the fire, apparently on the way to becoming friends. They both got up: Sybil's glance, I noticed, came straight to Guthrie; Christine's was lingering with something like puzzlement on Sybil. I remember wondering how we were all going to get on together without the help of eating and drinking.

Formality was our refuge. I was handed, more or less on a plate, to Christine, and presently found myself conscientiously developing a vein of subdued gaiety—embodied earlier in this budget, my dear—on my day's adventures. I don't think Christine is normally the sort that wouldn't relish a young man abruptly pitched out of the world into Erchany on a winter's night, or that she hasn't the wit and will to prick and quicken the gaiety of such a one with mockery. I am a sociable person; I meet dozens of young women in a year; and half a dozen, perhaps, are right for something like interesting personal relations. One knows at once, does one not? And Christine is right: very shy though she is, we ought to have been reacting to each other in from eight to ten minutes. Do you observe, Diana, the note of pique creeping in? She was quite charming, but if you imagine a political duchess thinking out a difficult manoeuvre at a party while being quite charming meantime to a stray young man who may be of middling importance in thirty years' time, you will get the effect almost exactly. Exactly—because Christine, though a slip of a rural lass, has an old-fashioned poise that is very engaging: I am consumed with curiosity as to how she has been brought up here. Point is, though, that there we sat, and that I went through my tricks, and that she registered just the right interest and amusement, and put in just the necessary number of words of her own—and that all the time she was profoundly unaware of me. Occasion, as I say, for slight pique.

Christine—I perhaps wearisomely reiterate—is *waiting:* waiting as brides must have waited when the world was younger. Undoubtedly, it is a lover!

And Guthrie is waiting too: only his waiting I just can't guess at—perhaps he has a date with the ghosts of Clerk of Tranent and Sir Mungo Lockhart of the Lea. But, in a way, he was putting up even a better show than the competent Christine; his taciturnity was gone, he was leading the conversation with Sybil and doing her really proud in point of courteous attention. I suppose his craziness to go with a great sense of what is owing in a laird of Erchany. When my attention drifted to them he was showing Sybil a case of curios—gold coins and medals mostly—which he had fetched from another room. Christine made an excuse of my momentarily drifting eye to move me across the room; I'm terribly afraid that—tête-à-tête—she'd had enough of me.

Guthrie was handing a little medallion affair to Sybil. "You recognize," he said, "the device?"

I recognized it at once from the creatures on the staircase. It was Guthrie's crest. Sybil took it, handled it delicately, and said nothing.

"The family crest," said Guthrie. "It has occurred to me, my dear young lady, to wonder if we may be related?"

Guthrie, of course, is the sort of old person who can say *my dear young lady:* nevertheless, I obscurely felt the bland phrase give—paradoxically—edge to the question.

Rather unexpectedly, Sybil gushed. "Mr. Guthrie, wouldn't that be just wonderful! I know my father was terribly proud of his Scotch connections. And I'd just love to think I was related to a romantic old place like your castle. It must be terribly old?"

You mustn't think Christine has extinguished my admiration for Sybil: I think Sybil quite remarkable, will-o'-the-wisp though she has been to me. And now I opened my eyes rather wide, for her reaction to Guthrie's polite suggestion was just a little too good to be true. But if my eyes opened I believe Guthrie's narrowed. Punctiliously, he answered his guest's question. "It is old. There are thirteenth-century foundations." And then he went on carefully: "We have connections, I know, in the United States. Families like ours do not care to lose sight even of distant branches."

"Mr. Guthrie—how exciting! And I am sure they love to come and visit Erchany."

"They have not visited me." And I think Guthrie smiled. "Not, that is, as far as I know." There was a pause. "But a year or two ago they sent—friends."

Christine was not rubbing shoulders with me; I must have sensed, rather than felt, her shiver. I know I glanced round at her quickly. And I believe I caught on her face what I had already caught on her uncle's: fear.

Guthrie waiting and Christine waiting—but not perhaps for the same thing. Guthrie afraid and Christine afraid—again not perhaps of the same thing. Here, in a word, is my preoccupation—almost my anxiety—of the moment; here—Diana—is the Mystery of Castle Erchany!

Sybil was not very oncoming about her family and Guthrie did not press her beyond his first polite suggestion of relationship. Instead his conversation drifted to his childhood, oddly, I thought—for though the picture of the elderly laird entertaining his guests with the golden memories of an Erchany infancy was pretty enough, it yet seemed false to the basic reserve of the man. Presently he was inviting Sybil's memories in exchange and it occurred to me rather sleepily that he was going after her family again in a ferreting way. But his interest seemed actually to be more general; he might have been a student of American social history, interested in the trend and tone of American life some twenty years ago. Sybil comes from Cincinnati, Ohio—I gathered that much—and I'm not sure there isn't something peculiarly hypnoidal about the words. Cincinnati, Ohio . . . Cincinnati, Ohio: beautiful, sleepy cadences I found myself drifting away on. And then I woke up with a jerk.

Guthrie had moved over to the dying fire and was standing before it with a small log in his hands: I think he didn't want to provide more firing than need be. And as he hesitated Christine said: "You seem to be in two minds."

Not much, you will say, to wake a chap up—rather less than the little crash with which the log immediately fell among the embers. But the remark held all the temper I had been expecting in Christine: into the words she was putting, I knew, a whole desperate situation and she was getting from them the fierce relief that a flash of wit can give. Whatever she felt Guthrie to be in two minds about was something that was vital to her.

And after this I remember, as they say, nothing more. We sat for some time longer, Sybil and myself waiting for bed and Guthrie and Christine waiting for I don't know what—but certainly something as immediate as a step in the corridor or a cry in the night. But by half-past ten the charm of the mysterious had waned and I was glad when we were reconducted up the great staircase to our rooms.

I spare you details of the horror of the night—the more willingly as Mrs. Hardcastle has just put her head into the room and said: "Won't you be wanting your breakfast?" The rats had certainly wanted their supper, as had a variety of lesser vermin too: meditate the discomposing effect of these before you judge hardly of my disjointed notes on Castle Erchany. I slept for a couple of hours or so and was awakened perhaps by a rat taking an exploratory nibble at my toe, perhaps merely by the owls in the snow-laden ivy by my window. Normally I rather dote on owls, but the owlishness of the Erchany variety is something overpowering. I counted several varieties, all hooting depression or despair, and at least one the note of which was strange to me—a high long-drawn-out *too-ee* that really froze the blood. The dogs threw in a howl from time to time; it was hard not to believe they were wolves—or werewolves, it might be, in the spell of the enchanter. And, always, there was the wind. In still weather Erchany must be full of whisperings: in a storm it is full of great voices, crying words and phrases one just can't catch. Perhaps after all I shall get away this morning, and to Edinburgh later in the day, and to town by an early train to-morrow.

Believe it, Diana, that the most heroical efforts will be made by your lover

NOEL.

2

Christmas Eve at night

NO go. Infuriatingly, I am hung up by blizzard for all the world like an antarctic explorer a march short of his depot. The village—Kinkeig—is just a short antarctic march away—nine miles or thereabouts—but the conditions are hopeless: the posts that serve to mark the track in common snowfalls will be most of them buried; a great wind and a steady fall between them surround one with a dizzying curtain of white the moment one steps beyond the door; and every hour the drifts must be becoming deeper and, I suppose, more dangerous. Even our prodigious Tammas—the Erchany odd lad, that is, who turns out to be a sort of low-grade moron (a nice finish, surely, to the amenities of the castle)—even Tammas is halted by this storm. So I must resign myself—Diana, maiden and mistress of the months and stars!—to your spending Christmas ignorant, alarmed and furious. That's the worst of being so closely netted round by civilization; it's hard to imagine a person dropping tolerably comfortably through and out of it without disaster suffered. I haven't broken a limb—or anything more than a nice young lady's baby car—and I haven't been put in gaol; I've simply got myself nine miles from the nearest telephone in a spot of dirty weather.

And I'm bored. After all my lucubrations in the small hours this is something of an anticlimax, but the mystery of Erchany fades away rather—as you might expect—in the light of common day. My host was the linchpin of my imaginings and to-day he has remained invisible, sending civil messages that he is a little unwell. Perhaps the caviare was too much for him; I don't believe somehow that caviare is a regular part of the Erchany diet. You know it *was* a mysterious supper. I believe the Erchany equivalent of the fatted calf would be a spot of stewed rabbit—and why even stew the rabbit without a prodigal son? Because Sybil may be all unknowing a prodigal second cousin thrice removed? Surely not. Or in honour of the favourite great-nephew of the deplorable Horatio? Surely, again, not.

We have been left to ourselves rather, Sybil and I. Christine has presided at two meals—simple enough this time—and vanished away on the plea of vaguely described duties. After breakfast she took us up to a long sort of gallery-place, full of dead Guthries and still-born theology, and invited us with downright malice to choose a book; after luncheon she bowed us into a billiard room, whisked a dustcloth off the identical table, one must believe, with which Noah beguiled the tedious hour, and said: All American women played? Tricks gaily and fantastically performed; the devil or an angel has entered into Christine to-day; she has put her fears—if I wasn't imagining them—behind her. And still she is beautiful..

So Sybil and I played billiards. There are no cues, one of the pockets is missing, and a fair part of the cloth has gone to nourish generations of moths; still, wrapped in our overcoats, we have played a sort of billiards and rather enjoyed it. Mrs. Hardcastle brought us two large cups of villainous tea and stood for about half an hour listening to the click of the balls as if it were something as good as a wireless set. We have even had some conversation with her—thanks to the initiative of Sybil, who suspected the old soul might want a gossip.

"Do you have much company at Erchany, Mrs. Hardcastle?"

Mrs. Hardcastle looked bewildered. "You're saying, Miss?"

"Do you have many visitors?"

Syllable by syllable Mrs. Hardcastle digested this. Then she shook her head with decision. "The laird's over narrow." She nodded with a sort of gloomy satisfaction. "There are few in these parts nearer-going than Guthrie of Erchany."

This was hardly a theme we could with propriety pursue—though Mrs. Hardcastle had rather the air of regarding it as a main asset of the establishment. And Sybil was just casting round for another theme when the old person sank her voice to an eager whisper and said: "It's the rats!"

"The rats, Mrs. Hardcastle?"

"The Guthries have ever had black imaginings. He thinks the rats are fair eating him up—him and all his substance. He's that near-going as he is because he thinks he's fighting the rats. If you please—there will be plenty of places with no rats—islands and such?"

We made embarrassed affirmative noises.

"They should get him away to an island. I told the doctors that when they came. He'd sleep of nights then and be fine, poor gentleman."

Sybil said awkwardly: "You think Mr. Guthrie is very worried by the rats?"

Again Mrs. Hardcastle gave her vigorous, senile nod. "And he won't spend his silver on the poison for them. He says he prefers his wee penknife."

So many bloodthirsty persons in the Scottish ballads perform unlikely feats of slaughter with their wee penknives that I suspected here a little literary joke of the laird's. But Mrs. Hardcastle went on seriously: "Real skilly he is at the throwing of it. And right loudly the creatures squeal."

Unedifying revelations these, I thought, of the perversion

of sporting instinct in the country gentry: Mrs. Hardcastle's confidences were making me distinctly uncomfortable. But Sybil was interested. "He goes about spearing the rats?"

"Just that. And now it's a hatchet. Sharpening and sharpening it yesterday he was in the court. And cried out at me right fearsome: 'To settle accounts with a great rat, Mrs. Hardcastle!' I wish he'd settle accounts with them all. I wish there were no rats. They squeal inside my head at night."

A cheery old soul. Sybil said rather feebly: "Couldn't Mr. Hardcastle get rid of them?"

Mrs. Hardcastle peered nervously about her. Her whisper grew hoarser. "Hardcastle's right unkind!"

I believed her. At the same time I felt that a recital of the domestic infelicities of the Hardcastles would be singularly lacking in charm and I banged the billiard balls quite violently as a possible distraction. Their music, however, had ceased to compel; the unsightly old person advanced unheeding and laid a claw-like hand on Sybil's arm. "And for why?"

Neither of us felt capable of dealing with this idiomatic demand. But Mrs. Hardcastle scarcely gave us time to answer. Her voice sank yet farther to an impossible croak. "It's the rats!"

We both said blankly: "The rats!"

Mrs. Hardcastle's affirmative nod this time involved not her head merely but her whole body: if I remember aright witches and bad fairies indulge just such emphatic bobs in pantomime. "I'm right fashed I didn't think to warn you last night. There's a terrible number of rats in Erchany."

Variations on a theme. Come, Muse, let's sing of rats. And Mrs. Hardcastle went on, a horrid and growing conviction in her voice: "It's the rats. For years now they've been working on my man. The rat-nature working on him! I think they go through his head at night, squealing—the coarse creatures. He's half turned to rat now and he feels it. It makes him right unkind. What will become of us? I lie in bed at night, Miss, and whiles the rats go squealing through my head and whiles my man. But more and more my man's like a great grey rat, and what will become of us when I can't any longer ell man from rat?"

Mrs. Hardcastle, you will agree, has a knack of posing awkward questions that would do credit to a nineteenth-century Scandinavian play. At the same time she plainly has, as an imaginative psychologist, a touch of genius and her conversation, if somewhat limited in range, has powerfully reinvoked the atmosphere that was so heavy about us last night. I was just going to explore her views on the influence of the Erchany rats on the moron Tammas when Sybil said abruptly: "Mrs. Hardcastle, has the doctor come?"

Interesting that the doctor had continued to puzzle Sybil as well as myself; more interesting that the question drew a complete blank. "The doctor, Miss?"

"I thought you were expecting a doctor last night."

"Faith, Miss, we never expect anyone at Erchany. Dr. Noble at Dunwinnie is the family doctor, but he hasn't been here these two years—not since Miss Christine sprained her wrist. There were some doctors a year or two back—the same I told you of—and it was but a sad welcome the laird gave them. Were *you* expected?"

The question suggested that outside the rodent sphere the good Mrs. Hardcastle's perceptions are dim. We said our arrival was singularly unpremeditated. Whereupon she looked from one to the other of us doubtfully before turning again to Sybil. "I just thought that seeing you are a kinswoman of the laird—"

But at this point Sybil, whose interest had been waning and who was rolling the balls vigorously about the table, hurled a ball clean over the cushion and into the pit of old Mrs. Hardcastle's stomach.

"Oh, Mrs. Hardcastle, I'm most terribly sorry—"

Mrs. Hardcastle picked up the ball and looked at Sybil with great respect. Her voice took on its familiar hoarsest tone. "Faith, Miss, were you after one of the rats? There's a terrible number of rats in Erchany."

With that, Diana, I think you've made the grand tour of

Mrs. Hardcastle: other facets there may be, but as yet they have not revealed themselves.

Which reminds me I rather want to make the grand tour of the castle. It seems a rambling place, added to from time to time in a fashion more or less in keeping with its mediaeval character. The oldest part, plainly, is the central keep or tower; I gather that the laird has his own set of rooms there and seldom comes out of them. So his indisposition may be a polite fiction. Still, if he is supposed to be keeping his own rooms, unwell, one can't very decently explore in that direction. It will be dinner or supper time presently, and I am waiting with the futile bored impatience with which one waits for a meal in a dull hotel. I look forward, it must be confessed, to another appearance of Christine, and perhaps I can make the beguiling mysteriousness of the place serve as amusement for another twelve or twenty-four hours. But I am so annoyed that I am not far on the other side of the Tweed!

Christmas Eve at night—and my birthday. Shall I hang up my stocking for the owls to nest in and the rats to gnaw? What sort of presents, I wonder, come to Castle Erchany this season? I look out of my window and see that there is a lull in the gale; the gloaming is falling over a landscape wonderfully still, peaceful, white. *Noel*, Diana, *Noel!*

Your

NOEL.

3

Christmas morning

HUNG be the heavens with black, yield day to night! My scribblings of the last two days have proved an induction to real tragedy. Mr. Ranald Guthrie of Erchany is dead.

It is all so fantastic—as well as rather horrible—that I

really doubt if I can change the key in which I have been writing. Erchany is still the enchanted castle; only the enchantment has grown murky as one of great-uncle Horatio's poems, and the enchanter—great-uncle Horatio's sometime crony—is with Roull of Aberdene and gentill Roull of Corstorphine. Strange that as he walked down the corridor the other night Guthrie was chanting his own lament!

> Our plesance heir is all vane glory,
> This fals warld is bot transitory,
> The flesche is brukle, the Feyind is sle;
> *Timor Mortis conturbat me.*
>
> Onto the ded goes all Estatis,
> Princis, Prelotis, and Potestatis,
> Both riche et pur of all degre;
> *Timor Mortis conturbat me.*
>
> He spairis no lord for his piscence,
> Na clerk for his intelligence;
> His awfull strak may no man fle;
> *Timor Mortis conturbat me.*
>
> Art—magicianis, and astrologgis,
> Rethoris, logicianis, et theologgis . . .

But to work—which is getting down on paper an account of what has happened. It may be useful; and it is still my journal for you, Diana. It will be some hours more before the world—doctors, police, lawyers—can get to Erchany; and I don't at all know how soon after that I shall get away. It is the unpleasant fact that I am involved in what may be an affair of murder. A strange Christmas Day.

I have first to persuade you—and myself—that while the sheets preceding have been an expedient for beguiling the time they are in no sense romancing. They give events accurately, and they give quite accurately too my own perhaps temperamental reactions to events. Nevertheless, I had better give a paragraph to recapitulating without fancy.

Miss Guthrie and I arrived at Erchany, unheralded and with every appearance of sheer accident, late on Monday evening. Hardcastle was rather stealthily on the lookout for a doctor. We were politely enough received by Guthrie into what appeared to be the household of a confirmed miser—though with curious elements of expense in the supper. The make-up of the household was noteworthy: the anomalous factotum Hardcastle a striking scoundrel, his wife weak minded, the odd boy half witted, the laird himself powerfully witted and perhaps powerfully made—I am over the line of facts here, for I would cut a poor figure trying to speak to Guthrie's mental condition in a witness-box. But an undoubted fact, if a mysterious one, is the sense of strain and waiting—a sort of electric current flowing round and between Guthrie, his niece Christine Mathers, and certain unknown outside persons or events. A further fact was Hardcastle's warning about the dangerousness of a certain Neil Lindsay. After that there are merely matters of impression. First, something about Sybil Guthrie's attitude to her kinsman's household and the way in which Guthrie told her his American cousins had "sent friends." To this, as you will hear presently, I hold a key. Second, the way Christine told her uncle he was "in two minds." And third, the way Guthrie said to me: "I am glad you found your way here." These utterances were *charged;* they stand—somehow—full in the picture; I give them the status of enigmatic facts. There may, of course, be other points of equal significance buried in my narrative but at the moment I can't dig them out.

And now the events leading to Guthrie's death. I don't know that you will be surprised to learn that the first matter to be recorded concerns a *rat.*

Christine appeared alone again at supper last night. I think she was rather stumped in the schoolroom afterwards for some method of entertaining us, and she ended by showing us a portfolio of her sketches that lay on a table as if in process of being packed up—rapid, economical impressions mostly of wild geese over Loch Cailie. But she was at once shyer and more secretly possessed than before and soon she slipped away. A few minutes later Sybil said it was cold—as indeed it was—and that she was going to read in bed. And a few minutes after that I went upstairs myself, having in my head the plan of a rat-proof tent on an improved model in which to spend the night. It was in furtherance of this ambitious project that I began studying the creatures.

The most obvious classifications were by size and colour. There were big rats and little rats, brown rats, grey rats and—what I feel vaguely is something very choice—black rats; and there were indeterminate rats of a piebald or mildewed sort. There were a few fat rats and a great many lean rats, a few lazy rats and a great many active rats—these categories overlapping substantially—and there was a possible classification too into bold and bolder. As far as I could see there were no really timid rats, despite the consternation that must sometimes be caused by the wee penknife of the laird. All this was more or less as one might expect in a mansion in which the rodent kind have it nearly all their own way. What really startled me was the sporadic appearance of *learned* rats. These are, I suppose, even rarer than the pink and blue varieties.

Learned rats. Rats, that is to say, lugging laboriously round with them little paper scrolls—rather like students who have just been given a neatly-printed degree. I am not sure whether I saw in all two or three of these learned rats.

My first thought was that Guthrie must be amusing his solitary days by conducting experiments—the business of tying labels on whales to discover how long it takes them to swim round the world. And I was sufficiently intrigued to go learned-rat hunting, getting quite worked up indeed and spending nearly an hour at it. A mad figure in the best Erchany tradition I must have seemed, stalking the creatures with the bedroom poker. The learned brethren were lazier, I think, and bolder than the others and I believe that the poker was probably a mistake; a skilled pair of hands could have caught one fairly readily. The poker, however, if not much good in attack, might be useful as a weapon of defence; when I abandoned the hunt and set about my fortifications for the night I kept it ready to hand.

Somehow I got to sleep. Twice I was awakened by the scuttling of the rats, twice I lammed out in the dark with the poker—and the second time there was a quite sickening squeal. Poor Mrs. Hardcastle: I know now just what goes through her head in the night. I lit the candle. Miraculously, I had killed a learned rat.

There was a nasty mess and it took me a minute to summon resolution to investigate. The scroll was a piece of fine paper—it might have been torn from an India-paper notebook—and it was tied to the leg of the rat, rather cunningly, with a fragment of cotton. I cut it free and unfolded it gingerly, for the creature's blood was on it. Neatly written in ink were seven words. *Bring help secretly to tower top urgent.*

I dressed. I don't think it occurred to me that the thing was melodramatic, or absurd, or a joke or fantasy of Guthrie's. A period spent at a considerable height will condition one to the job of going really high on a mountain and something over twenty-four hours spent at Erchany had conditioned me to taking the Appeal of the Learned Rat in my stride. I simply wondered how best to make the top of the tower.

The passage outside my room was pitch dark and I hadn't gone a couple of yards before my candle blew out. At that I remembered Sybil Guthrie's electric torch; it seemed a shame to arouse or alarm her—not that she is of a timid sort—but at the same time I felt the circumstances of the moment demand all the aids I could lay my hands on. So I turned back and knocked at her door. There was no audible reply; not surprising this, for the wind was rattling in a hundred places round about. I tried again and then I opened the door and went in. I called, struck a match, presently summoned hardihood to grope about on the enormous bed. Suspicion became certainty: there was no one in the room.

If leisure had been given me I believe I should have felt uncommonly apprehensive. But at this moment I caught a glint of light from the corridor; I went out expecting to find

Sybil and found instead the abominable Hardcastle, holding a lantern in one hand and thumping at my bedroom door with the other. He looked at me evilly—no doubt he was putting a construction agreeable to himself on my emergence from Sybil's room—and then he said the laird sent his compliments; he was better now and would I join him in a nightcap in the tower?

I looked at my watch—the refinements of politeness would be wasted on Hardcastle—and saw that it wanted five minutes of midnight. The very eve of Christmas.

"Yes," I said. "As it happens, I was just going there. Lead the way."

The lantern gave a jump in the brute's hand; I suppose I must have spoken about as grimly as his grim master. For the message that had come from the tower by Hardcastle—hours after it was known I had gone to bed—was scarcely less problematical than the one that had been brought by the rat: the two of them, coupled with Sybil's disappearance, were evidence of some devilment or other that I couldn't now do less than probe. So I tramped down the corridor after Hardcastle in a wrathful mood that probably concealed a good deal of trepidation. Whatever was happening, I had a good notion it was a trap. Some fly was walking into the spider's parlour. Was it Sybil? Or myself? It never occurred to me it might be Guthrie!

But it did occur to me that Hardcastle was one of nature's own spiders. Positively, I had told him to lead the way because I was not without anxiety about my throat and I kept a wary eye on him as we went down the great staircase and along what I rather uncertainly conjectured to be the schoolroom corridor. It must have been about half way that he hesitated and came to a momentary halt, as if listening. I drew up behind him and listened with all my ears too. At first I thought I heard hurried footsteps approaching us; I strained my eyes down the gloomy corridor and could see no one; then, hair-raisingly, the footsteps pattered past me without visible sign. Absurdly—for one can't brain a ghost—

I wished I had brought the poker which had accounted for the learned rat: then I realized that I had been listening only to the peculiar flap-flapping noise of that long tattered carpet that works like a sea on the corridor floor. At that I recovered my wits sufficiently to hear what Hardcastle was hearing: voices from somewhere near the far end of the corridor.

They were a mere murmur—until suddenly some trick of the fragmented Erchany winds caught them and we could distinguish the voice of Christine. I was rather relieved, for I presumed that Sybil was with her and that they were sitting up, perhaps, for Christmas. Hardcastle may have had the same thought; he looked at his watch as I had done a few minutes before; and then a further waft of wind brought us the other voice, a man's voice—elderly, I guessed, and very Scottish. A second later a door opened in the direction of the murmuring and we could just distinguish a figure slip out and disappear into the darkness in front of us.

The execrable Hardcastle hesitated a moment longer and then we went on. As you know, I hadn't so far had much chance of getting the lie of the remoter parts of the castle, and our progress now was quite bewildering. The tower is the oldest part, the original keep or donjon, and as we had descended from the bedroom floor I concluded it must be structurally distinct from the later buildings and connected with them only at ground level, making it an isolated place indeed. And presently I got the measure of this isolation. We passed through a small heavy door and then, not more than three yards on, a door that was exactly similar: the intervening space, I realized even in my rather rattled state, represented the thickness of the wall of the tower. And then we climbed a staircase.

I recalled, as one might recall something peculiarly absurd in a dream, that I was a chance guest going to welcome Christmas Day in the apartments of a friendly and courteous host. And again I wished I had brought that poker. We climbed steadily—Hardcastle in front moving with a sinister deliberation, like a warder setting a decent pace to the gallows—an unexpectedly broad staircase that went to and back in short flights, lit at every second flight by narrow windows. The skies must have partially cleared for the moment; through the windows came the faint pallid gleam of an uncertain moonlight reflected from snow; and it was this that gave the few seconds succeeding their most macabre effect. We had climbed it seemed interminably—I was just deciding that Guthrie must hold his vigils at the very top of the tower—when from above us there rang out a single fearful cry. A moment later the gleam from the window I was passing momentarily vanished as if a high-speed shutter had been flashed across the moon. And then—and after an appreciable interval—a faint, dull sound floated up from below.

We must both have guessed more or less what had happened. I felt that faint thud as infinitely more horrible than the cry which had preceded it; Hardcastle, three or four steps above me, called out: "Great God, if I didn't warn him!" And then we heard footsteps.

What happened then happened in a flash. A young man appeared at the turn above us. Hardcastle's torch caught him for a second and for a second only—nevertheless I received an extraordinarily vivid impression of passion: a dark skin drained of colour and stretched over a set jaw, an eye that smouldered like Guthrie's own. Hardcastle cried out: "Lindsay!" and made a lunge so clumsy it occurred to me to wonder if he were drunk; a second later the lad had slipped past us unheeding and was gone. Perhaps I ought to have grabbed at him myself; I suppose at the vital moment I felt the situation too obscure for action. Hardcastle seemed to hesitate whether to turn back; then he gave a curse and hurried on. I could only follow.

We were still a couple of storeys from the top, but now the staircase narrowed and there were no more windows. On each landing as we came up I had noticed a single massive door; we now passed one more of these and arrived panting together before the last of all, which was if anything more massive than the rest. Hardcastle threw it open. We were looking into a low, square room furnished as a study and lit as usual by a few candles. In the middle of it stood Sybil Guthrie.

For a moment we stood like actors holding a scene for the curtain; then Hardcastle bore down upon Sybil in a sudden unaccountable fury. "You wee limmer—!"

The phrase was no doubt insulting. I gave myself the satisfaction of taking the scoundrel by the shoulder—perhaps by the collar—and telling him to shut up. The action had a more decisive effect than I intended. Hardcastle at once became glumly and pertinaciously passive, with the result that from that moment I found myself saddled with the direction of affairs at Erchany. Willy-nilly, I am in charge until some competent and interested person arrives.

I turned to Sybil. "Where is Guthrie?"

For a fraction of a second she hesitated, looking warily but composedly from one to the other of us. Then quietly, a little unsteadily, she said: "He has fallen from the tower." And as if in explanation she pointed across the room to a door close to the one by which we had entered.

I took Hardcastle's lantern from him and explored. What I found was a small, narrow bedroom, with the same narrow slits for windows as in the staircase, and with a second stout door, now swinging open upon blackness, almost directly opposite the door in which I stood. I crossed the little bedroom to this further door and looked out. I had to clutch at the jamb as I did so, for the wind—though I believe it was moderating steadily—was terrific up here. Before me was a narrow platform of much-trodden snow, bounded by a low castellated parapet—the original battlements, I suppose, of the keep. I staggered cautiously to the verge and looked down. There was nothing to be seen but blackness, and nothing to be heard but the whip and sigh of the wind. I remembered the length of the climb I had just made up the tower staircase and knew that, however thick the blanket of snow beneath, the man who had gone over that parapet was now dead. My first thought—it shows how curiously practical one turns in a crisis—was of relief that there would be no agonized need of medical aid. My second and related thought was that we were most awkwardly isolated should it prove to be some deep mischief that was afoot. And my third thought was simply an image of the rascal Hardcastle, for in my mind already mischief and that ugly brute went together.

I turned back into the study doing my best to think fast. One thing was clear to me on a moment's reflection. Ranald Guthrie, unless drunk or really demented or walking in sleep or trance, was most unlikely to have taken that drop by sheer accident. It was with a shock that I remembered Sybil's flat words: "He has fallen from the tower." They implied—taken in strictness they positively stated—that the merest misadventure was in question. And suddenly I saw the full implications of such a violent and mysterious affair as this, and of the atmosphere in which I had been living these thirty hours past. Suspense, fear, black humours, learned rats, violent death: the sum of them gave one unescapable answer—suspicion. Erchany as the exclusive territory of a malign enchanter was a fantasy of the past; what had happened in the tower to-night made it the territory too of coroners and plainclothes policemen. And ten miles away over formidable snows there was no doubt a rural constable; twenty miles away a sergeant; and in Aberdeen or Edinburgh perhaps the sort of officer who would deal efficiently with such a matter as this. I must have looked from Sybil to Hardcastle and from Hardcastle to Sybil with an expression of positively virgin responsibility.

Guthrie was undoubtedly dead: nevertheless common humanity dictated that our first effort should be to reach his body. If, however, we were on the scene of a crime I felt that neither Sybil—whose presence in the tower was unexplained—nor the sinister Hardcastle had better be left in sole possession of it. Sybil could be sent to Christine—only the task of telling Christine what had happened I ought to perform myself, and it must wait until I had been outside and made sure. At the moment, therefore, the three of us in the tower had better stick together.

During these researches into the etiquette of violence I was looking around. I think you had better have the lie of the land as I made it out now and later.

This top storey of the tower is set back from the storeys below, and is in consequence completely islanded by a narrow battlemented platform—a parapet walk—from which there is a sheer drop to the house and the moat beneath. There are two staircases: one is a little spiral staircase that emerges through a trapdoor upon a corner of the open parapet walk; the other is the staircase by which I had come, and which opens within the topmost storey and directly upon the study. From the study one door gives upon the parapet walk and one upon the little bedroom—from which in turn another door gives upon the parapet walk. All the windows are of the narrow defensive sort.

I decided that if possible I ought to lock up. So I took Hardcastle's lantern again and went to explore the spiral staircase, as also the state of the snow on the platform. It was my impression that there was evidence of a good deal of coming and going about that wind-swept ribbon of battlement, but already the marks were everywhere indistinct and it would have been waste of time trying to direct on them the eye of an amateur detective. I noted the further fact that recently, within, say, the last half-hour—there had been something like commotion on this hazardous spot; then I went on to the trapdoor. And here the snow was disturbed in a way that afforded definite evidence; recently, the trapdoor had been open. A tug at a stout iron ring told me the door was now bolted from below; a moment's fumbling found me what I wanted, a bolt that could be pushed home from above. It moved easily; one entrance to the tower-top was secured.

I moved back as quickly as was prudent, pausing only for a glance at the sky. The moon was behind a rack of clouds, but here and there was a star or a group of stars: what must have been Orion's belt appeared as suddenly as a line of street lights while I looked. I guessed that daylight would see the snow stretched beneath a clear sky and that for the time being the last flakes had fallen.

I returned to the study and found Sybil and Hardcastle standing very much as I had left them. I said: "Now we'll go downstairs." We trooped out to the little landing and I locked the door and put the key in my pocket. Study, bedroom and battlements were inaccessible. Hardcastle muttered something indistinguishable—perhaps it was an attempt to vindicate his stewardship of Erchany—but I was already leading the way down at a run. When we got to ground level Hardcastle indicated another and smaller stair. I locked a further door giving access to the tower staircase and we went down further to a sort of basement. From the tower-top, I realized, Guthrie must have fallen clean into the moat. It was when we came to a little door giving on this that Sybil spoke for the first time since she had said: "He has fallen from the tower." What she said now was: "I'm coming too." And she produced her torch and switched it on with an air of such determination that I knew expostulation would be useless.

In the moat the snow was deep and so powder-soft that I wondered for a moment against my better knowledge whether Guthrie might not have survived. Our feet sank down to the knee as we rounded an angle of the tower, Hardcastle's lantern making a wavering circle of light around us and Sybil's torch exploring the moat in front. A moment later we saw ahead the expected dark splash on the snow. We hurried forward. My heart leapt. The dark splash had stirred.

There was a wild cry—Hardcastle's. I glanced at him; the sweat was pouring down his face in that icy ditch; he had completely lost his nerve. My glance returned to the vague bulk in front and I realized that what had moved was the figure of a man, crouched over the body. The figure straightened itself as we came up. A voice said: "He's dead."

When I wrote that Guthrie's end had been horrible I was thinking chiefly of the full, frank satisfaction in the deep Scottish voice which spoke these words. Dead men hear no curses and mundane mire and fury is nothing to a ghost; still

I hope that none will sound that note in my requiem. I said as sternly as if I had been owner of Erchany and chief constable of the county in one: "Who are you and what are you doing here?"

The stranger looked at me squarely in the lantern-light, an elderly handsome man with the life of the land writ large on his ruddy face. "It's Rob Gamley I am and I came maybe to have a word with the laird. But the laird's having a word by now with them are fitter to deal with him."

It occurred to me as I turned from this savage and unseemly speech and examined the body to wonder if Guthrie had left a single sorrowing heart behind him. Perhaps Christine's—I didn't know. Certainly he was gone to the judgment at which Gamley had hinted; his neck was broken and his death must have been instantaneous.

Standing in that little group of people round the dead man, I had to consider what was proper to be done. It may be that I should have insisted that the body be left where it was; one does this, I suppose, where there is suspicion of foul play. But was there, substantially and after all, such suspicion? On the one hand there was Sybil's statement that Guthrie had fallen from the tower; on the other hand there was only what must be called atmospheric evidence—violence and mystery existing merely in the air or uniquely embodied in the fantastic incident of the learned rat. In sum, I saw no utility and much indecency in leaving what was mortal of Ranald Guthrie in the moat—an indecency which the man Gamley's bitter speech had somehow underlined. So I said briefly: "Miss Guthrie had better go ahead with the torch and lantern and we will follow with the body. Mr. Gamley, you will please help."

Properly enough this time, Gamley took off his cap. The action attracted my eye and I saw that he was looking curiously and without friendliness at Hardcastle. And when I glanced in turn at Hardcastle I saw something extraordinary. The abominable creature appeared in mortal terror of Gamley and was keeping his distance as one might keep one's distance from a bear on a tether. At the same time he was peering at Guthrie's body with just the sort of excited, furtive interest I could imagine him giving to an obscene photograph. I had no notion what prompted either of these impulses, but the combination of them was somehow singularly disgusting. I much preferred Gamley's irreverence. Acting on impulse—and, I suppose, highhandedly enough—I ordered Hardcastle into the house to find a resting-place for the body. Gamley and I followed with our burden as well as we could.

We laid the dead man for the time being on a sort of stone table in a cellar hard by the door of the moat. Sybil played her part with the torch; then she said, "I guess I take the task of breaking this to Christine," and disappeared. It was good of her, I thought, and perhaps the best plan; I might have been clumsy enough.

I sent Hardcastle for a sheet. Gamley, still cap in hand, took one long searching look at the body. Then he strode to the door. "Steady on," I said. "Where are you off to?" For I thought he was due to give some account of himself. He looked at me squarely again. "Young sir," he said, "I'm off to advise the Devil lock up his spoons and forks." And with that dark jest he disappeared.

Here was the second mysterious visitor, I reflected, that I had let slip through my fingers that night. Erchany, well-nigh isolated from the world as it was, had proved mysteriously populous. Whence had Neil Lindsay come, and whence Gamley? Who had tied the messages to the rats? Who had been talking to Christine in the schoolroom? And had Hardcastle's doctor ever arrived? I turned from these riddles to contemplate the larger riddle of death.

Diana, a man can cry out in agony or fear, fall two hundred feet through the air, break his neck and much else, and look at the end of it all like a child asleep in a cradle! A trick of the muscles at the ultimate moment, no doubt, but something strange and terrible to contemplate nevertheless. Guthrie in his dust had returned to innocence; that sinister face, with the strongly marked features that speak of race, was stronger and purer, as if some artist had taken a sponge and swabbed the baser lines away. One reads of death showing such effects; to encounter them at such a violent issue was disconcertingly moving. I composed the body as I could, brushed the snow from face and hair, and waited.

Presently Hardcastle returned with a sheet. Reasonably or unreasonably, I had formed the opinion that in his attitude to the dead man there was something positively indecent, and I found myself instinctively blocking his way at the door. He handed me the sheet sulkily, peering past me in the same absorbed way as before. "I suggest," I said, "that you go and tell your wife to make some tea or coffee. Something of the sort will be needed."

The unsavoury brute gave a gulp as if he were swallowing his true reactions to me. Then he said with a sort of elephantine cunning which I was at a loss to fathom: "Mr. Gylby, you'll have had a look at the body? It might have been robbed or the like?"

"The police will enquire into that?"

"But, sir, we might just give a bit look and see?"

My anger against the noisome creature grew. I turned round and rapidly shrouded Guthrie's body. "And now, Mr. Hardcastle, we must get a message off to Kinkeig. The snowfall is over and there's a drop in the wind. You must see if your odd lad can set out at daybreak." And I pushed the factor out of the cellar, locked the door and pocketed the key. I can only assure you that there is something in the atmosphere of the place that confirms me in my self-appointed role as warden of Erchany. Fortunately the minutes are flitting past as I write and presently I expect to resign honourably on the arrival of the law. Meantime, there is still a shock or two to record.

On my locking the cellar door Hardcastle went off down the corridor in a huff and I was left to debate my next move. Nothing would have persuaded me to rummage about the body like a police-surgeon, but Hardcastle's talk of robbery did put one idea in my head. It had taken me some time to hut up at the tower-top and get the little party to the moat; vhen we arrived there we found the mysterious Gamley rouched beside the body. His identity would no doubt ppear in good time, but might there not be evidence in the now—perishable and best investigated at once—of how he ad got there? I took up Hardcastle's abandoned lantern and, efore returning upstairs, slipped once more out to the moat.

The wind which had so quickly obliterated intelligible races on the battlements had been without force in this deep rench; every mark since the snow had ceased to fall heavily vas legible. And the remoteness of Erchany was curiously rought home to me here; everywhere the snow was patterned ver with the tracks of wild creatures that had sought shelter rom the storm: the incisive pad of a fox, the little long-jumps f weasels, hither-and-thither scurryings of rabbits crossed nce by the steady march of a pheasant upon some invisible nark—and once a little splash of blood and fur. The moon vas now coming and going in the clouds with the regularity f a neon sign and the moonlight passed in waves over this rabesqued carpeting of snow; it was something to stop and ook at with disinterested pleasure; I had to conquer this nseasonable aesthetic impulse before I pushed ahead with ny investigation.

Where Guthrie's body had fallen the snow was splayed up s if a great meteorite had fallen to earth and round about vas the confused trampling of our feet as we had raised the ody. But beyond this circle every footprint was distinct. And the story told was clear. Gamley had dropped—hazard-usly—into the moat about fifteen yards from where Guthrie ad fallen and gone straight to the body. When he left me e had exactly retraced his steps to the wall of the moat and hen, finding it difficult perhaps to get up where he had come lown, he had worked round to that little bridge by which Sybil and I had first crossed to the postern door. There he ad been able to climb from the moat without difficulty, and he purposefulness of his progress plainly argues him familiar vith the ground. I climbed up after him and followed his tracks—with difficulty now—away from the castle. And presently they converged with the faint remains of tracks coming the other way. Gamley had simply come out of the night and returned to it; presumably he had been making for the little postern door when he had been diverted by Guthrie's fall.

I returned to the moat and laboriously made the circuit of it. The final picture was perfectly clear: Gamley coming to the body from one quarter; Sybil, Hardcastle and myself from another; our all moving on a line to the house; Gamley making off as he had come. Perhaps my reconnaissance was wasted labour but it gave me a comforting sense of tidying up behind me.

Hardcastle was hovering at the end of the basement corridor; I think he may have been hopefully trying the door of the cellar—if his wife is a witch he himself is certainly a ghoul. And now he came up to me and said hoarsely: "It's murder."

"That remains to be seen, Mr. Hardcastle. Come upstairs."

"I tell you the tink-loon Lindsay's mischieved and murdered him. Didn't I tell the laird devil the good could come of traffic with one of that name? He's mischieved and murdered him, and now he's away with the girl."

I had been tramping firmly in front of the brute; now I swung round on him. "What's that you say?"

He gave an evil grin that might have signified "I've pricked you at last"; then, as once before, his dirty hand came from behind his back to stroke his chin. Incredible the slow, stupid malice with which he went on: "So you want to know?"

Whatever impertinent effect of suspense Hardcastle designed was marred at this moment by the outburst, just above our heads, of a quite spine-chilling howling and wailing. A hard-fought battle between wolves and hyenas might, I fancied, have produced a somewhat similar impression; it was a few seconds before I realized that I was hearing at least Erchany's lament for Ranald Guthrie—a lament which was about two-fifths Mrs. Hardcastle, two-fifths the moron odd-boy, and one-fifth dogs in the background. Its composition changed as we reached the stairhead, Tammas—the odd boy—sinking his ululations to a whimper and Mrs. Hardcastle achieving something like articulate speech. Sybil was standing between them, looking so determinedly cool and severe that I suspected the night's events were really beginning to get on top of her at last.

"Woe the day, woe the day! The good laird's dead, the good laird's dead, and the lassie's away with a Lindsay!"

Oddly and movingly, the old lady chanted her woes in rhythm. And grotesquely Tammas, swayed by the singsong of her voice, began to mumble verses of his own:

> *"The craw kill't the pussy-oh,*
> *The craw kill't the pussy-oh. . . ."*

It was an uncanny dirge. But I have had my bellyful of the uncanny of late, and I thumped upon an old baize door beside me like a chairman calling a rowdy meeting to order. Presently Tammas subsided into mere whisperings and Mrs. Hardcastle, after an unpromising excursus on rats, fell into a vein of simple sense. What light I got on the situation in the next fifteen minutes I had better compress into a few sentences.

Neil Lindsay, the lad who thrust past us at that dramatic moment on the staircase, is, as I guessed, Christine's lover—and one whose suit Guthrie was absolutely opposed to. He is of crofter folk—tenants of a very small farm—in a neighbouring glen; and this social disparity is complicated, according to the Hardcastles, by some species of hereditary feud—I suppose that in these parts such a picturesque absurdity is still possible. There has been tension for some time and recently Lindsay has been coming about the castle at night in a threatening way. Neither Guthrie nor Christine had said anything about the inwardness of the matter, so the Hardcastles are somewhat in the dark. But Hardcastle professes to believe that Guthrie had decided to buy Lindsay off, and that it was for this purpose that he had been ordered to send the young man up to the tower upon his next appearance.

Lindsay came shortly before half-past eleven, was admitted by Hardcastle and sent straight up to the tower. Shortly before midnight Guthrie rang a bell—he seems to have had both the Hardcastles at his beck and call—and when Hardcastle mounted the stair shouted down to him the message about the nightcap which eventually brought me on the scene.

It was at this point that I really had to interrupt. "But, Mr. Hardcastle, can you explain why I should be summoned to celebrate this painful business of buying off the young man Lindsay? Wasn't it rather a private affair?"

"By your leave, Mr. Gylby, I'm thinking the business would maybe be over and the bit dram with a stranger a way of getting the unchancy loon quietly away."

I need hardly tell you there was scarcely a word of this story that I was in the least anxious to believe. In estimating its credibility, however, I have to remind myself sharply that on Hardcastle's lips the multiplication table would soon become, as far as I am concerned, suspect at once. And now he was a less prepossessing figure than ever: his surliness was uncomfortably laced with servility and I was aware that he was intensely uneasy. I had contrived to get part of the narrative from his wife and I think he may have been in terror lest she should say the wrong thing—let the wrong species of sinister cat out of the bag. Or he may simply have been scared of me. Or of Sybil.

One fact has emerged clearly. Lindsay and Christine—unless they have been conveyed to some hidden dungeon of the castle—really have gone away, singly or together. Mrs. Hardcastle, whom I am increasingly inclined to believe an honest woman, professes to have seen Christine running down the schoolroom corridor with a suitcase, and a hunt by lantern light at the main door of the castle has revealed two half-obliterated tracks leading off into the darkness. The elopement, I believe, is a fact—and a strange season they chose and a hard trek they've had. Lindsay when we met him on the staircase must have been making straight for Christine; a few minutes later they must have departed. But what had happened in the few minutes preceding? What happened in the tower?

On one of these questions Sybil was a witness. She had

been—and quite mysteriously—in the room from which Guthrie had gone to his death. But so far she had been all but mum and I was reluctant in the presence of the Hardcastles to embark on what might appear an interrogation. Hardcastle himself, I could see, was consumed with curiosity about Sybil, and this alone would have inclined me to hold off. But in addition I thought I read an appeal or warning in Sybil's eye, as if she would tell me that before pressing further a private conference would be best.

Another problem came into my head. I turned to Hardcastle and asked as abruptly as I could contrive: "Did your doctor ever come?"

It was a hit. Had I clapped on an executioner's mask and incontinently invited him to lay his head on the block the horrid creature could not have been more taken aback. I have a fancy that a criminal lawyer could have got a lot from him in that moment—a moment in which he was floundering out of his depth. He didn't know what it was I knew. And it must be confessed that, like a fool, I promptly told him.

"You called out to ask if it was the doctor, you know, when you opened the door to Miss Guthrie and me."

"And didn't you know, Mr. Gylby, that one of the dogs is called Doctor, and that I was but thinking he'd got loose?"

I was rather taken aback myself this time by so neat, if evident, a lie. The fellow possesses the cunning that his face claims for him and for the moment I gave him best. It occurred to me to attempt some sort of communication with Tammas—who was to be our first link, it seemed, with the world.

"Do you think," I said, "that you can get down to Kinkeig?"

Tammas, realizing that he was addressed, blushed in the uncertain lamp-light like a girl. And then he murmured softly:

> *"There's nae luck aboot the hoose,*
> *There's nae luck at a',*
> *There's nae luck aboot the hoose*
> *When our goodman's awa' . . ."*

In the Elizabethan drama, you will remember, fools and

idiots constantly express themselves in snatches of obscure song. Tammas's habit suggests that the convention has some basis in pathological fact. At any rate, experimental transmission had failed, and I may say I haven't succeeded in getting across to him yet. Most irritatingly, Hardcastle is a necessary intermediary. I now had to listen to an unintelligible dialect conversation from which there finally emerged the report that Tammas was ready to set out for Kinkeig at once.

And presently set out he did, with instructions simply to announce the death of Guthrie and the need of a doctor and a policeman. I rather expected Hardcastle to be all for raising an immediate hue and cry after Lindsay and Christine, and I was surprised at his good sense in agreeing to reticence for the time being. I wrote out a telegram or two, including one that you will have had by this time. Then I watched him set off, ploughing powerfully through the drifts in the moonlight. In a few minutes he had disappeared; only in the stillness that had come with the drop in the wind I could hear him—uncannily again—singing to the moon. His progress would be dreadfully hard; with good luck he would make the village, I reckoned, about dawn.

It is two hours past dawn now and we may expect help soon. Through the small hours I have kept my lyke-wake in company with this narrative; it has grown to an unconscionable length and I don't want to run on into embroidery. But there is one further matter on which to report. You will guess that it is an interview with Sybil Guthrie.

After Tammas's departure there seemed little or nothing that could be done. Sybil and I had big cups of Mrs. Hardcastle's tea in the schoolroom—strangely desolate that pleasant, simple room now seems—and Mrs. Hardcastle, standing respectfully by and snivelling, told us that until recently Guthrie had never allowed tea in the house—a beautiful trait in the good laird's character, it seems, from which she is disposed to draw the comfort of pious contemplation.

When we got her out of the room there was a little silence. Sybil's affairs, I felt, were no business of such a casually-met companion as myself, and remained essentially no business of mine even when they brushed against mystery. Still, I thought it fair to say nothing and look ever so faintly expectant. And sure enough, Sybil presently said: "I think I want to talk to you, Mr. Gylby." And at the same time she nodded significantly towards the door.

Taking the hint, I strode over and opened it. There was Hardcastle in his favourite lurking role, a sort of adipose fox outside a hen-run. "Mr. Gylby, sir," he said with a fantastic attempt at a solicitous air, "I'm thinking you might like a bit more fire in the grate?"

I saw that for the time being there was only one possible working arrangement between Hardcastle and myself—a couple of stout doors securely locked. So I said we didn't want the fire stoked; we were just going up to the tower. And up we went, Hardcastle looking after us rather as if we were a couple of cockerels scrambling to safety on a tree. I imagine he is still guessing—goodness knows about what—and that this is making his unbeautiful personality somewhat ineffective. I turned round and called to him, perhaps with a spice of malice, that we should be down to breakfast and could Mrs. Hardcastle manage boiled eggs? Then, silently and still by the light of a lantern, we climbed and climbed.

Ever since I so neatly demolished her car Sybil and I have been as matey as could be; we cannoned into each other—literally, need I laboriously point out?—from contexts thousands of miles apart and straightway trickled together into an environment almost equally unfamiliar to both of us, a process well calculated to the formation of a close alliance. But during the last couple of hours—ever since Sybil's unexplained appearance in the study—we had rather drawn apart. Now as we climbed into the solitude of this dark tower, and quite apart from Sybil's implied promise of explanations, our alliance reasserted itself. I don't think I feel romantic about this quite unromantic young person but as we came to the locked door of the study I saw that she might have got herself into a fix in which I should have to stand by. "Sybil," I said, "hold the lantern while I find the key." She laid her hand on my arm and then on the lantern; in a minute we were standing once more in Ranald Guthrie's study.

Rather idly I said: "The scene of the crime."

"But, Noel, there was no crime. I told you he simply fell."

"However did he manage that?"

I suppose I must have looked at Sybil doubtingly or doubtfully as I spoke. She flushed and repeated: "He simply fell."

There was a little silence. Perhaps I rumpled my hair in perplexity; anyway, I became aware in that little silence of the ticking of my own wrist-watch. And powerfully there came back to me the slow tick of the clock as we had sat at supper the night before last, the slow tick of the clock upon which I had projected all the intolerable strain of waiting that had been about us. Had we been waiting only for Ranald Guthrie to tumble accidentally from his tower? At two o'clock in the morning one's mind is not in its best logical trim: I was suddenly convinced that the atmosphere which had been about us was incompatible with Sybil's assertion. It was a sheer mental failure; I was seeking quite unwarrantably for some simple melodramatic pattern to impose upon a most confused series of events; and Sybil caught me nicely by asking: "Do you insist on something more lurid?"

I said evasively: "There will be a tremendous number of questions asked, you know."

"I guess so."

"They'll want to know all about everybody: where one was and why—all that."

"And I should practise my replies on you?"

I said soberly: "I should like you to."

Sybil walked to the far end of the study and turned round. "Noel, you are a nice young man despite your airs. But I wish I knew something of your abstract principles."

"Take it that they are orthodox and severe."

"A pity." Sybil looked at me perfectly gravely as she spoke and I knew that somehow she meant what she said. She paused for a moment, knit her brows, from somewhere produced cigarettes. I struck a match, she gave two puffs and went on carefully. "Mr. Gylby—Noel—you are entitled to the whole story as I can tell it. Listen." Again she strode to the end of the room and this time spoke before turning. "I was up here spying around."

"Enterprising of you."

I'm afraid my tone of casual admiration wasn't a success. When Sybil did turn round it was with a satirical smile for the outraged Englishman. "I said I was spying around. This household kind of got me curious and I just felt like hiding behind doors and listening. That's why I was so quick on the draw with friend Hardcastle a few minutes ago in the schoolroom. I've got the instinct to prowl and hover."

"Very well, Sybil. You have been peering and listening about. Go ahead."

Sybil glanced at me doubtfully and went ahead with an apparent struggle. "This tower has been intriguing me most. It's so romantic—"

"Cut out the ingenuous tourist, Sybil. Or keep it for the dumb Dicks."

"I thought I had to practise on you! Well, listen. When I went to my room I just lay on my bed and read—and the longer I lay the less I felt like getting my clothes off and trying to sleep. Once or twice I got up and peered out of the window. That was just restlessness, of course; there was nothing but blackness to be seen. Or nothing but blackness until some time round about half-past eleven: I became aware then of a moving light high up across the court I look out on. I guessed it must be Guthrie up in that gallery-place, and it occurred to me that while he was there this tower might be open to inspection. I thought, after all, there wouldn't be much harm in exploring the—the other public rooms of the castle."

"Quite so. As a matter of fact, I set out for the tower myself just a little after you did."

"You mean when Hardcastle summoned you?"

"No. I was going on my own initiative when Hardcastle happened upon me."

For a moment Sybil seemed to concentrate on an attempt to get behind this statement. Then she continued. "I took a candle and matches and went downstairs. I had already given some thought to the plan of the castle and I reckoned with luck to find my way. All the same, I wasn't awfully hopeful of a successful prowl; I thought it very likely that Guthrie kept his tower locked up. So I was pleased as well as a mite scared when I found I could get through and up the staircase."

"You didn't meet anybody or hear anything? They'll ask questions like that."

"Nobody and nothing. I tried one or two doors on the way up. They were all locked. So I just went on climbing till I came to the top and walked straight in on this."

Sybil paused and we both looked about us. A sombre room, full of dark woodwork and simply crammed with books; Guthrie was presumably by way of being a learned man as well as a songster. I began to browse around, partly out of curiosity to see which way his tastes lay, partly because I didn't want to seem impatient for Sybil's confidences. At one end of the room the bookshelves ran out in bays; I went and peered into these; then I came back and asked Sybil: "You poked about?"

"I didn't. I hadn't time. I wasn't in the room a minute when I heard footsteps mounting the way I had come. It was Guthrie returning."

"A moment not without its embarrassment, Sybil."

"I'll say. I knew I really hadn't any business to penetrate to this remote study. It was frightfully ill-bred. And I was kind of scared of the old gentleman when it came to the point of facing him with grovelling apologies. I saw that in venturing into his den I'd done a silly thing. And I lost my head."

Sybil's head, I reflected, was now happily restored to her shoulders; she was as cool as could be.

"It was quite mad, but I just cast about for somewhere to

hide! There were two possibilities: that door near the staircase door, and that other one over there that is a sort of French window on the parapet walk. The first—the one we now know gives on the little bedroom—proved to be locked; I just had time to make for the other and get through. It wasn't at all comfortable; I found myself out in the open, on a narrow platform, hundreds of feet in the air and buffeted by a howling hurricane."

"Between the Prince of the Air within and his attendant spirits without."

"Exactly. I dropped my candle in the snow—it will be there still—and stood clinging to the handle of the door. It was pitch dark and the wind simply caught at my wits and numbed them. Minutes must have passed before I realized that a door meant some sort of security beyond and that I was on something more than the merest ledge. I couldn't quite get the door shut and I was frightened to risk my balance with a really stout tug. So there I was on one side of the thing and there was Guthrie, moving round lighting a few candles, on the other. I had either to recover my good sense and face him, or stay tucked away. I stayed tucked away.

"Guthrie went over to the desk there in the middle of the room, sat down and buried his face in his hands. A couple of minutes later—no more—he straightened up and called out something I didn't catch. The staircase door opened—it was just within my field of vision—and a young man came in, ushered, I think, by Hardcastle, though I didn't see him. Guthrie rose, pointed to a chair, and this time I heard him speak quite distinctly. He said: 'Mr. Lindsay, sit down.'

"Unfortunately—I suppose it must be said—those were the only words I made out. The wind was howling so that the rest of the interview was simply a dumb-show. They talked earnestly for some time—"

I interrupted. "And angrily, Sybil?"

Sybil shook her head. "Definitely not. It occurred to me they weren't good friends—it had the appearance of rather a formal parley—but there wasn't anything that looked like heat. They might simply have been settling something up."

"Like the buying-off business Hardcastle told us of?"

"I suppose so." Sybil had paused for a moment as if to inspect my question. Then she went on. "Presently they both stood up and Lindsay shook his head—a curiously gentle, curiously decisive action it seemed to me. They moved towards the door—"

"They were in view all the time, Sybil? They hadn't moved, for instance, to the other end of the room?"

"They were in view all the time. They moved towards the door and there shook hands—formally, I should say, rather than cordially. Lindsay went out and Guthrie turned back. I got a shock when I saw his face. He looked—I don't know how to put it—tragic and broken. I saw him only for a second. He took a key from his pocket, unlocked the bedroom door and disappeared inside, shutting the door behind him. It seemed about a minute or half a minute later that I heard a faint cry. I waited another minute and then decided to make a dash for the staircase. I was in the middle of the room when you and Hardcastle came in upon me."

"And when I asked you about Guthrie you said, 'He has fallen from the tower.' Forgive me, Sybil, but this is what they will ask. How on earth did you know?"

Sybil Guthrie looked at me in silence for a moment. Then she said: "Yes, I see." There was another silence. "Noel, it was a sort of intuition."

"Didn't you tell me once you weren't psychic?"

I ought not to have brought that in; I wasn't a prosecuting barrister. But I felt it extraordinarily important that Sybil should realize certain dangers in her situation. And suddenly she blazed out. "I tell you I knew, Noel Gylby! That interview had somehow crushed the man. I saw imminent death in his face. And your rushing in on top of that cry just *told* me. Guthrie was next to mad anyway and when his plans went wrong he made an end of himself."

"He had failed, you mean, to buy Lindsay off, and couldn't bear the thought of losing his niece?"

"Something like that. And it should be lurid enough for you."

We were sitting now perched side by side on Guthrie's desk. After a time I said: "Well, that's been a useful trial spin, Sybil."

She turned her head and gave me a quick glance. "Just what do you mean by that?"

"I mean," I said gently, "that we must have a revised version."

"In other words, I'm lying?"

"Not at all. What you have said may be gospel. But it's just too awkward to be safe. Your piece of intuition is perfectly possible. But it's the sort of possibility that looks perfectly awful in a court of law."

Again Sybil said: "Yes, I see."

"You are lurking here, Guthrie goes into the bedroom, there is a cry, we rush in, and then your mind takes a great leap in the dark—a leap to the truth, maybe. But you see how strange it could be made to look? Only the fact that you have no real connection with Guthrie is between you and positive suspicion."

Sybil stood up and faced me. "Noel, shall I tell you the truth?"

"For goodness' sake do."

"Behold the chatelaine of Erchany!"

I jumped up. "What do you mean?"

"I mean I'm Ranald Guthrie's heir."

. . .

The row of little dots, Diana, means that you are invited to be staggered. Perhaps you won't be—if only because I wasn't myself. That there were wheels within wheels in Sybil Guthrie's relations with Erchany is something that I've had a dim sense of for some time, and that sense has probably got into my earlier narrative. If I was decidedly taken aback it was by the sudden vivid image of Sybil and myself sitting each on a wing of my car in the snow and my seeing the Erchany light and saying so importantly that we would make for *that*. For I had come upon her, in fact, in the middle of a more than ingenious plan to gate-crash on Erchany—a plan into which she had incorporated me magnificently and in her stride. Some refinements of the scheme—the artless requests for guidance south, the resolute driving her car over a bank—I recall with positive awe. And did she not, in the very critical moment of her plot, stand idly making quiet fun out of the text of Coleridge's *Christabel?* As I think I discerned—a formidable young woman.

As yet I have got only the outline of what it is all about. The American Guthries—Sybil and her widowed mother—were served some dirty financial turn by Ranald Guthrie; they heard rumours that he was mad and irresponsible; and having an interest in his estate they have been trying in various ways to discover the true state of affairs. Sybil, being in England, decided to discover for herself. She explored the ground some weeks ago and when the snow came she saw her chance. What she didn't see, poor child, was the awkward scrape into which her irresponsible jaunt was going to lead her. She really is a bit scared now—which only shows her common sense. It is a most extraordinary position.

But if she's scared she's also full of fight. Standing before the empty fireplace in Guthrie's study and looking down on her as she perched once more on the desk, I thought of the motto that I now knew was hers by right. *Touch not the Tyger*. It was not inappropriate: the beast was lurking there truly enough and I felt that I had neither touched nor scratched it—I knew, in other words, very little about Sybil. Only I guessed that she would leap at danger if she felt the call; and I knew that there were ways in which she could be quite, quite ruthless. Observe, Diana, that the attraction of Miss Sybil Guthrie is a lunar echo of the attraction of Miss Diana Sandys: observe this and hold your peace.

She perched there full of fight, scarcely needing my prompting that her situation was awkward. I was puzzled, indeed, by an obscure feeling that she was planning ahead further than I could see—a feeling prompted, I knew, by some association in the recent past. A second later I got it: it was Sybil's eye. She was looking at me, and about the study, with the very glance that Ranald Guthrie had bent upon his unexpected guests. I could scarcely have had a more dramatic reminder that there was a Guthrie at Erchany still.

"What is known," I asked, "of your earlier reconnoiterings here?"

"I don't know. Not much. I sent a telegram from the pub in Kinkeig saying I expected to get something soon."

"Whom to?"

"Our lawyer. He was in London then but he's sailed for home now. Noel, I think I'd better have a lawyer or someone."

"I think you better had. As a matter of fact, you have. I wired."

"Noel Gylby! Explain yourself."

"I didn't like it at all: Guthrie dead and Hardcastle muttering murder and you being found up here. We must protect ourselves, mustn't we? And I have an uncle in Edinburgh just now; he's a soldier and has the Scottish Command. He'll see the right sort of person is despatched."

"I'll say you have a neck."

"So have you, Sybil. That's the point."

"Yes, I see."

So that was that. I didn't think anyone would really want to hang Sybil; I rather hoped they would be able to hang Hardcastle, though I couldn't see just how. The thought prompted a question. "Sybil, you say Guthrie and Lindsay were in view all the time? What about Guthrie's ringing a bell and going to the door and shouting to Hardcastle to invite me up?"

Sybil for the first time in our acquaintance looked really startled; I saw that I had brought forward a point that had escaped her. She said: "Where is the bell?"

"Over here by the fireplace."

"Then Guthrie rang no bell. And he certainly didn't go to the door and shout. Hardcastle lied."

"And Hardcastle was next to livid at finding you here. In

fact Hardcastle had a game. Come over here."

I led her across the room to one of the bays into which I had been peering earlier. There was an old bureau in which a drawer had been violently broken open. It was empty save for a few scattered gold coins. "The miser's toy cupboard," I said, "and the toys are gone."

I glanced at Sybil as I spoke and saw that she had turned pale. For a long moment she was silent; then she said, in odd antithesis to what had been her most familiar phrase hitherto: "No—no, I don't see." She knit her brows. "And even if—" She broke off and I could see that she was searching desperately in her mind, perhaps in her memory. "I couldn't be mistaken on that." And she turned away from the rifled drawer. "Of course, Noel, it adds to the puzzle, but no further problem is involved."

I must have looked my bewilderment at this outburst of riddling speech, for Sybil laughed at me as she walked across the room and rather wearily threw her cigarette into the fireplace. "Noel, what will your lawyer be like? I'm rather wanting to see him." She stretched herself with an engaging affectation of laziness and added: "And I'm rather wanting to go to bed and sleep."

"Then off you go. You have some hours before the rumpus. I'll see you to your room."

But Sybil gave a dismissive nod. "You needn't come down, Noel Gylby. Ranald's ghost won't trouble me; as you know, I'm not really romantically inclined. But I'm glad you smashed my car. Good night."

And so I was left in possession of Ranald Guthrie's tower. And here I have sat scribbling away like Pamela—who, you remember, wrote home thousands and thousands of words on every attempt of her master's on her virtue. I always liked Pamela and now I know why: I have that itch—hers, I mean, not her master's. As they said to the Historian of the Roman Empire: "Scribble, scribble, Mr. Gibbon?" The story's a good one, but I forget it. I'm tired. Take it these last few lines are sleep-writing absolute.

Very presently, I suppose, Tammas will bring back a few hardy representatives of order and sanity to this crazy castle. Crazycastle, Dampcastle, Coldcastle, Hardcastle. Hardcastle—grrr!

Good night, lady, good night, sweet lady, good night, good night.

Quoth

NOEL YVON MERYON GYLBY.

III

THE INVESTIGATIONS OF ALJO WEDDERBURN

1

I MUST begin my contribution to this record of the curious events at Castle Erchany with a confession. From the very beginning I had the gravest doubts—doubts which I cannot conscientiously say subsequent events resolved—as to whether, in the large utterance of the young man Gylby, "the right sort of person had been despatched."

It will doubtless be within the knowledge of readers familiar with the legal institutions of these Islands that the society of Writers to the Signet in Edinburgh is for the most part happily associated with the quieter, the more spacious, the truly learned aspects of the law. And I can modestly say that the firm of Wedderburn, Wedderburn and McTodd has amply contributed to this respectable tradition. Our clients are never harassed by importunate endeavours to bring their affairs to an issue, for the passions of to-day are the forgotten follies of to-morrow and procrastination in consequence is of the essence of soundly conservative legal practice. Again, they are seldom exposed to the uncertainties of litigation, for the harmonious and profitable commerce between solicitor and client can only be disturbed by the intrusion—not unaccompanied by heavy demands of a pecuniary nature—of our learned brethren of the Faculty of Advocates. The pleasures of conveyancing—a science often of the greatest antiquarian interest—together with the discreet superintendence of bankruptcies, alimonies, insanities and irresponsibilities among the best Scottish families has made the major part of our professional activities for some generations. Especially have we been reluctant to engage ourselves in the lurid limelight of the criminal law!

With this preliminary observation—which I trust will obviate any misunderstanding that may arise—I will plunge, in the phrase already employed by my worthy friend Ewan Bell, *in medias res.* On the afternoon of the Christmas Day upon which this chronicle centres, having despatched my family to the pantomime—a mode of entertainment which has for me, I fear, a very limited appeal—I walked up the Mound and let myself into the Signet Library, proposing a few hours' quiet study: some of my readers at least may not be uninterested to know that I hope shortly to publish a monograph entitled *Run-rig, In-field and Out-field in the Scottish Land Courts of the Eighteenth Century.* I was in the act of consulting a valuable article by the learned Dr. Macgonigle in the *Scottish Historical Review* when I was interrupted by the appearance of my chauffeur with the news that General Gylby had called at my home on a matter of considerable urgency and was now awaiting my return.

Gylby and I had shot together in Morayshire and he had some claim upon my friendship; I was aware, moreover, that his wife's sister was engaged to the young Earl of Inverallochy: I therefore commended my man's intelligence in summoning me and drove home.

It is scarcely necessary to inform the reader that General Gylby's business concerned a telegram he had received from his nephew: this young man, together with a female friend, had become involved in an episode of a violent and mysterious sort—and in such a way as to make immediate legal advice desirable. The telegram was brief and necessarily obscure, and but for the risk of offending the General I believe I should simply have recommended him to some competent young solicitor unconnected with our firm. As the matter stood, however, I determined to turn to my nephew Aeneas. Aeneas has now been some years my junior partner, and it must be avowed that during this period he has shown a very considerable flair for just those over-colourful branches of the law which we have always been concerned to eschew. When Mrs. Macrattle of Dunk poisoned her head keeper by injecting sheep-dip into a haggis with the local doctor's hypodermic syringe it was by Aeneas that the matter was adjusted; when the Macqueady was sensationally arraigned for discharging an extensive land-mine under an entire house-party organized by his wife it was Aeneas who instructed counsel in the successful plea that nothing but a geological experiment of a purely scientific kind had been intended. Aeneas, in fact, seemed just the man for General Gylby's nephew; and on the evening of Christmas Day he set out for Dunwinnie. My perturbation may be imagined when I received a telegram early next morning to say that while hastily changing trains at Perth he had slipped on the ice and broken a leg. I need not detail the alternative arrangements I endeavoured to make. They failed; we were pledged to General Gylby; that afternoon I set out for Dunwinnie myself.

It must not be concealed that I climbed into my carriage at the Caledonian station in a mood of considerable annoyance—nor indeed that this annoyance was increased rather than diminished by the discovery that I was to have as travelling companion my old schoolfellow Lord Clanclacket. With all proper deference to a Senator of the College of Justice it must be frankly said that Clanclacket is a bore. Not only a bore but a chilly bore: the last man one would choose to sit opposite to on a journey uncommonly dull and chilly in itself.

We were on the Forth Bridge before Clanclacket spoke. He then said: "Well, Wedderburn, you're going north?"

It is with questions of just this degree of perspicacity that Clanclacket is wont to entrap unwary young advocates from the bench. I briefly agreed that I was going north and ventured to suppose that he was in much the same case.

"A week's quiet in Perthshire," he said. "It is a holiday you are taking, Wedderburn?"

"A professional journey—a little matter of family business. Notice, Clanclacket, that the fleet is in. I wonder, can that be *Renown* just opposite Rosyth?"

My companion made what I fear was but a decent pretence of being diverted for a moment to these naval matters. We were still rattling through the cantilevers of the bridge when he resumed: "What's your station?"

"I change at Perth. Let me offer you *Blackwood's*."

Clanclacket took the journal—an offering made, I may say, with considerable reluctance—and studied its cover much as if it had been an unfamiliar document put in evidence. Then he said heavily: "Ah, *Blackwood's*. Thank you. Excellent. Very good." And at that he tucked it firmly away—so firmly, indeed, that it would not be seriously inaccurate to say he sat on it. "You were saying, Wedderburn, that you change at Perth for—?"

"Dunwinnie."

"Your business is there?"

"*My* business, my dear Clanclacket, is there or thereabouts."

For a few minutes the emphasis of my remark did hold him up, but we were scarcely through North Queensferry before he was employing another tactic.

"Um, yes—Dunwinnie. A bonny spot. I don't know, though, that I know many people in that neighbourhood. Do you know the Frasers of Mervie?"

"No."

"The Grants of Kildoon?"

"I believe I have met Colonel Grant. But we are not acquainted."

"The Guthries of Erchany?"

"I have never, I think, met a member of that family."

"Old Lady Anderson of Dunwinnie Lodge?"

"She was a friend of my father's. But our firm has never done business for her and I do not know that we have met."

Clanclacket relapsed for some minutes now into baffled silence. I had got past the danger-point, I congratulated myself, by a neat formula enough. Presently he tried another shot. "I wonder about the other families thereabout. Do you know who they are?"

With great satisfaction I replied: "I am acquainted with none of them."

That—as Aeneas is accustomed to put it—really fixed him.

And balked in his endeavours to acquire information he presently fell back on imparting it. "About the Frasers of Mervie," he said. "I could tell you of certain curious episodes—"

This is Clanclacket's customary proem to extended dissertation; for over an hour we pursued the eccentricities of the Frasers of Mervie and all their kin about the globe. In these matters Clanclacket is notoriously encyclopaedic and as the Frasers began to show signs of exhaustion it occurred to me that this knowledgeableness, if tactfully exploited, might have its immediate utility for me. "Clanclacket," I said as if with sudden interest, "the Grants of Kildoon—do you know much about them?"

He looked at me suspiciously. "No," he said. "No! Nothing at all. But if you had happened to ask me about the Guthries of Erchany—"

I endeavoured to assume the identical expression with which I had listened to the vagaries of the Frasers, though with quite other feelings. My knowledge of Mr. Guthrie of Erchany, the dead man to whose late seat I was now travelling, was confined to the intelligence, gleaned from a corner of that morning's *Scotsman*, that he had fallen from a tower on the night of Christmas Eve in circumstances that awaited investigation. Any information that I could glean from the anecdotal habit of Clanclacket as to the character and connections of this unfortunate person was likely to be serviceable. I confess to simulating a yawn as I asked indifferently: "They are interesting folk?"

"They have been interesting folk for centuries! Take Andrew Guthrie, known as the Gory Guthrie, who was killed at Solway Moss—"

There was no doubt, I reflected as some forty minutes later my companion's chronicle was approaching the fringes of the eighteenth century, that these Guthries of Erchany were interesting folk enough; it was doubtful whether one could find a more picturesque record among the minor families of Scotland. But my interests were on the present occasion contemporary and I possessed my soul in patience until Clanclacket should come down to the present generation and its immediate predecessors. As evening fell and we ran further north through a countryside submerged in snow I was not inclined to feel the mission on which I was engaged the less uncomfortable and wearisome; nevertheless, I almost regretted the speed at which we were travelling, being apprehensive lest we should arrive at Perth before we arrived at Mr. Ranald Guthrie.

". . . And take Ranald Guthrie, the present laird. Once more, the same morbid constitution—I believe in an aggravated form. I believe"—and here Clanclacket sank his voice and glanced into the corridor to make sure he was not overheard—"I believe he is artistically inclined."

"Dear me!"

"But we must be accurate, Wedderburn; we must always be accurate. I hasten to add that this inclination may be a thing of the past."

"I am sure it is, Clanclacket."

"Eh—what's that? You know nothing about it, man. I'm telling you that as a lad this Ranald ran away from home and went on the stage."

"Ah!"

"Exactly. A thoroughly unstable stock. But we must be fair, Wedderburn; we must always be fair. He was then exceedingly young. And he was reclaimed. After some months—a year maybe—he was reclaimed and, of course, sent abroad. Colonial life was plainly the only thing. They chose Australia; it has the advantage over Canada in such cases of being three or four times as far away. But Ranald didn't like it. On first seeing Fremantle harbour he endeavoured to commit suicide."

"Dear me! I suppose this is all ancient gossip now? It would be difficult to have that attempted suicide, for instance, sworn to?"

"Really, Wedderburn, you should know I never gossip. These are facts confidentially communicated. Long-past history though the incident be, and remote as is the site of it, I could as it happens put my finger on an eye-witness tomorrow. Ranald Guthrie, I say, attempted to drown himself and his life was fortunately saved by the bravery of his elder brother."

"So a brother went to Australia with him?"

"Ian Guthrie. He too had given a little trouble. Not, I think, anything serious: I have no evidence of artistic temperament in Ian. Possibly merely a matter of young women; we must be fair. And I believe that no scandal circulated. Both these brothers were generally thought to have gone abroad because they were reluctant to enter the ministry. Of course when Ranald inherited he came home."

"Ian had died?"

"Yes. There was some tragedy. I believe both went prospecting or exploring and that Ian got lost. His body was later recovered by a rescue party. Ranald, who is as I say an unstable person, was upset."

"Upset?"

"*Greatly* upset. When he came home he lived in a very peculiar manner. I understand that he still does and that he is, in fact, a miser and a recluse."

"Was."

"I beg your pardon, Wedderburn?"

"Ranald Guthrie has just died. And here is Perth. I am afraid I must hurry. Pray, Clanclacket, keep *Blackwood's*. Good-bye."

2

FROM Perth to Dunwinnie the railway line had as yet been but imperfectly cleared of snow and as a result my train ran over an hour late. Once arrived, moreover, I had the utmost difficulty in securing a conveyance the driver of which was willing to undertake the perils of a night drive to Kinkeig. I was told that Dr. Noble had been through, as also the police and the sheriff, and that word had come back of the sheriff's judging it necessary to hold an inquiry into the manner of Mr. Guthrie's death. I saw that it was necessary to push forward and, having secured some modification—though a mere *solacium* indeed—of the first exorbitant tariff proposed, I succeeded in reaching Kinkeig without notable hazard just short of eleven o'clock. It is the merest hamlet and I counted myself fortunate in securing simple but adequate accommodation at an inn laconically known as the Arms.

My client, whom I supposed to be the young Mr. Gylby, was still at Erchany and thither I proposed to proceed—I had better, perhaps, say penetrate—on the following morning. Precise information would then be available. Meanwhile I did not think it wise altogether to neglect the voice of rumour. I proceeded to the parlour—the bar being of course closed—and rang the bell. The mistress of the house, a Mrs. Roberts, answered, and to her I said: "Would you be so good as to bring me—"

"What you'll be in need of," interrupted Mrs. Roberts firmly, "is a nice cup of malted milk."

It is a maxim of sound forensic practice that to give play to the eccentricities of a witness's character is the surest technique for landing fish. I said: "That is exactly what I was going to ask for. Please let me have a nice cup of—ah—malted milk."

Mrs. Roberts hurried away and it is proper to testify that the potation with which she returned was not unpalatable. Moreover she was disposed to be talkative, and for the next half-hour I listened to information about the affair at Erchany which in places made me open my eyes very wide indeed. Little more than twenty-four hours before I had been absorbed in the tranquil study of in-field and out-field in the eighteenth century. Now I was confronted with a story having all the characteristics of what students call the Senecan Drama: revenge, murder, multilations and a ghost. Must I confess to a trick of my nephew Aeneas's temper coming upon me as I listened, and to an unwonted quickening of the pulse of the senior partner of Wedderburn, Wedderburn and McTodd? I have always felt a curious attraction in romances of detection—a species of popular fiction which bears much the same relation to the world of actual crime as does pastoral poetry to the realities of rural economy—and now as I listened to the good Mrs. Roberts I seemed to be faced with a rank confusion of kinds. Mr. Guthrie's death was actual enough but it was set in just such a context of fantasy as might have been woven round it by the operation of a wayward and irresponsible literary mind. Or perhaps it was rather the folk-mind, with its instinct for bizarre elaboration, that I had to deal with. In listening to Mrs. Roberts I was listening to the voice of rumour, perhaps to the lingering mythmaking faculty of simple people. Revenge, murder, mutilations and a ghost—these, it might be, were but adding one more to the romantic legends of the Guthries with which Clanclacket had been entertaining me earlier that day.

Revenge and murder. A certain Neil Lindsay, a young man of loose principles and a cruel heart, had taken upon himself to revive and prosecute an immemorial family feud with the Guthries. This he had done by hurling Ranald Guthrie from a high tower at midnight on Christmas Eve, stealing a large sum of gold, and making off with a young woman variously reported as his enemy's ward, niece, daughter and mistress.

Mutilations and a ghost. Not content with these abominable deeds the young man Lindsay had paused in his flight to inflict a most horrid outrage upon Guthrie's dead body, chopping a number of fingers from the corpse in macabre requital of some savage incident between the families five hundred years ago. And this lurid and perverted deed was in its turn crying out for vengeance; at the midnight of Christmas Day Ranald Guthrie's ghost had been abroad in Kinkeig, waving its maimed hands to the moon and crying out awfully of that hell from which it had been a few hours released to walk the earth.

I have here compressed the narrative of Mrs. Roberts into a few sentences; rumour is invariably diffuse. But I was, as I have intimated, curiously compelled by her wandering recital; the story had a measure of imaginative coherence which evoked something like conviction; I found a positive effort was required to view it critically—to note, for instance, the interesting rapidity with which the legend had been enriched with supernatural accretions. As a humble student of folklore I thought this aspect of Kinkeig's reactions to the death of its laird worth some further enquiry. "Mrs. Roberts," I asked, "have many folk seen the ghost?"

"Faith, yes."

"You yourself?"

"No, faith!" Mrs. Roberts looked quite scared at the mere suggestion.

"Then who?"

Mrs. Roberts considered. "The first would be Mistress McLaren, the smith's wife. The pump in her yard was frozen fast and she was going down the road for water when she saw the uncouthy thing right afore her in the moonlight. She gave a scraitch, poor creature, that was heard by half Kinkeig. And you couldn't have better proof than that." Mrs. Roberts must have detected a sceptical temper in my enquiries, for she produced Mrs. McLaren's conclusive scream with a good deal of triumph.

"No, indeed, Mrs. Roberts. And what happened then?"

"The McLaren body was just outside Ewan Bell the sutor's. She ran in to him fair terrified and he took her home."

"And did Mr. Bell see the ghost?"

"That he did not."

"Does Mrs. McLaren often see ghosts?"

My hostess was much struck by this question. "Fancy your asking that, sir! A Highland body she is and second-sighted; it's her that says she foresaw the Erchany daftie come louping through the snow with news of the Guthrie's death. And it was her that knew the Guthrie had the evil eye."

"Well, in your own words, Mrs. Roberts, you couldn't have better proof than that. And who was the next to meet the ghost?"

Mrs. Roberts looked at me rather suspiciously. "The next would be Miss Strachan the schoolmistress."

"Miss Strachan. Now do you happen to know if this Miss Strachan had any reason to have Erchany and its affairs much on her mind?"

Mrs. Roberts's suspicion became plainly tinged with respect. "Faith, and that's unco strange to ask! It was the Strachan woman that had a right awesome meeting with the laird at Erchany a while back."

"Quite so. And who else saw Mr. Guthrie's ghost?"

Mrs. Roberts looked doubtful. "Well, I don't for certain know that—"

"In fact, nobody else? Just those two and not, as you suggested, a number of people?"

I was really quite remorseful over this examination, Mrs. Roberts looked so dashed. "No," she said; "I suppose no one else really. Except, of course—"

At this point we were interrupted by the entrance of the lady's husband, who appeared to be going round shutting up the inn for the night. "Mr. Wedderburn, sir," he said, "you'll surely be wanting a nightcap? And it will be a toddy, I'm thinking, in this dreich weather?"

Mrs. Roberts seized my empty cup. "Mr. Wedderburn, you'll take another malted milk?"

I divined here some conjugal friction which I had no desire to exacerbate; murmuring an indistinguishable word I picked up my candle and betook myself to bed. But I verily believe that, for all my satisfactory demolition of the supernatural element in Mrs. Roberts's story, I half-expected to meet the ghost of Ranald Guthrie of Erchany in the corridor.

I was awakened in the morning by clamour; hastening to the window, I found this to proceed from the assembled young of Kinkeig, and to be occasioned by the appearance at the tail of the village of a tall and slender youth, armoured in the species of exquisiteness that defies exhaustion or disordered attire, and bearing on his shoulder—the prime cause, this, of the juvenile excitement by which I had been disturbed—implements which I presently identified as ski sticks and skis. It was to be conjectured that here was a visitor from Erchany; I dressed and hurried downstairs. As I had anticipated, the young man was awaiting me. He came forward and said: "I am Noel Gylby. I think you must be—" I rather expected him to add "the person sent by my uncle." Instead, he concluded: "—the gentleman who has been good enough to come and help us?"

"My name," I said, "is Wedderburn. And I have come to give what help I can."

Warmly, but not without the deference proper in the young, Mr. Gylby shook me by the hand. "Then, sir," he said, "begin by offering me breakfast!"

In the course of the hour ensuing I found Noel Gylby—though not perhaps without a due sense of his own charm—an agreeable and intelligent youth. His account of the events at Erchany was lively—in places, indeed, what Aeneas would call "hard boiled"—but it was also confident and clear: I noted that if and when the time came here would be an excellent witness. And by extraordinary good fortune he had kept a journal at Erchany. He was good enough to hand it to me and I read it at once. I will here merely add a note on the events subsequent to his last entry.

The Erchany odd lad—orra lad, to give the phrase its local flavour—had reached Kinkeig, as Gylby predicted, shortly after dawn on Christmas Day. His exhaustion was such that it was some time before he could give an articulate account of himself; and it must have been between nine and ten o'clock before anything effective was done. A volunteer had to be found to struggle into Dunwinnie for the doctor, the telephone line having come down in the night. Even then there was likely to be delay; Dr. Noble's most practicable route to Erchany would be along the frozen length of Loch Cailie, and it would be unlikely that a vehicle could be prepared for him under a matter of hours. A similar delay marked the immediate relief of Castle Erchany. The Kinkeig constable was justifiably doubtful of keeping his bearings without Tammas, and so Tammas had to be given time to recover. Eventually the constable, Tammas and two strong lads set off some time after noon—the escort being occasioned, it may be suspected, by the constable's sense that he was about to storm a citadel of the blackest magic. Making remarkable time, they reached Erchany soon after four. The constable inspected tower and body, took statements, pocketed keys and drank tea—by which time the hour was too advanced for any sort of safe return. One of the lads, however, was resolute to get back that night—he had a tryst, Gylby imagined, with his lass—and he eventually set out alone and had the good fortune to reach Kinkeig safely at about nine o'clock, bringing with him the constable's preliminary report. By this time the telephone line had been repaired and the police at Dunwinnie were provided—apparently by Mrs. Johnstone the postmistress—with all the information that was available. Meanwhile Dr. Noble had reached the castle by way of the loch; like the constable and the second strong lad he spent the night there.

Thursday the twenty-sixth December—the day of my own journey north—was distinguished by the appearance of senior police officers and the sheriff of the county, a person of adventurous disposition who was attracted by the notion of a mystery buried so deep in snow. He came by way of Kinkeig, set out accompanied by his clerk to tramp to Erchany, abandoned the clerk half-way, arrived at the castle, took notes and announced that he would hold an inquiry, turned back, found the unfortunate clerk in a critical condition and carried him on his shoulders back to the village. He then ate a supper the proportions of which I was later to hear graphically described by Roberts, excruciated Mrs. Roberts by drinking a bottle and a half of bad claret, and was finally driven off to Dunwinnie, promising to arrange for a fleet of snow-ploughs next day. I should say that I recount these circumstances not as being strictly relevant to my narrative, but simply as likely to reflect credit on the legal profession in the northern part of these Islands.

Gylby then went on to explain his own appearance that morning. He had noticed the skis among some lumber in the little bedroom in the tower and recollecting that the route to Kinkeig was largely downhill over not too heavily-timbered snow slopes he had persuaded the police to let him borrow them. The proceeding had been successful and had given him, he complacently remarked, a capital appetite. He only regretted that there had not been a second pair of skis for my client Miss Sybil Guthrie—who, as the heiress of Erchany, was expecting the arrival of her legal advisor with some impatience.

I was just resigning myself to the prospect of a journey altogether more arduous than suited my years when a further and greater commotion in the village heralded the arrival of the promised snow-ploughs. Two motor contrivances of a modern and powerful type, they passed us with a muffled roar and disappeared up the road to Erchany. I had retained my hired car overnight; we had nothing to do but step into it and follow comfortably and at our leisure. Learning that the body was to be brought down that afternoon and that the inquiry would be held at the manse immediately before the interment, I judged it prudent to proceed to the castle at once. I had instructions to receive and observations to make before I could confidently face the afternoon's proceedings. Gylby, who had something the air of a lighthouse-keeper who has successfully handed over in trying circumstances, seemed disposed to linger over the oatcakes and marmalade; with some persuasion I managed to get him on the move a few minutes before half-past nine. We were about to leave the inn when Mrs. Roberts appeared and asked me—with the most evident interest—if I would see a caller, him that Mistress McLaren had taken refuge with, Ewan Bell? I could hardly refuse; Gylby politely proposed to take a walk down the village and buy tobacco; the visitor was presently shown into my private sitting-room.

Mr. Bell will forgive me if I venture to describe him as venerable and magnificent. An athlete who had retired in his later years upon the profession of Biblical patriarch is perhaps the best image to offer the reader: his shoulders might have been those of a smith rather than of a cobbler; his features had the benign severity of some pillar of the Kirk from the pencil of a Wilkie. He bowed to me gravely and said he understood I was to represent the family interest in the probing of the sad affair at the big house?

"I am giving legal advice to Miss Guthrie, Mr. Bell. As you may know, she is the American lady who happened to be staying at the castle at the time of Mr. Guthrie's death."

"And no doubt, sir, a relation of the laird's?"

I considered Mr. Bell shrewdly. He seemed a most responsible old man and not at all likely to have called merely out of a thirst for gossip. "Miss Guthrie is a relation of the dead man and has a near interest in the estate."

Ewan Bell again gravely inclined his head. "What I've ventured in about, Mr. Wedderburn, is the young people that have gone away—Miss Mathers and the lad Lindsay. I have a thought that if there's any talk of its being other than an accident that's befallen at Erchany it will be the strangeness of their going that's the reason."

"Their disappearance is certainly a striking circumstance."

My visitor weighed this non-committal answer carefully. Then he said: "What I've come to say is, their going was at the bidding of the laird."

"You interest me, Mr. Bell. May I invite you to take something against this very trying weather?"

With a severity which contrived to give all the effect of stern refusal Mr. Bell agreed to a dram. This was presently brought by Mrs. Roberts—I fear it confirmed her in the evil opinion of lawyers which the sheriff's tolerance of claret had begun—and Mr. Bell paused only for a ceremonial word over his glass before producing that letter of Christine Mathers' which has been reproduced on an earlier page. I read it through twice with the greatest attention before I spoke. "Mr. Bell, this is a most significant document. You have no doubt shown it to the police?"

"I thought, Mr. Wedderburn, I'd like the counsel of a well-reputed person like yourself first."

"A perfectly proper feeling. But you must take it to the police before the inquiry. And now perhaps you can give me some account of the circumstances in which the letter was received?"

Briefly, Bell outlined that interview with Christine Mathers which is fully described in his narrative. I was a good deal impressed both by the facts and by that interpretation of them which seemed to lie at the back of the Kinkeig shoemaker's mind. If Guthrie's final interview with Lindsay in the tower had been arranged not with the purpose of buying him off but of dismissing him in the company of Miss Mathers, then the tone of the interview as reported by Miss Guthrie was a perfectly natural one. And it was conceivable that Guthrie, a highly unstable man unable to reconcile himself to losing his niece to an enemy, had simply committed suicide as Miss Guthrie apparently maintained.

But undoubtedly there was some sort of case against the lad Lindsay. His known enmity towards Guthrie, his dramatic appearance on the tower staircase a minute after Guthrie's fall, the rifled bureau, his flight with Miss Mathers: these as counts in an indictment were clear enough. He was protected, indeed, chiefly by my client Miss Guthrie's categorical statement that he had left Guthrie alive and well in the tower. This statement Bell's testimony and the letter he had produced now reinforced, for they indicated that the difficulties over Lindsay's suit had been in process of settlement—a settlement the final stage of which Miss Guthrie had witnessed just short of midnight from her hiding-place outside Guthrie's study. No doubt a person concerned to suggest a case against Lindsay could attempt to place the letter as part of an elaborately contrived plot against Guthrie, but unlikely ingenuity of this sort I did not think it necessary to explore at the moment. I turned to another point.

"Mr. Bell, we have here a very extraordinary situation. Miss Mathers' letter suggests that she was to be packed off quietly—apparently with the unkindest implications of ignominy—at Christmas. She and her future husband were simply to emigrate and go out of Mr. Guthrie's life. That is strange and harsh enough and would convict the dead man of being more than eccentric in character. But what are we to think of this departure being fixed for the dead of night—and moreover actually insisted upon when that night proved as wild as it did? It is difficult to believe that these young people could have got through the snow alive."

Bell nodded his head and was silent for a moment. Then he answered my last point first. "They took a chance their spirit would drive them to take, setting out in the smother of the storm. But you'll know, Mr. Wedderburn, the wind had dropped within minutes of their leaving, and a bittock moon was coming through forbye. Lindsay, that's a stout and skilly chiel, would get the lass safely over to his own folk in Mervie. And the next day they'd be at Dunwinnie and away."

"It hasn't been heard if they've been traced at Dunwinnie?"

"That I couldn't say. But with all the stour and confloption of the curlers there it's likely enough not. And as for the laird driving them out in secret and at midnight into a storm, it's just what would fit the black humour of the man."

"You think he really did that?"

"I do."

"And that the laird then committed suicide in some sort of despair?"

"I think that's the conclusion will be come to, Mr. Wedderburn."

I looked at Ewan Bell curiously. "Then how would you account for the gold that has disappeared?"

He was plainly startled. "The gold, sir? I know nothing of that."

"A drawer in the corner of the study, I understand, has been violently broken open and gold apparently taken from it."

"That's not so hard to explain as you might think, Mr. Wedderburn. You'll notice Christine says Guthrie was going to give her a sum of money—her own—and as for a drawer being opened with violence the laird himself was a right violent man. You'll be hearing a story soon of the senseless fury he put to the breaking down of a door a while back."

That Guthrie had himself taken the money from the drawer and given it to Miss Mathers again dovetailed, I noted, with Miss Guthrie's statement that neither the laird nor Lindsay had moved in the direction of the bureau while Lindsay was in the tower. And once more I was confronted with a hypothetical sequence of events that had marked imaginative coherence: the final and harshly contrived parting, the bitter plunge to death almost as the hour brought in peace on earth and goodwill among men. I contemplated this in silence for some moments . . . and knew I was dissatisfied.

I rose. "Mr. Bell, I must be getting up to Erchany. As yet I know far too little to judge of the matter. But I am very grateful to you for coming in. You are an important witness and I shall no doubt see you again this afternoon."

"And you think, Mr. Wedderburn, it will be suicide proven?"

"I think the police, or others, must find Lindsay and Miss Mathers. And for the rest—that truth lies at the bottom of the well. By the way, can you tell me anything of a man called Gamley? He was the first to find Mr. Guthrie's body in the moat."

"He was grieve at the home farm once, but left after having words with the laird."

"Harsh words?"

Bell smiled. "It would be hard to find any in these lands that couldn't remember harsh words with Guthrie of Erchany. But I judge he comes little into this story. He would be but with the lad Lindsay and waiting to give him a hand away. They met in together some time back and had become fast friends."

And here my interview with Ewan Bell ended. I rejoined Gylby, who had returned triumphant from the stationer's with a tin of John Cotton, and we went out into the nip of the winter morning. The skis were piled on the roof of the car, certain parcels requisitioned by Mrs. Hardcastle were deposited with the driver, and we drove off for Castle Erchany amid the universal curiosity of Kinkeig. As Mrs. Roberts confided to me at parting, there had been nothing like it since the medicos—the reference being doubtless to the unfortunate London physician and his colleagues who had visited the dead man some two years before.

"Mr. Gylby," I said as we crept cautiously over the surface exposed by the ploughs, "I take it that nothing"—I hesitated—"untoward was discovered about Guthrie's body?"

"I don't understand."

"Well, as the story runs in Kinkeig, this desperate Lindsay had chopped off a number of the fingers."

Abruptly, young Gylby stopped stuffing a pipe. "I really think the Scotch are—"

"The bloody limit?"

My young acquaintance, I believe, had placed me comfortably as a person of somewhat ponderous utterance; it gave me considerable pleasure to see him positively jump as I thus briefly expressed his thought. "I was going to put it," he said, "that they are people with a developed taste in the macabre. Guthrie's fingers are intact. It's his gold that's gone."

"Quite so. . . . I understand that it is definitely for Miss Guthrie that I am to act?"

"If you are going to be so good."

"Very well. Let me put it to you that you have made a statement in contradiction to certain apparent testimony of my client." And I tapped Gylby's journal which I was still holding. "Miss Guthrie states that between Guthrie and Lindsay there was nothing like heat; that they shook hands and parted quietly; even that Lindsay spoke or comported himself 'gently.' You state that at your own view of Lindsay little more than a minute later you received 'an extraordinarily vivid impression of passion.' Now this discrepant evidence may be important. Are you sure that your impression was accurate?"

"Yes." Gylby's answer was at once reluctant and convinced.

"Miss Guthrie was observing those people more or less at leisure. You, on the other hand, speak of what 'happened in a flash,' and of 'a second and a second only.' Are you not more likely to be mistaken than she?"

I thought it wise to let my tone suggest to this slightly airy young man the manner in which an inquiry of the sort impending might have to be conducted. But he was perfectly serious and perfectly forthright. "There seems to be such a probability, Mr. Wedderburn. Nevertheless I don't think my impression is wrong."

I believe it was at this point that I made up my mind—if in a preliminary way—as to what had really happened at Erchany. And my conclusion, I saw, was likely to make my position delicate. I turned to another topic.

"Mr. Gylby, about the man Hardcastle. You are something of a prejudiced witness? It would be possible to suggest, on the strength of your journal, that your attitude to him has been quite venomous from the moment of his first unkind reception of you at Erchany?"

Gylby contented himself with saying: "You wait till you see him."

"And you are inclined to credit him with some hidden motive in the affair?"

"He was up to something. Guthrie never gave him that message to me."

"Certainly that appears to be Miss Guthrie's impression."

With unexpected heat Gylby said: "Sybil was speaking the truth."

"You cannot suppose me to be suggesting otherwise. Have you any notion of why Hardcastle should give you the false message?"

"I have some notion it might be an act of stupid malice against his master. He stumbled against the wall of the staircase once or twice as we were going up and it occurred to me he was acting in some sort of random, fuddled state. I think he may be not only a rascal but a drunken rascal."

"And not a man engineering some complicated deception?"

Gylby shook his head. "He's cunning, all right. But he couldn't see far enough ahead for anything like that."

"Another point. You thought Guthrie was mad? And you formed that impression before hearing Mrs. Hardcastle speak of doctors who had apparently come to inquire into his sanity some years ago?"

"I thought him mad from the first few minutes. Only you must understand, sir, that I use the word very loosely. I don't know that his was the sort of madness they certify; I rather suppose not. It was more as if he lived in the shadow of something that no man could remain quite sane while contemplating. He was broken, fragmented. He was mad as the heroes were mad when the Furies were hunting them down."

I looked at my companion with a new interest. "A most illuminating remark, Mr. Gylby. I have always maintained against our educational reformers that there is the greatest utility in the grand old fortifying classical curriculum."

3

THE road from Dunwinnie to Kinkeig and the road from Kinkeig through Glen Erchany to Castle Erchany form with the long line of Loch Cailie a rough equilateral triangle. In the centre of this soars the bulk of Ben Cailie, buttressed to the south by the smaller mass of Ben Mervie and skirted to the south again first by Glen Mervie and then by the precipitous Pass of Mervie. The panorama of this on our right as we drove—peak upon peak of virgin snow soaring into a bleakly sunlit winter sky—was a spectacle well-calculated at once to soothe and elevate the mind. The latter part of our journey was performed in silence, broken only by an involuntary exclamation of my own when we finally turned a bend and sighted the castle across a final arm of the loch. As a historical monument it is, I suppose, of quite minor importance, and additions in the later seventeenth century have somewhat modified—though they have not destroyed—its stern mediaeval character. But my first impression of it was of something so darkly powerful and so inviolably lonely—like a monster of the most solitary habit half couched in a lair of larch and snow—that I could not have been more struck by the sudden appearance of the original Tintagel itself. Particularly impressive was the tower, massive but remarkably lofty, and built, it may be supposed, for observation as well as defence. Looking at the sheer lines of it from a distance I could understand Gylby's instant knowledge that the man who had fallen from that height was inevitably dead.

We drove over a drawbridge and pulled up in the central court. Young Gylby said cheerfully: "Home again!" and assisted me to alight.

My first awareness—like that of Erchany's unbidden guests a few nights before—was of the dogs; confined in a system of kennels at the farther end of the court, they were signalizing their disapproval of our advent in no uncertain terms. I was next aware of an elderly and infirm old woman in a shawl and snow-boots, hobbling towards us with every appearance of haste and anxiety. For a moment I was almost afraid we were to hear the announcement of another fatality; then she called out eagerly: "You'll have minded my poison? You won't have disremembered it, Mr. Gylby, sir?"

"Here you are, Mrs. Hardcastle." And Gylby handed her out the parcels from beside the driver. She was about to make off with them as hastily as she had come when she became aware of the presence of a stranger. Not—as I imagine—without some discomfort in the joints, she made me a ramshackle curtsy. Gylby said politely: "Mr. Wedderburn—Mrs. Hardcastle."

"Sir," she said, "you'd best know at once what Mr. Gylby knows. There's a terrible great number of rats in Erchany." She tapped her parcels and looked fearfully about her. "But

I'm enduring it no more! I'm an old body grown and now I'm going to sleep of nights." Her voice sank hoarsely and she nodded her head to where the figure of a man had appeared beside the kennels. "But don't tell my man! He's right unkind. Whiles he sets them at me."

"The dogs, Mrs. Hardcastle?"

"The rats."

And Mrs. Hardcastle, concealing her parcels beneath her shawl, hurried away. I turned to Gylby. "That is Hardcastle over by the kennels? It occurs to me to have a word with him before we go in."

I crossed the court. The late laird's factor was giving the dogs a more than meagre meal and cursing them heartily the while. "Down, Caesar," I heard him call as I came up, "down, you tink cur!"

My approach in the snow had been quite unheard. I said pleasantly in his ear: "Bonny beasts, Mr. Hardcastle."

He swung round and glared at me suspiciously—not, I fancy, merely because of the obvious irony of my remark. His villainy as sketched by Gylby was apparent enough. But it was not an assured villainy; he seemed, indeed, wofully lacking in confidence. He said now with a sort of surly uncertainty: "Maybe so."

"And this is Caesar? I should be inclined to give him a powder and follow it up with a little red meat. Now pray, Mr. Hardcastle, which is Doctor?"

Rather weakly, Hardcastle pointed at a recumbent animal. "That's him."

"Is it indeed? Let's have a look at him. Doctor! Hey, Doctor! You know, Mr. Hardcastle, I think Doctor must be deaf."

Hardcastle positively brightened. "He *is* deaf."

"Really now? That is a little unusual in so young a dog. I wonder, can you be mistaken? It should be easy to devise a test."

"Damn't to hell!" cried Hardcastle. "Will you leave the beast alone?"

"Certainly if you wish it; I believe my interest in the

animal is exhausted. A dumb—and deaf—witness, is he not? I am solicitor to Miss Guthrie, the incoming proprietor. I should be obliged if you would take me to her."

Gylby's estimate of the factor, I reflected, had been remarkably accurate. A cunning ruffian, but one whose cunning was soon exhausted. I was not displeased to find him fitting neatly enough into the picture that was forming in my mind of the events of Christmas Eve. This picture was as yet far from complete; only the cardinal pieces—if I may use an image suggested by what I had heard of Ranald Guthrie's jigsaws—were as yet in place. But these gave me—unless I was greatly mistaken—the first outlines of a very curious situation. Inevitably, there was a great deal that was still obscure and invited the most careful and cautious investigation. I pause on this word. I had come to Erchany in my professional character as a solicitor; it will be not without amusement that the reader perceives me, while yet standing but on the threshold of the castle, as lured into the undignified role of a private detective agent!

As I entered the great hall of the castle a uniformed police officer stepped forward, introduced himself as Inspector Speight, and invited me into a small and bare room in which he had apparently established his headquarters. I might properly have insisted on being conducted to my client before assisting at any conference with the police; there seemed, however, to be no necessity for this and I accepted the invitation. I found Inspector Speight a civil and intelligent officer and judged it might be useful to show him I already had some grip of the situation. After a few preliminary remarks I therefore said: "I suppose you've found Gamley?"

"Yes, there was no difficulty in that. We have a line on him for this afternoon."

"And you have no doubt traced the young people who were packed off by the late Mr. Guthrie?"

"Packed off? I don't know about that."

"A point that will emerge, inspector. I think it will be found to be of some importance. And where had they got to?"

The inspector shook his head. "Strangely enough, Mr. Wedderburn, we've had no word of them yet. But then they had good reason to lie pretty low."

"I wonder, inspector, I wonder. It is possible that now Mr. Guthrie is dead the necessity for their departing unobtrusively is over. I venture to think it is very possible."

"If I may say so, Mr. Wedderburn, that seems a singularly wrong-headed way of looking at it."

"That depends entirely on the point from which one looks, does it not? Perhaps you have grounds for believing that the young Mr. Lindsay has committed some crime?"

I had reckoned accurately in counting on a streak of irritation latent in Inspector Speight. My bland manner drew him at once. He said abruptly: "The lad pitched Guthrie to his death. I haven't a doubt of it."

"Perhaps so, inspector. I would say myself it is a little early to cherish convictions. And I think there may be some evidence in direct rebuttal?"

"To be sure, there's Miss Guthrie."

So Miss Guthrie had already told the police her story. I rose. "I think, inspector, I must now seek my client."

Inspector Speight made a protesting gesture. "You mustn't be taking it, sir, I think it necessary to discredit what the young lady has told us entirely. But she was scared and confused out there in the storm and she wanted to see as little ill in the business up there as might be." The inspector paused. "Perhaps she'll come to a clearer recollection, though, on thinking it over."

I was again aware that Inspector Speight was an intelligent man. And for a moment I wondered if he might not be positively guileful. Miss Guthrie, who had been mysteriously on the very battlement from which the dead man had fallen, was it appeared that dead man's heir. Of the delicacy of this position Speight had given no hint.

"So you think, inspector, that it's either Lindsay or nothing?"

Speight nodded emphatically. "An old feud, a new quarrel, a witness that he was in blazing passion, the gold broken into, him and the girl gone. One could hardly ask for more."

"Unless, perhaps, the chopping of the fingers from the corpse."

The inspector stared. "You've heard that? It but shows the daft and dirty gossip that countryfolk will seize on. Never heed their foolish claik, Mr. Wedderburn. You and I are concerned with facts."

"A healthy reminder, inspector. It frequently falls from my friend Lord Clanclacket on the bench. And you think there is no other direction in which the facts can point?"

Almost happily, Speight smiled. "Mr. Wedderburn, I'll give you something away. The American lassie didn't do it. There's such a thing as experience in the ways of crime. And thirty years of that tells me not to waste time that way. The lassie's real nice."

"I need hardly say that your impression is a most welcome one. Of course Neil Lindsay may prove real nice too."

Speight chuckled. "Time enough to decide that when we lay hands on him. I say it's Lindsay or nothing. And I think you really agree with me, sir."

"No, inspector, I don't agree. I cannot claim your experience of crime. But I have another opinion."

"Mr. Wedderburn, it would be a real privilege to have it."

"If, as I hope, it turns to conviction you shall have it before the sheriff this afternoon. But—as I said—it's early for convictions yet."

4

I WAS received by Miss Guthrie in what is referred to throughout these narratives as the schoolroom. She struck me at once as possessing that blend of elegance and *élan* which gives many of her cultivated countrywomen their slightly baffling charm; I was inclined to think that Inspector Speight, in finding her "nice" had displayed at once an accurate and unexpectedly sophisticated taste. She was evidently determined to be businesslike. I judged her to be a person familiar with the elementary proprieties of legal business; nevertheless I thought it proper to say a few words on the relations generally presumed to exist between solicitor and clients in these Islands. She listened with a very becoming attention—the reader must not think me unaware of a slight tendency in myself to what might be unkindly termed pomposity on such occasions—and presently we were seated comfortably together on a sofa. Miss Guthrie, indeed, was so kind as to give me permission to smoke a pipe.

"So far," I said, "I have interviewed only a certain Mr. Bell, our friend Mr. Gylby—from whom I have had a very full narrative both orally and in writing—and the Hardcastles. Gylby's character-sketch of Hardcastle seems to me penetrating."

"Noel," said Miss Guthrie briskly, "is quite an able youth."

"No doubt. He has also given something of a character-sketch—writing, you will understand, to a most confidential correspondent—of yourself."

Perhaps a shade blankly, Miss Guthrie said: "Oh!"

"He has recorded the opinion that you are not romantically disposed."

"I call that a mite unkind of Noel. All nice girls are romantic."

I smiled. "But some perhaps conceal it."

Sybil Guthrie lit a cigarette. "Mr. Wedderburn," she said, "is this the right way about our business?"

"I conceive it," I replied gravely, "to be a suitable approach."

"Very well. And I am a romantic girl and Noel was wrong. Will you tell me just why?"

"Consider the manner of your coming to Erchany, Miss Guthrie. Mr. Gylby, who was involved with your plan at the very closest quarters, is chiefly impressed by its ingenuity and efficiency. But to one like myself, at some distance from the affair, it is its aspect as a romantic prank that is most evident. You had eminent medical testimony, I gather, that Mr. Guthrie was in no sense certifiably insane, and your own covert visit to him could be of no practical utility. But you liked the excitement—the romance and excitement—of besieging the castle, of carrying it not by storm but by a ruse. You even sent a slightly flamboyant telegram to your American lawyer in London. What were you fundamentally engaged in? Family business? Not a bit of it. You were simply after adventure—and adventure seasoned with at least an appreciable spice of danger, for Mr. Guthrie was a very eccentric man. Noel Gylby has been so struck by what I may term your executive ability that he has quite missed what must be called the romanticism of the underlying motive."

Miss Guthrie manipulated a delicate veil of cigarette smoke between us. "And then, Mr. Wedderburn, what?"

"I am wondering whether this same impulse has not made you manipulate a little what you witnessed in the tower."

"You mean that Ranald Guthrie didn't commit suicide at all?"

"On the contrary, I am quite sure he committed suicide. Believe me that if I thought the account you gave to Mr. Gylby a fundamental perversion I could not possibly consent to act for you. And now, Miss Guthrie, we had better hold the rest of our consultation on the site of the incidents involved."

"You mean the tower? Must we? I hate the place now."

"Nevertheless I think that if you will be so good, and if the police will permit us, it will be a useful move."

My friend Inspector Speight proved good enough simply to hand me the keys of the staircase and the dead man's study; I rejoined Miss Guthrie and together we made the laborious ascent of the tower. Once entered, I looked about me with the liveliest curiosity. Flush with the door by which we stood, and but a few feet away, was what must be the door to the little bedroom. Half-way along the left-hand wall was the French window to the battlements. In the middle of the room was a square table serving as a desk. And everywhere were books.

I was struck by the agelessness of the place: not a thing but might have held its place where it stood for generations. The late Mr. Guthrie, it was to be concluded, had been of more than conservative temperament—in addition to which, of course, he had spent no penny that he could help. Half idly, I cast round for some sign of the nineteenth or twentieth centuries, and found it abruptly in the form of a hand telephone on the desk. I glanced at Miss Guthrie in perplexity. "Surely," I said, "Erchany isn't on the telephone!"

"Of course not, Mr. Wedderburn; we weren't as dumb as that. The machine here must be some sort of house-telephone to the offices. I haven't seen another in the castle."

"An interesting innovation of the penurious laird's. The police, I suppose, have been most efficiently over these rooms; nevertheless I suggest that before further talk we make a little inspection of our own. Let us begin with the rifled bureau."

The piece of furniture to which my client led me would have delighted a connoisseur, but it struck me as a most improperly fragile strong-box. Its single drawer had been broken open—a single powerful wrench would have sufficed—and in the bottom there still lay the few odd coins that had been noticed by Gylby. I stared at them, I suppose, in a sort of absent perplexity; Miss Guthrie seems to follow my thought. "I reckon," she said, "the tower itself is a sufficient strong-room."

"Perhaps so. Nevertheless it was a deliberate establishing of temptation. Do you think Hardcastle, for instance, would be so faithful a retainer as to resist it?"

Miss Guthrie wrinkled her forehead. "It is rather perplexing."

"Not at all."

"Mr. Wedderburn!" The sincerity of my client's astonishment was a pleasure to mark.

I gave a chuckle which oddly reminded me that I was Aeneas's uncle. "No perplexity, my dear lady, was intended: and—what is much more—none exists. Though I am bound to say you have done your best."

"Mr. Wedderburn, you are making quite unprofessional fun of me."

"Then let us be grave again and pursue our inspection. Among other things, I should much like to find the poems of William Dunbar."

I fear I was excelling in a rather childish species of mystification. I turned to the book shelves without more ado and began very seriously to search for the publications of the Scottish Text Society. Guthrie's books were most methodically arranged and I came upon them without difficulty. Taking down the three volumes of Dunbar, I found myself quite smothered in dust. "Our friend the poetical laird," I said, "knew his favourites. He had no need to refresh his memory on the poem he seems to have been so fond of." And I turned to the *Lament for the Makaris.*

"He takis the knychtis in the feild,
Anarmit under helme et scheild;
Wictour he is at all melle;
Timor Mortis conturbat me.

"He takis the campion in the stour,
The capitane closit in the tour,
The lady in bour full of bewte;
Timor Mortis conturbat me. . . .

"Well, Death has certainly taken the captain from his tower." I laid down the volume. "And there seems to be only one interpretation, does there not? But if Guthrie has not been reading Dunbar recently, let us see what he has been reading." And I moved over to a pile of books, still in their dust-covers, on the desk. Ewan Bell had omitted to tell me, at our interview a few hours earlier, of Guthrie's sudden interest in medical studies as reported by Miss Mathers, and I was therefore surprised as well as puzzled by the pile of medical literature which I found confronting me. Letheby

Tidy's *Synopsis of Medicine.* Osler's *Principles and Practice of Medicine.* Muir's *Text-book of Pathology*—I turned them over one after another in some perplexity. "Now where," I said, "does the science of medicine come into the picture?"

Miss Guthrie picked up Dunbar. "Well, it comes for that matter into the poem." And she read:

> "In medicyne the most practicianis,
> Lechis, surrigianis, et phisicianis,
> Thame self fra ded may not supple;
> *Timor Mortis conturbat me.*"

"That is very interesting. And if I may make the remark, Miss Guthrie, you have considerable facility in Middle Scots. You studied it at college?"

"Why, yes, I did."

"May I ask if you have taken your Ph.D.?"

"Yes, Mr. Wedderburn, I have."

"Then are you quite sure that you are not the 'doctor' for whom Hardcastle was on the lookout?"

Miss Guthrie flushed. "What an extraordinary piece of ingenuity! Of course I'm not. He knew nothing about me. And one doesn't arrange to be called 'Doctor Guthrie' all one's days because of a roaring piece of pedantry in youth."

"I suppose not. Well, let us search further. I only wish that my own 'youth' were as little behind me as yours."

I found little more to interest me in the study. Books apart, it carried only a few traces of the career and interests of Ranald Guthrie: a boomerang and a native food-carrier from his Australian days, a few sketches by Beardsley to mark his contacts with a past generation of writers, a case or two of Pictish and Roman remains in token of his interest in archaeology. I moved into the bedroom. Here too there seemed little of interest. Guthrie had slept in a room immediately below. Except for a stretcher bed used perhaps for an occasional siesta this was little more than a lumber-room: a broken chair, a pile of old canvas, rope and sticks in a corner, a cracked mirror hung on the wall, a scrap of tattered curtain over the narrow windows. Much of Erchany, I gathered, was in just this state of dilapidation; I was turning away when my attention was caught by a book lying on the floor. I picked it up. "More medicine, Miss Guthrie. *Experimental Radiology* by Richard Flinders." I put it down again. "We are here by courtesy of the police and had better leave things as we find them. And now, perhaps, it is time to return to our discussion."

Back in the study, Miss Guthrie took up what I knew to be her characteristic position perched on the desk. It was uncommonly chilly and I so far consulted the halting circulation of age as to talk while pacing about. "Miss Guthrie, I dare say you have read stories in which all sorts of revelations are effected by what is called a reconstruction of the crime?"

Obliquely but positively Miss Guthrie answered: "There was no crime. You've agreed to that yourself."

"I think you mistake me. But for the moment we will say 'the events of Christmas Eve.' And I invite you, here in this room, to consider the probable results of the police attempting a reconstruction of those events."

"I don't quite get what you mean."

"I mean simply that such a reconstruction would at once shake your testimony as it stands at present; and that it would shake it for a very good reason. The account you gave to Mr. Gylby was as much coloured by your own desires as it was illuminated by the clear light of objective fact."

Miss Guthrie stood up. "If you believe that, Mr. Wedderburn, I really don't think—"

"But what I can see that the police might not see is that you are placing yourself in a hazardous and disagreeable position to no purpose at all. I will not presume, as a man, to judge your attitude, though as a lawyer I must think it wrong. The relevant point is this: romantic perjury can only embarrass us. And all we need is the facts."

Miss Guthrie inspected the tips of her fingers. Then she said: "Please explain what you mean about a reconstruction."

"Imagine this room lit by two or three candles. The French window is not quite shut, there is a gale outside and the light is not only dim but uncertain and flickering. You are outside the window, peering in. Just how much could you see?"

"Quite a lot—in a flickering way. And no reconstruction could prove that I saw just so much, no more and no less."

"Very true. But it is much easier to demonstrate that neither you nor anyone else can see round a corner. And I put it to you that without thrusting your head into the room it is impossible from that French window to see those two contiguous doors—to staircase and bedroom—*fully and clearly*. If either were opened *wide* you would no doubt be able to see the movement. But if one—or both—were opened only *slightly*, so that a man might slip through, you would see nothing. In other words, Miss Guthrie, your testimony translates an impression quite illegitimately into a certainty. The staircase door opened wide and you saw no more of Lindsay. The bedroom door opened wide and you saw no more of Guthrie. But Lindsay might in the moments following have slipped through the two doors—from staircase to bedroom and back—without your being any the wiser."

Still perched on the desk, my client looked at the doors long and thoughtfully. "I suppose," she said, "that is so."

"I think you liked Miss Mathers?"

"I did."

"And this young Mr. Lindsay, from what you saw of him?"

Miss Guthrie's chin went up a decisive inch. "I thought him quite beautiful, Mr. Wedderburn."

"And you had further formed the opinion that your kinsman was an almost wholly unbeautiful person?"

"Very decidedly."

"Then we begin to see where we are. You were going to stick to these young people—whose circumstances are romantic, touching and beautiful—let the worst betide. All that stood between Lindsay and the gravest suspicion was your *knowledge* that he had gone out for good while Guthrie was alive. Therefore you have deliberately given your impression the status of knowledge . . . Miss Guthrie, have the police recorded your statement?"

"No. Inspector Speight said he would take it formally later."

"Speight is a most circumspect officer. Now let me most

earnestly tell you that you must go back to your mere and honest impression about the doors. You will lose credit if you don't. And the one vital necessity is that your testimony should be seen to be reliable."

"Mr. Wedderburn—I don't understand. Vital to what?"

"Vital to the safety of the quite beautiful young man Neil Lindsay."

My client jumped up and approached me in considerable agitation. "You must tell me more of what is in your mind, Mr. Wedderburn. You *must*."

"Simply this. That you couldn't really and truly see the doors clearly is a thousand pities—still, it is not fundamentally important. What is fundamentally important is what took place between Guthrie and Lindsay. And that is where you have actually lied."

Miss Guthrie was very pale and I thought I detected a rising tide of passion which might at any moment usher me from her presence for good and all. I therefore went on as hurriedly as was consonant with the impressiveness I knew to be necessary if I were to get my way with her. "You say Lindsay left quietly. Gylby says he left in a passion. And Gylby is speaking the truth. Now if Lindsay is to be vindicated we must have a clear picture of what actually happened. And that clear picture requires the truth—Gylby's truth. Do you understand me?"

Miss Guthrie passed a hand over her forehead and sat down rather limply on a chair. "I don't understand you at all."

"Let me then assure you of this—and I speak with nearly fifty years' experience of the law. Neil Lindsay is safe. I have a picture of the case now which no prosecution could break through. Guthrie committed suicide. But that is far from implying that there has been no crime. A few hours ago I thought your evidence about the doors might be vital to him. I know now that all he needs is your simple story of what happened in this room. Please give it to me."

Miss Guthrie rose, walked to the window and scanned the

snow as if there might be counsel in it. "I find it," she said presently, "terribly hard to believe you." There was a silence. "But it is clear I must do as you say." And she turned and came back to her old position on the desk.

"Of course you are right about the doors. I didn't realize it, but I see it's something they could demonstrate as a fact simply with a scale plan. I couldn't be certain Lindsay hadn't slipped back and through the bedroom to the battlements for the necessary half minute—though I *knew* he hadn't." Miss Guthrie looked at me squarely. "I *knew* Lindsay hadn't killed Guthrie. And everything followed from that."

"Inaccurate evidence never follows legitimately from anything, my dear."

With a sober nod Miss Guthrie acknowledged this final fatherly rebuke. Then she went on. "Everything I have said about the interview between Guthrie and Lindsay is true—except right at the end. They sat and had that formal parley. Guthrie never went and shouted to Hardcastle about asking Noel up. Neither of them could have gone near the bureau—"

"Exactly. That is vital and they can't shake you on it."

"But at the end they got up and walked about halfway to the door. I could still see them clearly and I thought they were going to part with formal civility—like I made up for Noel—when I suddenly saw that something had gone wrong. Guthrie was talking and though I couldn't hear a word I could *see* just what he was doing. He was lashing the boy—the young man—Lindsay with words. It was as if he knew he had some hold on him—some hold that made it safe to be briefly and hideously cruel. I knew in that instant that I just hated my kinsman and I felt—horribly it now seems—a fierce longing that the boy should kill him there and then. That was why I felt afterwards that I must—"

"I see. Had Lindsay actually killed Guthrie you would have been spiritually an accomplice."

"Something like that. It was a piece of obscene cruelty on Guthrie's part, and it was over in a few seconds. I had just drawn breath from it when I saw that Lindsay was gone."

"And that is the whole story? Then you have nothing to do but come downstairs and repeat it formally to Inspector Speight."

Miss Guthrie gave a sigh of relief. Then she hesitated. "Mr. Wedderburn—you are sure? It's terribly hard to believe."

I smiled at the reiterated phrase. "You need have no doubts."

"You know, Noel said there was another thing. He said it would be thought very strange that I should *guess* on that cry that Guthrie had—"

"My dear young lady, Mr. Gylby's experience is no doubt curious and extensive. Nevertheless I venture to assure you that you need have no apprehensions." I consulted my watch. "And now there will just be time to send post-haste to Dunwinnie for an electrician."

"An electrician!"

"Precisely. And one, if possible, with an impressive and venerable exterior. Much depends on little matters of that sort. And now, Miss Guthrie, for Inspector Speight."

We went out and I locked the study door behind me. I felt, I believe, much as I feel when I lock up a family deed box with the knowledge that its affairs are comfortably settled for a generation. In silence we descended the long staircase and made our way to the police inspector's room. We found Speight consuming ham-sandwiches in meditative solitude.

"May we interrupt you, inspector? My client Miss Guthrie would like to make a formal statement. And I don't think we shall have much more trouble over the Erchany mystery."

"You think not, Mr. Wedderburn? I'm real glad to hear it. Come away, Miss Guthrie, and we'll have your bit story down on paper for the sheriff."

"There is one other matter before we begin. I propose to send my car into Dunwinnie to find a competent electrician. I believe he may be useful to us."

Inspector Speight put down his sandwich. "Mr. Wedderburn, did you say an electrician?"

"Just that. And if they have a stop-watch at the police station I believe that would be useful too."

5

WHEN my client's statement had been taken I excused myself and sought out Noel Gylby. I saw that I should presently need an assistant, and realizing that Miss Guthrie's considered evidence on the doors had confirmed Speight in his suspicions of Lindsay I judged it imprudent to attempt taking him into my confidence at this point. Gylby, I thought, would be reliable as well as intelligent, and he would certainly relish the business of unravelling a mystery. Together we found Mrs. Hardcastle, who was creeping somewhat eerily about the castle in furtherance of her furtive warfare with the rats, and persuaded her to cut us some sandwiches for an early luncheon. I then suggested that we find a quiet spot for a talk and Gylby, after a moment's thought, led the way up to the long winding room known as the gallery. I paused to view the demolished door in some astonishment—I had not yet heard little Isa Murdoch's story—and then we passed inside. After a cursory view of the family portraits and the mouldering theology we made ourselves as comfortable as we could in an alcove.

"Mr. Gylby, you will have some idea of what the police have in mind about this affair?"

"Hanging the elusive Lindsay."

"Quite so. And have you any opinion of your own?"

"Nothing so clear-cut as an opinion. But I have one or two feelings—the principal one being that there are too many pieces. It's as if a couple of the laird's famous jigsaws had got mixed up and one found oneself, as the picture progressed, with an *embarras de richesses*."

"I find myself in agreement with you, Gylby. Pray go on."

"Too much villainy about. Active villainy in Hardcastle and a sort of lurking, prospective villainy in Guthrie himself. My idea rather is that Guthrie was up to some dirty game, that Lindsay was somehow too much for him and that in consequence he got what he more or less deserved. I have felt that Sybil has some suspicion or knowledge that it was that way—and that she has been trying to shield Lindsay as a result."

"A most interesting theory. Can you push it further?"

"Well—it sounds fantastic and squalid and horrible—but what about this. Consider the apparently rifled bureau. Guthrie was proposing to plant a fake robbery on Lindsay at the very moment he was going off with his niece. Lindsay spotted the plot while up in the tower, slipped back without Sybil seeing him and sent Guthrie over the battlements. Then he simply made off with the girl."

"Excellent up to a point. But I think it has a psychological flaw. Such a plot against Lindsay implies a twisted mind of the perpetrator. We may grant that; it is evident that Guthrie was a most peculiar person. But what of Lindsay? Guthrie was in a sense his enemy, and that he should kill him in passion upon the discovery of such a plot is possible enough. But would he thereupon—as you put it—'simply make off with the girl'? I think that would almost imply another twisted mind in the case. The impulse of a normal man, killing his enemy in passion and upon the discovery of a dastardly plot, would be to face it out. Particularly, he would not make off as a fugitive with a girl he loved. Is that sentiment, Gylby? I am inclined to call it sound mental science."

"I rather agree."

"Moreover we should still be left with far too many pieces—have fitted in, indeed, little more than the rifled bureau. So let us go back and glance at what appears to be Speight's present case. Lindsay kills Guthrie, steals his gold and runs off with his niece. What do you think of that as a picture?"

"First of all, that Christine Mathers isn't the sort to fall for that kind of chap. And that it's lurid and crazy."

"And if Lindsay could be shown to have paused in his flight, and in requital of some legendary injury to have chopped a few fingers off the corpse?"

Gylby stared at me. "A madman's dream."

"Exactly—a madman's dream. And your first impression of Ranald Guthrie was that he was mad."

"Good God!"

"Your ejaculation is almost justified. It is a most horrid picture. Ranald Guthrie committed suicide—and in the same instant an abominable crime. Having got that we have got to the core of the mystery. It remains to work it out in detail.

"Guthrie would not let Lindsay have his niece: we must begin, I think, with that as a fact of pathological intensity. And for some reason his hatred of the young man was so extreme that he plotted—having failed, perhaps, to achieve his end in other ways—to prevent the thing by Lindsay's death—and his own. Remember he was of a more than melancholic temperament, with that deep will-to-death which is the ground of so many apparently unmotivated suicides. Actually, he once attempted suicide—I was fortunate enough to secure evidence of that yesterday—and we must imagine him contriving an act in which these dominant impulses would be telescoped. He would rob Lindsay of his niece by a method that meant nothing less than Lindsay's ignominious death at the hands of the law; at the same time he would satisfy his own obscure and profound craving for self-destruction. You can see why he chanted Dunbar's poem and why the fear of death was upon his face: he knew he was going to die. You can see why he gave signs of struggle; why, as Miss Mathers said, he seemed 'in two minds.' No man could meditate such a deed without moments of terror and revulsion.

"There was to be a crime—and a witness. There was to be the best sort of witness—a medical witness."

"Hardcastle's doctor!"

"I think so. The first thing that went wrong was that this doctor—whoever he be—failed to turn up. You and Miss

Guthrie turned up instead. And Guthrie decided that you would serve. Hence his look of calculation as he considered you. Hence his significant remark that he was very glad you had come.

"I believe there is another trace of the original plan in the circumstance that Guthrie feigned illness next day. That was somehow to be exploited to get the doctor to the right place at the right moment—everything was to turn on that—and it was a fragment of the plan which for some reason he adhered to even when the doctor—daunted, we may guess, by the snows—had to be replaced by yourself.

"And now the plan. It was really very simple. Lindsay was to come on Christmas Eve and take Miss Mathers, together with her dowry, quietly and indeed secretly away. Guthrie's eccentricity, his insistence that the marriage was disgraceful and so on, was enough to give a natural colour to this. Lindsay and Miss Mathers would see that he was determined to humiliate them by such an arrangement, but they would suspect nothing more. Nor should we at this moment have the least notion of what had been arranged but for the chance of Miss Mathers having managed to send a letter to an old friend in Kinkeig. Save for this circumstance, which Guthrie didn't reckon on, there would only have been the word of the fugitives that Guthrie had ever sanctioned their departure, or that he had given Christine a sum of gold.

"Lindsay was to be brought up to the tower for a final interview with Guthrie—and at a set moment he was to be dismissed. And dismissed in a particular mood. I suppose Guthrie knew the lad's temperament, and knew how to lash him—Miss Guthrie's word—into a flaming passion before telling him to go."

"Mr. Wedderburn, the man was a fiend!"

"You barely exaggerate. And you see what actually happened. Summoned by Hardcastle, you came up the tower staircase just in time to meet that very angry young man face to face. He pushed past you unheeding—you remember that Hardcastle made a noticeably ineffective attempt to stop him—and suspecting nothing. Then he simply joined Miss Mathers and together they shook the dust of Erchany from their feet. And meantime—the moment, indeed, that Lindsay was through the study door—Guthrie had dashed through the little bedroom and over the battlements to his death."

Gylby had got up and was pacing up and down the gallery. Now he stopped, the plainest excitement on his face. "It fits—yes, Mr. Wedderburn, it all fits! Only I can't just see how the times—"

"An important point. We shall presently suggest with a stop-watch, I hope, that Lindsay could not have killed Guthrie; that between the moment of your hearing the cry and seeing Guthrie fall and of his appearing at the turn of the stair there was not sufficient time for him to have come all the way from the battlements. But Guthrie did not expect a matter of half a minute to be important there. He did not expect the witness on the stair to *see* his body fall. And, overestimating his own nerve, he did not expect to give that cry. It was to be enough that, hard upon Lindsay's descending in a passion from the tower, Guthrie's body should be found at the bottom of it.

"Nevertheless we must return to the matter of timing in a moment. But meanwhile note this. Guthrie's nerve failed him in that final cry. But it also failed him in a more vital particular. He was unable to lop himself of a finger or so before he fell."

"Mr. Wedderburn, I can't believe it all. It's the most horrible thing I ever heard."

"But it is so. Guthrie sharpened a hatchet to deal, he told Mrs. Hardcastle, with a great rat: it was undoubtedly his underlying thought that the rat was Lindsay and that the hatchet was to be used to incriminate him. Again, Hardcastle displayed a curious eagerness to get at the body; he declared that Lindsay had 'mischieved' the body; as soon as the lad brought here by the constable got back to Kinkeig the rumour spread that the body had been mutilated. Only Hardcastle could have set that story going; he believed the thing had happened simply because he knew it was to be part of the plan; and if he has been in some puzzlement and uncertainty recently it is because he is bewildered at having heard no authentic news of it. If the thing had actually happened the point of evidence against Lindsay would have been, in the popular mind, overwhelming. And the popular mind is not to be disregarded when you are out for a criminal conviction. Macabre as Guthrie's abortive plan was, it was by no means unintelligent."

Gylby produced a handkerchief and mopped his brow. "Mr. Wedderburn, I most frightfully admire your unruffled calm. Guthrie must have been horribly and obscenely mad."

I shook my head gravely. "No! In all this there is nothing that is not perfectly logical and clear-headed, nothing that would incline a court for a moment to allow that Guthrie was insane. He knew what he wanted and how to achieve it. And he emerges from your own narrative clearly enough as one who knew right and wrong. Mad he was in the loosest sense. Strictly he was sane, wicked and fantastic, and even his fantasy was perfectly efficient—was all calculatingly directed to a rational if perverted end. Only once did he topple over into extravagance—a flourish of fantasy that positively told against his game."

Gylby slapped his hand resoundingly upon the faded surface of Africa on an adjacent terrestrial globe. "The learned rats!"

"The learned rats. His plan for getting the witness up the tower stair was upset by the non-appearance of the doctor, and before settling on the further perfectly rational plan which he finally employed he indulged the fantasy of luring you to the tower through the messages tied to the rats. I believe a court would accept that as fragmentary evidence of real craziness. But it was only a momentary aberration. And all the time the prosaic and efficient machinery for getting you to the tower on time was waiting to be set in motion."

"You said you would come back to the timing. And that was surely the difficult thing—getting me near the top of the tower staircase on the dot."

"Undoubtedly it was. And it was there that the conservative

laird had recourse to the resources of modern technicology. That is why I have sent for an electrician. Notice that it was unimportant that you should be at this or that point at a given moment by the clock. What was important was that Guthrie should know just where you were at a given moment. He could then time his conversation with and dismissal of Lindsay. You remember saying that you had wondered if Hardcastle were drunk—because once or twice he stumbled against the wall of the staircase as you went up? And you have noticed that Guthrie had a little house telephone on his desk? No doubt there is no bell but merely a muted buzzer of the modern type. And no doubt Hardcastle could send signals of your progress by some such simple action as momentarily contacting two wires. He led you upstairs, you will recall, 'deliberately.' The picture seems complete. Your visit to the laird was timing itself with all the accuracy of a royal procession."

"It all means that Hardcastle was privy to the whole unspeakable plot?"

"I do not think you were mistaken, my dear Mr. Gylby, in your estimate of the very great depravity of the man Hardcastle. I only wish that his neck, in our good Scots phrase, could feel the weight of his buttocks. But unfortunately he is not an accessory to actual murder."

"But he will be convicted? I mean you can put all this across the sheriff or whoever it is, and see that the man is tried?"

"I haven't a doubt of it. And now I wonder if there are any loose ends? Guthrie's random efforts to break momentarily from his own extreme miserliness—the efforts that had the odd consequence of presenting you with a supper of caviare—were an attempt, no doubt, to make colourable his treacherous gift of gold to his departing niece. If she had reason to think his miserly habits were breaking up she would be the less likely to suspect that there was anything wrong. And the sudden interest in medical studies I am inclined to put down to a morbidity arising from the knowledge of what was in front of him. Indeed, here perhaps is another glimpse of real craziness in the man: Guthrie turning to medical science for companionable reading on amputations and broken necks. A poor preparation for eternity, Gylby. I fear he little heeded the last verse of Dunbar's poem.

Gylby rose. "What a comfort orthodoxy can be! It's nice to think that the soul of Ranald Guthrie is fairly roasting."

"I fear that is very much the sentiment you justly censured in the man Gamley. And now—"

I was interrupted by the appearance of Inspector Speight in the demolished doorway. "Surely, inspector, that is not my electrician yet?"

"No more it is: he'll be a good hour more. But there's a message up from Kinkeig I thought you'd like to have. They've found Lindsay and the young lady at Liverpool. The two are on their road back now, with a lad from Scotland Yard to help them find their way. They set off yesterday afternoon and will be in Kinkeig in time for the sheriff."

"Splendid, inspector. Their return is most timely. I think we can undertake to settle the matter of Mr. Guthrie's death quickly enough and leave them to their happiness. They will deserve it."

Speight stared, shook his head dubiously and went away. I turned round and discovered Gylby gazing absently at the long line of cracked and browned Guthrie portraits, a curiously perplexed look on his face. He caught my glance. "Mr. Wedderburn, Guthrie's death is settled—but somehow I don't feel there is any happiness for Christine Mathers. Something about her, some obscure awareness she can't bring to consciousness . . . I don't know."

"My dear Gylby—more mystery?"

"I don't know. Tragedy perhaps." He passed a hand through his hair. "Erchany must be getting me. I am not gay."

This was Noel Gylby in an unsuspected character, and I was about to probe into the basis of his feeling when we were again interrupted. The Kinkeig constable, considerably out of breath, had appeared in the doorway. "Excuse me, sir, but would the inspector be here about?"

"You have just missed him. Is anything the matter?"

"By your leave, sir, it's the coarse creature Hardcastle—"

I jumped up. "He's bolted?"

"No, sir. But he's drinking like a fish."

"Is that all? Save your breath, man, and let him drink. It's no business of yours." I turned to Gylby. "He'll cut all the sorrier figure this afternoon."

"But, Mr. Wedderburn, sir, you don't understand. And I don't know what to do. The daft creature's drinking water!"

For a moment I thought the man was attempting an unseasonable jest; then I saw that he was not only agitated but positively shaken. I said: "Explain yourself."

"Sir, it's the most uncouthy sight. The gomeril chiel's down by the cattle-trough in the back court, whiles roaring and scraiching like Judas Iscariot at the Judgment, and whiles fair wallowing in the sharrow sharny seip."

"God bless me! Gylby, come." And we all three hurried from the gallery and downstairs.

The spectacle with which we were confronted in the back court may justly be termed extraordinary. Hardcastle, his body hideously swollen and bloated, was lying by a low trough in a corner, screaming horribly and fighting for water amid a multitude of hideously swollen and bloated rats. A few seconds more and his screams died away. Even as we ran up he rolled on his back in a final convulsion, his limbs twitching faintly in ghastly correspondence to the weakening reflexes of the already dead vermin about him. And he was not unattended in his agony. On one side stood his wife, crying out: "He took the poison for his porridge, 'twas the rat-nature lured him to it, woe the day!" On the other side stood—or rather pranced—the daftie Tammas, clapping his hands and casting a wild laughter against the very face of death.

6

WE did what we could but it was plain that Hardcastle had gone to his account. I suppose he had been drinking in verity: he could hardly otherwise have mistaken a mess of poisoned meal for his dinner. Mrs. Hardcastle had been merely negligent—no more; I saw clearly enough after the event that so slender-witted an old person ought never to have been entrusted with large quantities of poison. Speight sent a message to Dr. Noble—who could do no more than certify the cause of death—and then Erchany, with its two dead men, settled down to mark time. It was a dreich wait and I for one, taking a breath of chill air in the snow before the dark and mouldering castle, felt the fatality of the place heavy upon me. I thought with what must have been akin to pity and awe of the strange childhood and youth of the girl Christine Mathers, and for a moment I felt with Noel Gylby that no one could break through to happiness from such an environment. It was with positive relief that I saw the arrival of the motor hearse that was to take Guthrie's body to Kinkeig. A few minutes behind it came my own hired car with a most respectable elderly electrician from Dunwinnie. Gylby and I had then work enough until it was time to return to the village.

I ought here to say that a sheriff's inquiry, while it takes the place of a coroner's inquest in England, is a less formal and at the same time a more restricted affair. The English coroner's court has gradually come to usurp many of the functions that properly belong to the police court, and is in consequence frequently the scene of elaborate and prolonged investigation and argument. The Scottish sheriff, who has more varied duties than the coroner, confines himself to the investigation of accidental fatalities; when the appearance of criminal matter emerges the case passes at once to the Procurator Fiscal, who may then institute proceedings before the courts. I need not enlarge on the superiority of the

Scottish practice: it is sufficient to indicate that in England a man may virtually be put on his trial before the coroner, and often without the safeguards of good criminal law. I venture on this note the more willingly in that I do not intend to embark upon an account of the afternoon's proceedings in Kinkeig. The reader is now familiar with the facts educed, the opinion of the good Inspector Speight, and my own discoveries. It will be sufficient to say, with modesty, that I carried all before me. The case was clear: moreover, as both Guthrie and his accomplice Hardcastle were dead, it was virtually closed. The papers which recorded Guthrie's highly criminal conduct would pass immediately to the Procurator Fiscal, but unless the weak-minded Mrs. Hardcastle could be indicted as a second accomplice it seemed unlikely that any proceedings could be instituted. What actually followed, including the further clarification afforded by the young people who had now been brought back to Dunwinnie, I will therefore leave in what I may confidently term the capable hands of the next narrator.

IV

JOHN APPLEBY

1

THEY were not yet married. Perhaps they were to have been married before sailing that afternoon: I made no inquiries for it wasn't my business. It was in no sense—it never in any sense became—my case: I had simply found them and I was ordered to get them back to Kinkeig—tactfully and if possible without producing the warrant with which I had been provided for Neil Lindsay. If I became interested in them in the course of the journey, if I subsequently became more interested still in the events with which they were involved, that was matter of my own curiosity and not of official instructions. Until they were under the eye of my Scottish colleagues I was a watchdog; after that the merest busybody. This is my preface to what I have to say: I am afraid it is not so impressive as Mr. Wedderburn's.

"May I speak to you for a few minutes in private? I am a detective-inspector from Scotland Yard."

They looked at me with wonder but, I thought, without apprehension. They were anxious—an elopement in any circumstances must be an anxious business—but my announcement had not increased their anxiety more than by the expectation of some vexatious official delay in their affairs. It was Miss Mathers who responded first; if she had seen even less of the world than Lindsay she was nevertheless the more competent in dealing with it. I felt that even in his own environment he would be half lost, a creature brooding fixedly on some abstract, imperfectly understood purpose to be achieved. Miss Mathers said: "Please come in."

"I understand that you have both come from Castle Erchany in Scotland? And that you are the niece, madam, of Mr.

Ranald Guthrie? I am sorry to have to tell you that Mr. Guthrie is dead."

An exclamation broke from Lindsay. Miss Mathers said nothing but only turned away for a moment into a darker corner of the dingy little room. Presently she turned again, very pale but quite composed. "He is . . . dead, you say?"

"I am advised that he died suddenly and in obscure circumstances on the night of Christmas Eve. And that it is desirable you should both return to Kinkeig."

"Neil, we must go at once. As quickly as can be arranged." She turned to me. "What will be quickest? We have money."

They had money: it did not seem strange to them that it was largely in gold. I said: "There is a train to Carlisle in twenty minutes. I have a taxi at the door and we can just catch it."

Miss Mathers turned to Lindsay, who stood immobile regarding me with dark dilated eyes, and shook him gently by the shoulder. "Neil, hurry." And swiftly she gathered up her things. It was not until we were on the train that she said, with the implication of a most substantial question in her voice: "You are coming too?"

"There is to be a legal inquiry. As a matter of routine, Miss Mathers, I am asked to travel north with you."

At last she looked at me with something like fear in her eyes. "Was my uncle—"

"You must understand I know little about it. I have come from London, not Scotland."

Lindsay spoke, suddenly and harshly. "London?"

"It was important to find you. I was put in charge of the search."

From Liverpool to Carlisle, and from Carlisle over the moors and through the border towns to Edinburgh, I spent most of my time in the corridor, cursing my trade. I think I had fallen under the spell of the girl. I knew nothing of her past, and of her future I could guess only ill. But racing through that wild and lonely country, that seems to cry still to the imagination of the old bitterness of foray and feud and

Covenant, and that lay now as in a penance under its garment of snow, I felt obscurely that she was part of these things and that in the most real sense I was bringing her home. Once, just short of Moffat, she came into the corridor and stood beside me, and her look was so far away that I thought she must be searching her memory or her fears. But in a minute she said softly: "The peewits." Straining my eyes I could just see them wheeling in the gathering dusk. Birdlife, I have been told, is scanty in Canada; I suppose she may have thought never to see the lapwings again.

From Carlisle they had sent a telegram; at Edinburgh they were met by a young solicitor called Stewart, who had made commendable haste from Dunwinnie. I made the best arrangements I could for the night and the next day we continued our journey. It was inevitably a constrained and uncomfortable affair and I was afraid that Stewart might try to take a firm line and order me out of the picture. He proved however discreet: he may have guessed that I had an emergency card in my pocket. Lindsay never spoke, burying himself in a textbook of geology. Geology, I discovered, was his passion; coming of folk who were bound down, generation after generation, to the ceaseless turning of the soil, he had made the barren and unchanging rock the symbol of his revolt. Lurking in him was the character of genius that lifts a man out of the categories of class; without having exchanged a dozen words with him I realized that Miss Mathers was not proposing a mere misalliance with a green and handsome country lad. Handsome he was—beautiful, in Sybil Guthrie's word—and the eye saw no reason to dispute that he might have reckless violence to his credit. But I was less interested in what crime might have been his than I was held by the intense relationship that was his and Christine Mathers'. The old high way of love—in our modern world fragmented into sensuality and affection—was in that railway carriage: passion too sheer and taut to be embarrassing or even pathetic, and that evinced itself—though they allowed each other scarcely a word or glance—as clearly as some massive atmospheric pressure upon a barometric screen. And the simple pressure was not the less compelling because somewhere I felt the needle tremble, as if all but invisibly deflected by an alien force. I wondered if suspicion, or a suspicion of suspicion, was hovering between them.

Miss Mathers had some code, not unimpressive in itself, that made her deny the mere constraint and awkwardness in our journey. She spoke to me occasionally of things seen in passing, but most of the time she spent gazing thoughtfully out of the window, her eye searching the turbulent snow-swollen waters of the Forth or absorbedly watching the hovering of a hawk over the Carse of Stirling. At Perth I exercised a certain primitive professional skill in detecting and avoiding a couple of newspaper-men who had got word of us; at Dunwinnie a magnificent and anxious old man—his name Ewan Bell—was waiting with a large car. They all held some sort of conference while I foraged cups of tea: and then we drove to Kinkeig.

By this time I wanted to know what it was all about. I listened attentively and with proper admiration to the facts and theories in the possession of Inspector Speight; I inspected the bodies—the so-dramatically poisoned Hardcastle's with particular interest; and I broke what I believe was fresh ground by interviewing the small person called Isa Murdoch. It was then time for the inquiry.

The inquiry was, in its somewhat gruesome way, a treat. I had no notion of the identity of Mr. Wedderburn and for some time I was under the impression that Stewart must have brought down the ablest advocate in Edinburgh. He made no attempt to smother the plain beginnings of a case against Lindsay. He spoke only once while Miss Guthrie was giving evidence, and that was to draw attention to the cardinal fact that Lindsay, during all the time that he was in the tower, could not have got at the bureau. He then bided his time until the appearance of the witness Gamley, and here he succeeded in emphasizing another significant point. Lindsay and Gamley had become friends, and Lindsay had confided to Gamley that he was taking Miss Mathers away, with her uncle's consent, on Christmas Eve. He had then asked Gamley to be present at his final interview with the laird, feeling reasonably enough that the support of a friend might be desirable. Gamley had actually accompanied him to the castle for that purpose but had been refused admission by Hardcastle. He had waited, had seen Guthrie fall and hurried to help. Lindsay and Miss Mathers, finding him gone, had concluded that he had returned home and gone off without further waiting. Unless Lindsay and Gamley were in a conspiracy it was thus evident that Lindsay had at least not premeditated any violence.

But it was after the available witness was apparently exhausted that Wedderburn played his single decisive card. For the guidance of the sheriff he begged leave to call a certain Murdo Mackay, who proved to be an elderly and impressive working electrician. This person swore that there had been installed—and unmistakably recently installed—an electrical contrivance for the sole purpose of sending signals to Guthrie's study from various points on the tower staircase. The apparatus was perfectly simple, a matter of two wires that had only to be pressed together to activate the buzzer of a small desk telephone—a buzzer that had been so muffled that it would be audible only to a person actually sitting by the desk. The whole contrivance could have no other purpose than that which he had described; moreover it was so set up that it could have been removed without leaving a trace by anybody with five minutes' leisure in the study and on the staircase. The existence of this device the police, whose attention had been called to it by Wedderburn at the last moment, had to confirm.

After this Wedderburn's road was clear. He built up an unshakable case. Guthrie, while affecting to give his niece away to Lindsay under eccentric and humiliating circumstances, had actually plotted that rarest of human achievements, a truly diabolical crime.

I followed all this with sufficient interest—it was an anatomy of wickedness beyond my considerable experience—but nevertheless I believe I was still primarily interested in the young people with whom I had travelled. As the story grew Lindsay's eyes darkened; he gave no other sign of whatever emotions possessed him. He was, I suppose, relieved—and yet I doubt if throughout he had ever thought of his neck. He was of the secret kind, with that almost maiden's shyness which often marks in a man the union of simple breeding and sensibility, and the light that had come to beat on Christine Mathers and himself was a sort of death to him. There was a sense, I felt, in which Ranald Guthrie had triumphed. Though not lacking in manners, Lindsay had to be prompted by the girl into some expression of thanks to Wedderburn; after that it was clear he only wanted to get away.

But it was in Christine Mathers that I was most interested. She had not the mask or shell of Lindsay, and wonder, horror and thankfulness were evident in her by turns: to have her lover cleared at the cost of her uncle and guardian's infamy must have been a harrowing and bewildering experience. But her responses were far from being emotional merely; she followed the course of the inquiry syllable by syllable with her whole mind, as if she were preparing to fight every word if need be. And I noticed—what nobody else in court, I believe, troubled to notice—that as Wedderburn's story grew so did a look of puzzlement on Christine Mathers' face. Through all the interplay of her emotions—anxiety, abhorrence, relief—was this constant and growing thing: an intellectual doubt. Speight might have taken heart had he observed it, but Speight was fully occupied with the task of retreating in good order.

Sybil Guthrie—felt by Speight to be "real nice"—had also captured something of my attention. If Miss Mathers was relieved and puzzled Miss Guthrie was exultant and—indefinably—something else. When Wedderburn began to speak she had watched him much as I have seen women watch an unlikely fancy in a horse race; when he had finished and it was all over I thought I could discern some faint light of mockery or irony on her face. She was tasting, it occurred to me, some delicate flavour in the affair that others were unaware of—and a flavour, maybe, not without its astringency or even bitterness. But when the sheriff had pronounced his findings and withdrawn she was the first person to hurry to Miss Mathers. Standing at the back of the minister's library in which the inquiry had been conducted, I saw her kiss Christine, shake hands awkwardly with Neil Lindsay and then turn and go briskly from the room. An interesting girl: I felt sorry I was unlikely to see more than a glimpse of her again.

The transition from inquiry to funeral was a difficult business during which I felt a considerable admiration for the minister, Dr. Jervie. He might have been moving among the relatives of the most beloved and pious of his parishioners; and his control of the situation was the more remarkable in that he was not, I thought, one to whom pastoral contacts came easily—rather he was a shy, scholarly, and, it might be, visionary man. Perhaps because I was attracted by his personality, I felt some desire to attend the funeral myself. But it seemed scarcely an occasion for curious strangers, and after some conversation with Speight I set off to find myself a room at the inn.

The manse is some way from the village; I had to tramp about a quarter of a mile in the heavy and now melting snow. That day had seen a rapid change in the weather: a stiff, mild wind had blown the sky almost clear of clouds and there was every indication of a rapid thaw. Beside me as I walked was the splash and gurgle of a torrential little stream; at the tail of the village it went to swell the ice-green waters of the Drochet, a small river that was already risen high on the piers of an old stone bridge I presently crossed. In front of me, at a distance difficult to assess in the now failing light, was the shadowy whiteness of Ben Mervie, with the summit of Ben Cailie still clear-cut in brilliant sunlight beyond. Over the village the blue peat smoke was drifting on the wind, and already in some little shop there was the yellow light of a lamp. It was cold, peaceful, lonely, compelling; I walked for some time merely submerged in the spirit of the place. But presently the tug of the snow at my shoes brought me back to the fact that there was matter tugging too at my mind. I had just set myself to explore it when there came a hail behind me. It was Noel Gylby.

I should explain that Gylby and I were old acquaintances, having met in a setting of some excitement a year before. He takes rather a glamorous view of criminal investigation and I believe he was sorry I hadn't arrived in time to make spectacular gestures in the Erchany affair. He called out now: "Appleby—I say—I've got my journal back!"

I stopped. "You what?"

"Didn't you know? I wrote a whacking great account for Diana of what was going on at the castle. Old Wedders"—he meant the eminent Writer to the Signet—"had it and now he's returned it. Would you like to read it?"

"Very much."

Gylby thrust a small sheaf of papers into my hand. "You may find it a bit literary"—he said this with complacency—"but all the facts are there. Are you going to the pub? You know, I think you might do something about ordering a meal. The sheriff has told Wedders there's a claret would go splendidly with a piping hot curry or a tart really stuffed with strawberry jam. I'm going back for the last act."

"The funeral baked meats shall be ordered. And thank you for your notes."

I went on to the inn, secured a room and sat down to Gylby's journal. Perhaps it stands to the credit of his literary style that I quite forgot my promise about ordering a meal. When he returned with Wedderburn and Sybil Guthrie a little more than an hour later there were introductions and we sat down to a supper of cold roast mutton. It was singularly tasteless and I don't doubt threw the execrable claret into the highest relief. I drank beer.

Old Wedderburn seemed disposed to expand; indeed he

beamed on me so cordially that I ventured to congratulate him on his conduct of the case.

"My dear Mr.—um—Appleby, it was my good fortune to listen patiently to the gossip of the hostess of this inn. Everything followed from that."

"Indeed?"

"The fantastic rumour about the mutilating of the corpse! Could such an extraordinary story start up unbidden, or as the result of some mere misapprehension? For a little time I was dull enough to think so. Then I saw that it must have its source in malice—malice that was either stupid or calculating. I tested the theory that it might be calculating—and what did I find? That the rumour, if it were to be really damaging, must be true. And to that I knit the remarkable fact of Hardcastle's curiosity about the body and the statement he made—without having had the opportunity to investigate—that Lindsay had 'mischieved' Guthrie. That took me straight to the heart of the plot."

"A strange plot, Mr. Wedderburn. I doubt if there is anything closely analogous on record. Men have killed themselves to incriminate others before this, but they were not men of what appears to have been Guthrie's type. They may have had his melancholy verging on madness, but they have been lacking in his intellectual vigour."

"I am without your familiarity, Mr. Appleby, with the archives of the criminal mind. But we must frame our psychologies to fit facts, and not vice versa."

I reminded myself that that afternoon Wedderburn had annihilated his adversaries, and that nothing was to be gained by setting myself up as a cock-shy for his very efficient forensic method. I said: "Very true. And the fact of the abominable plot against Lindsay is unshakable."

"You know—" It was Gylby who spoke, and he looked rather warily at Wedderburn before continuing. "You know, Christine said a queer thing. I hung about a bit at the manse and made helpful noises. And suddenly she said quite out of the blue: 'I can't believe it; my uncle had a finer mind than that.' And then she looked at me as if I must have an alternative explanation in my hat."

Wedderburn peered severely at the sediment in the bottom of his glass. "I do not see it as a queer thing. Such a sentiment in the scoundrel's niece and ward is a very proper and becoming one. But we are not concerned with family piety."

"I'm afraid, sir, she didn't mean quite that. She wasn't denying that Guthrie was capable of great wickedness. She meant that his mind was subtler—more ingenious—than the story shows."

"*More* ingenious? Bless my soul!"

"And she said: 'He had a level head really; he would pit extremes only against extremes.' "

Sybil Guthrie crumbled bread, made a wry face over a mouthful of claret and broke in: "Will she brood over it? I suppose she will. Mr. Appleby, how do people's minds behave when they have been through a horrid thing like this?"

I avoided generalization. "I think, Miss Guthrie, she will brood as long as she feels she hasn't got the truth."

"She has the truth! We all have."

"It is scattered among us. But I don't know that we have pooled it all yet."

Very deliberately, Wedderburn put down his glass and folded up his table napkin. "Mr. Appleby, Gylby assures me that your opinion in matters of this sort has great weight. Will you be so good as to explain the statement you have just made?"

"Miss Mathers herself has one piece of information which has not, I think, been pooled. Who was with her in the schoolroom, and who emerged from it and disappeared into the darkness, just before Gylby and Hardcastle went up the tower staircase?"

"Dear me—an interesting point. She has no doubt told Stewart. I fear I rather took charge from him this afternoon; otherwise the explanation would no doubt have emerged."

"It is more than an interesting point. Here in Erchany on this isolated night is another man—and we are told nothing of him. Unless indeed it could have been the boy Tammas."

Gylby shook his head at this. "Not Tammas; he wasn't let into the house till long after. And not, of course, Gamley either."

"Very well. And the matter gains much greater significance from the fact that there was in all probability—and despite Miss Guthrie's impression to the contrary—another visitor to the tower. Somebody must know who it was that opened the trapdoor on the battlements, passed through it, and bolted it on the lower side. Gylby's record tells us that the snow provided the most conclusive evidence on that point. The door had been opened not long before. By whom? Why?"

They were silent for a moment and then Wedderburn said, with unexpected humour: "Mr. Appleby, this is a slaughter of the innocents. And I fear they include both myself and your colleague Speight." He paused. "However clear the main features of the situation, there are undoubtedly factors we have overlooked. And I will say that they call for investigation."

"I think they do—and that there is yet truth to come. Miss Guthrie, you agree?"

She eyed me thoughtfully before replying. "If you find real evidence of another person in the tower I agree there is yet truth to come. Mr. Appleby, come to Erchany."

Wedderburn rose. "Miss Guthrie and I intend to go up now. The dead man appears to have had no legal representative and in the circumstances we judge it proper, along with the young man Stewart, to search for what papers there may be. You will come along with us? But first, perhaps, we should go to the manse, where Miss Mathers is staying for the time being, and ask her to explain her nocturnal visitor."

"I will come up—though you will understand that I have no official standing. Anything we discover may have to go to Speight. As for Miss Mathers, I think it would be wise to wait until later. There is another question I am saving up for her."

Wedderburn turned from helping Miss Guthrie with her coat. "And that is?"

"Whether her uncle ever went in for winter sports."

"A most enigmatic inquiry."

Noel Gylby looked up from stuffing his pockets providently with buttered biscuits. "You'll find," he said, "that Appleby has questions like that for us all round. What's mine?"

"Just this. We've had the message of the Learned Rat. But what was the message of the Unfamiliar Owl?"

2

STEWART, we found, had been called urgently to Dunwinnie and had left with a promise to follow us presently to Erchany. During the drive through the darkness I got from Wedderburn most of that information embodied in his narrative that I did not already possess, and I believe my ideas were in tolerable order by the time we arrived at the castle. From fragmentary evidences of what had happened here on Christmas Eve Wedderburn had that afternoon built up a picture that was coherent and convincing. Only he had failed—in the image drawn so significantly from Ranald Guthrie's jigsaws—to use all the pieces and his picture was therefore necessarily incomplete. Despite every appearance to the contrary, it was possible that the pieces yet to be fitted would confound or reverse the meaning of those outlines which were already clearly established—much as the figure, say, of an assassin, belatedly discovered in some shadowy corner of a painting, will give sudden sinister significance to what may have appeared a merely sentimental or spectacular composition. The Erchany affair could scarcely become more sinister, but I was fairly sure that as more pieces were added the composition would deepen and complicate itself. What I could not tell was that the jigsaw metaphor was wholly inadequate;

that we were confronted rather by a chemical mixture, complex and unstable, ready to take final and unexpected form only at the adding of the last ingredient of all. Perhaps it was because I had the jigsaw metaphor fatally in my head that in looking back on the Erchany mystery I have to remind myself of Ewan Bell's words: there's ever a judgment waits on arrogance.

Both Mrs. Hardcastle and the lad Tammas had been taken in by kindly or curious folk in Kinkeig and the castle was deserted when we drove up to it. The moon had not risen but the sky was clear and starry; driving over the drawbridge and into the central court I could distinguish first the vague bulk of the main building, encircling and menacing us, and then, soaring into increasing definition where the sky grew more luminous towards its zenith, the strong sheer lines of the tower. From his boyhood, I reflected, Ranald Guthrie must have been familiar with that great drop to the moat; time and again, leaning over the parapet more or less venturesomely according to his temperament, he must have tested his nerve against the dizzying sense of it. And for how many years, perhaps, had he been fascinated by the thought of a body swaying, toppling, falling—finally hurtling with the velocity of a projectile to the hard stone below? I said to Wedderburn: "I should like to begin by visiting the moat."

Gylby got a lantern and together we climbed down by Gamley's route. The snow was soft and watery in the thaw and we made a thoroughly uncomfortable progress. We found the little crater made by the body—it was still readily distinguishable, such had been the force of the impact that created it—and we looked at it for a few moments in silence. Then I said: "All those pieces of the puzzle—there's a missing piece we ought to find hereabouts. Could you get a spade?"

Gylby went off and returned presently through the slush with two spades. "Here you are," he said happily. "And now for the skull of Yorick."

We prodded and dug about—the job would have been much better performed by daylight—and by mere good luck my spade eventually rang on something deep in the snow. A minute's digging and I had uncovered a small, sharp axe. Gylby studied it carefully. "It will make a nice present," he said, "for Speight."

"It wasn't Speight's fault it wasn't found. There was no occasion to suspect its existence till this afternoon. And of course it fell from that height clean and deep into the snow. But it will please Wedderburn: a suitable finger-lopping implement is a most desirable accessory to his case." I fingered the edge of the axe. " 'To settle accounts with a great rat.' I cannot say that the character of friend Ranald grows on me. Let us go in."

We found Wedderburn and Miss Guthrie in a little island of candle-light amid the gloom of the great hall or chamber of the castle. I suppose that a few days before the place must have given some impression of a dwelling. Now, though it had been empty but a few hours, there hung heavily about it the atmosphere of an ancient monument. The tenancy of Ranald Guthrie had been a thread holding it to the present; that thread broken, it had slipped into the past as inevitably as a ripe apricot falls to the ground. We might have been idle tourists on some nocturnal sightseeing had we not carried with us our own heavy sense of fresh mortality. The clock of which Gylby had become so sharply aware still ticked, but with the sinister pulse of a watch in a dead man's pocket.

I took a deep breath of that chill, dank air. Here surely rather than in Kinkeig was the right haunt for Guthrie's wraith, fitly attended by the shade of Hardcastle and a scampering wreath of ghostly rats. And though I did not believe that these spirits walked I yet found myself almost yielding to a sudden and powerful impulse of superstition. That afternoon Wedderburn had laid the Erchany mystery to rest: it were better not to agitate it anew, lest worse might befall. So strong was this feeling that I had to summon the abstract principle of my profession—the principle of justice—before I could shake myself free of it and say to my companions: "May we go up to the tower at once?"

In silence we traversed a long corridor and passed through the first of those doors the timely locking of which by Gylby had foiled Hardcastle in any attempt to remove the tell-tale telephone equipment. Then we climbed. The tower, psychologists tell us, is a symbol of ambition—of perilous altitude, like the apex of Fortune's wheel. And the solid earth—the humble *below*—is a symbol of safety. And the man who feels a mad impulse to hurl himself from one to the other seeks only to pass from danger to security; he is betrayed by the treacherous logic of the buried mind. No doubt it was Guthrie's ambition that had obscurely driven him to fix his quarters in this laboriously attained retreat. Might the psychologist's theory of symbols illuminate what had happened on Christmas Eve? At some deep level of the mind had the ruining plunge held the significance of security gained or granted—of rescue—for Guthrie? Was there here, as it were, a subconscious piece in that biggest of all the jigsaws of which he had darkly announced the completion to Christine Mathers? I docketed the somewhat academic questions for consideration later: we had come to the study door.

The room has been described and I need add few details. Many towers of the sort have been added to storey by storey—building upwards being the most economical way of getting extra space. But this topmost storey of Erchany was clearly an integral part of the original structure. The walls, being set back some four feet in order to give space for the parapet walk surrounding them, could only be about half the thickness of their immediate foundations: nevertheless I was chiefly impressed by the strength as well as by the isolation of the place. These two rooms—study and adjoining small bedroom—belonged to a period when castles were true strongholds and not mere manifestoes of rank. And they preserved their character of inviolate mediaeval fastness.

The study was now embellished with a number of dead rats: otherwise nothing had changed since Gylby first locked the door on it. I had a good idea that Speight, when he had digested the afternoon's proceedings, would be up and poking about again on the morrow, and I was glad of the opportunity of a quiet survey first. The rifled bureau, the bogus telephone—it was amateur work but a neat and simple job nevertheless—and the books on the desk: I examined them carefully before turning into the bedroom. Here I rummaged about among the lumber in the corner and then returned to the study with the book already discovered by Wedderburn: Flinders' *Experimental Radiology*. "An interesting book," I said. "Or rather an interesting fly-leaf. You noticed?"

But nobody had noticed the fly-leaf and I now laid it open on the desk. Neatly written in ink was this inscription:

Richard Flinders
Fellow of the Royal College of Surgeons
Born in South Australia February 1893
Died at

Wedderburn stared at this abrupted memorial in considerable perplexity. "Dear me! I ought not to have missed that. A most mysterious inscription. Can it be connected with Guthrie's colonial days?"

I pointed to the second line. "Born 1893. Can we learn anything from that?"

There was a baffled silence and then Sybil Guthrie spoke.

"Christine told me her uncle came home and inherited Erchany in 1894. Just a year after this person's birth."

I nodded. "Good. A significant fact—and one that doesn't fit! Often the most useful sort of fact. Gylby, will you see if Guthrie's recent purchases include a medical directory? I rather fancy they must."

A brief search proved me right and I quickly turned the pages. "Here we are—and the sort of long entry they give to very big guns. M.B., B.S., Adelaide; worked there, then in Sydney, then a long spell in the United States. It's on the strength of that, no doubt, that he has just been appointed emeritus fellow and pensioner of an American learned society. Then back in Sydney, with various short periods in London. A tip-top surgeon, apparently, who turned to experimental work—hence the need, I suppose, of a pension. Two standard text books, including the one before us. Any amount of communications to journals and about a dozen monographs. Listen. *Radiology of the Cardiac Region. Radiology and the Differential Diagnosis of Intestinal Maladies. An Historical Outline of the Medical Use of Radium. Analysis of a Case of Long-term Amnesia. Syringomyelia: the Radiological Approach. The Technique of Rapid Screening: A Contribution to Contemporary Radiology. Radon—*"

Wedderburn interrupted. "My dear Mr. Appleby, is this really interesting?"

"Interesting? Well, there's another point that might interest you more. The distinguished Flinders is not merely a big gun; he's a prodigy."

"A prodigy?"

"Definitely." I pointed to the inscribed fly-leaf. " 'Born in South Australia February 1893.' If we accept that statement we have to believe that he graduated in medicine at the age of seven."

Wedderburn exclaimed impatiently. "This is nonsense!"

"On the contrary, it is the first glimpse of the truth. And now we had better aim at the truth all round. Miss Guthrie, I think these developments take you somewhat out of your depth?"

"Indeed they do."

"Then listen. I give you the same promise about Lindsay that Mr. Wedderburn gave. We have the truth of his position in the story. He is out of it. So now let me ask you the question Gylby asked. *However did you know Guthrie committed suicide?*"

"I didn't. In fact I saw him sent over the parapet."

Wedderburn sighed and fell to polishing his glasses. "I think," I said, "we might usefully go up to the gallery."

3

THE faded terrestrial globe stirred, revolved: my finger traced the long route from Australia through Suez to Southampton.

"It's in the blood, and by the great God he will . . . !"

We walked down the gallery, our lanterns and torches playing before us on the long line of dead Guthries. I paused, picked out a sixteenth-century portrait by a Flemish artist, then swung round to a late eighteenth-century laird by Raeburn. It was the same face looked down on us. Softly I said: "What for would it not work, man? What for would it not work?" We stood in silence for a moment. "Gylby, can you repeat the end of Dunbar's poem?"

And Noel Gylby recited:

"Gud Maister Walter Kennedy
In poynt of dede lyis veraly,
Great reuth it wer that so suld be;
Timor Mortis conturbat me.

"Sen he has all my brether tane,
He will nocht let me lif alane;
Of force I mon his nyxt prey be;
Timor Mortis conturbat me.

"Sen for the deth remeid is non,
Best is that we for deth dispone
After our deth that lif may we;
Timor Mortis conturbat me."

There was another and longer silence. "Ranald Guthrie," I said at last, "has a pretty art in turning mediaeval piety to irony. *Death threatens; best so to arrange for it that one continues to live.* That's his reading of Dunbar. And, somewhere, Ranald is alive now. It was his brother Ian—Richard Flinders the Australian surgeon—who died. Ranald's story we shall piece together. But the whole story of Ian we shall never know."

Wedderburn seemed to struggle for words—was forestalled by a startled cry from Sybil Guthrie. There was a scuffle in the darkness; I lowered my lantern and saw that Mrs. Hardcastle's all too potent poison had accounted for yet another rat—a great grey creature that had grotesquely dragged itself to die at our feet. For a moment I thought it was one of Gylby's learned rats, with its little message attached. Then I saw that it was a rat more learned than that. Clutched in its mouth, as if seized to staunch its final agony, was a small black notebook.

V

THE DOCTOR'S TESTAMENT

1

AS consciousness came to me I was aware that the landscape was unfamiliar. And this awareness was for a space like Adam's in the Garden: I recognized novelty without the aid of any of those contrasting memories which would seem essential to the formulation of the idea. More strangely, I was unperplexed by this. I suppose my mind had vigour only for the business of survival.

Before me was a rolling immensity of dark green vegetation, its dull lustre fading into purple distance under a vibrant blue sky. Behind me, I thought, was the roar of breakers, and heat as if the breakers were lava beating up from a subterraneous sea of fire. I struggled round. The sea was an illusion; the reality was a sweeping curtain of veritable flame, a great sickle of flame that reaped the tinder-dry vegetation with a motion perceptible as I watched. For a moment it was a spectacle only; then it realized itself as imminent peril. I got to hands and knees and saw, bounding before the blaze, a scattering of miniature prehistoric creatures—one grotesque form reproduced on every scale from the human to the rodent, like a child's nest of bricks. Kangaroos and wallabies: with an immense effort my blood-soaked brain gave them their names. And at that much of my local knowledge returned to me; I saw that I was in the path of a bush fire and that I must find a break or be overwhelmed.

I was crouching where I must have fallen, half way down an out-crop of limestone rock from which a dry gully dropped to lose itself in the scrub. Here and there the scrub gave place to a sparser growth of ti-tree, prickly bushes and salsolae, which in turn exhausted themselves round arid islands of sand. But nowhere was a denuded area large enough to promise security; my only hope was in a single massive ridge of rock that showed not more than two miles away, in startling isolation amid the low and endless undulations of green. It swayed and quivered as I looked—partly from refraction in the heat, partly perhaps to my own impaired sense—and I could be certain neither of its size nor of the practicability of ascent. It rose in sheer lines accentuated by an occasional perpendicular funnel or cleft. Up one of these I might scramble to safety.

I got to my feet and found myself—with a sort of detached surprise—not without considerable physical strength. The fire was partly checked by a veering wind; had it been sweeping directly towards me I should have had no chance at all. As it was, it was a grim race and I wasted no time. But before striking down the gully it occurred to me to discover if I had any possessions. There was evidence of a little encampment: a dead fire, an overturned billy, horse-dung. These meant nothing to me. But I found a haversack which I knew to be mine and took up. I knew too that there ought to be a water-bottle. In a swift and desperate search I failed to find it. Then I set out. The scrub was low and, when entered, not actually dense; I got forward without difficulty and with my mark always before me. A mile on I found a water-bottle—mine or another's—three-parts empty. This strange chance gave me a sort of irrational or superstitious confidence without which I should not be alive to-day.

By the time I reached the foot of the ridge there were already little fires about me. The heat of the conflagration was attracting a light headwind that blew in my face but through this the main blast was carrying forward showers of sparks that in places kindled flaring outposts of fire hundreds of yards ahead. Once I was nearly trapped by a sudden line of flame that leapt to life in a clump of yaccas about me—stunted spearlike growths of which the resinous butts will kindle with the force and rapidity of an explosion.

For agonizing minutes I explored the rock-face in vain for cleft or foothold: it seemed that my back, in a most horrible sense, was to the wall. But presently I found a possible chimney and began to climb. It is interesting that in that crisis I commanded all the lore though nothing of the memories of a mountain youth. And perhaps it was because my memory was like a freshly sponged slate that I can recall now with an almost hallucinatory power every step and strain of that desperate ascent. I emerged at length some nine hundred feet above an inferno of fire, and sufficiently shaken to fear that I might only have attained to a species of monstrously elevated grid-iron where I should perish like a martyr in a mad painter's dream. I was however perfectly safe.

For over an hour I watched the fire sweep past. Though powerless against the barrier of rock it yet added appreciably to the burning heat of the sun and the scorching breath of the dry north wind that fanned it behind. The climb and the heat and the terror of the scene had momentarily exhausted me; I drank charily from my water-bottle and concentrated all the resources of my will on the next and all-important battle—the battle against mere despair. Many men who have wandered in wild places have found themselves in just such a perilous pass but few, except perhaps in some ultimate stumbling agony, can have experienced my peculiar distress. With my senses in fair order and almost unimpaired physical strength, I yet found myself void of all memory of my own identity or of my whereabouts. Below me, I was massively aware, was a landscape not native to me—the landscape of Australia in one of its most appalling manifestations. I had plenty of knowledge—I could have read Latin or recognized the Parthenon or selected a fly for trout—but of knowledge organized round the fact of personality this was my whole store: I was a stranger lost in Australia. Beyond this I found it impossible to struggle. My consciousness of myself had no wavering boundaries which effort could push back: I was imprisoned in ignorance by walls as sheer as the rock up which I had recently climbed.

The fire had rolled away—by watching the dropping sun I judged roughly to the south-west. It had left behind it a smoking vastness which would be dangerous to traverse before a night had passed; my only present course was to take what bearings I could, find shade, and rest.

I estimated my horizon at about fifty miles. And in all that vast circle, save for the eminence on which I stood, was nothing but the empty and featureless bush, scarred by one long and diminishing trail of fire—a rolling and planless dapple of scrub and sand, diversified only by a sporadic growth of timber or by the swell of some undulation slightly more pronounced than the rest. Of clearing or settlement or homestead, white man or blackfellow, there was no slightest sign; the scene was void, sullen, and sinisterly waiting in a way that caught and haunted the nerve. Only on the very verge of the southerly horizon lay a single level pencilled line. Long and anxiously I studied it through the treacherous heat. And finally I decided to call it the sea and make it my goal.

I turned to reckon needs and resources. Tied to the haversack was a hat, the primary need of all. Inside were a shirt, oatmeal, some biscuits, matches and a few personal belongings at which I could only gaze in perplexity. I had no compass. But in my trousers pocket I discovered a watch. And I had a two quart billy-can without a lid.

In the bewildering country below me I believed that the watch and the sun alone would be useless. I needed the watch roughly set at noon, a clear star-lit sky, country sufficiently open and a surface sufficiently safe to traverse in the cool of the night. I needed water within twenty-four hours, and food within three or four days. These points determined, I found a patch of shade, lay down and was almost instantly asleep.

I awoke in the brief Australian dusk to see below me a hundred points of smouldering fire. But the main conflagration had disappeared, caught and smothered perhaps in some chance funnel of sand, and I decided to descend and at least test the possibility of beginning my journey that night. The route down the chimney was doubly hazardous in the failing light but I was in the mood for taking chances. The decision nearly cost me my life. It also saved it.

Before I was half-way down the light had failed badly. Near the bottom the chimney forked; I misjudged a foothold in attempting to take the route by which I had come and fell perhaps fifteen feet down the other branch of the cleft. I lay at once dazed and in a curious agony of calculation: a broken limb or a bad sprain and I was done for. I felt no pain—but pain often comes later. I moved my limbs; they answered my will and a wave of relief passed over me. It was followed by a wave of fear. My legs were soaked in what I thought was blood. It was water. The discovery changed all my plans. I must carry with me every ounce of water that I could, half of it in an open billy. Until the billy was exhausted I must never once stumble. Such a strange variant of the egg and spoon race could be accomplished only in daylight. I judged that the gain in water would outweigh an extra twelve hours' strain on my food, as also the risk of my not being able to hold a fairly straight southerly course by the sun. This decided, I lay down once more to sleep or rest. The night was cool but without extreme cold or frost. This encouraged me in the belief that I had seen the sea: it was unlikely that I was either at a considerable altitude or islanded in a great land-mass.

I was up at dawn and, accepting the dubious analogy of the camel, drank a good deal more water than was comfortable. There was a difficult climb from the spring by which I had fallen to the open ground and I found that my mind, though tolerably clear, had alarming blind spots in addition to that of memory. I wearied myself with trying to climb free with a brimming billy before I saw that I could fill the billy in the open from the water-bottle and then return to the spring and replenish that. Apprehending this aberration, I spent some bad moments in sheer fear of fear—in panic lest I had discovered in myself a first symptom of that paralyzing panic that can come on men who feel themselves bushed. Concentration on the first miles of my egg and spoon race conquered this feeling. The scrub was fairly open and the undergrowth too sparse to be treacherous. I allowed myself a pint of water that day and brought the rest safely to my evening halt. During the march I had eaten a few biscuits; I now kindled a fire and cooked myself a species of oatmeal bannock on a flat stone. I felt far from hopeless. Throughout the day I had been troubled by intermittent but piercing headaches; otherwise my physical condition was good. And that night I slept dreamlessly. But in the morning I was so stiff that I guessed my muscles had been more accustomed to riding than tramping.

On the second and third days I must have made some twenty miles a day. Thereafter, the billy being empty, I travelled by night. That I was moving almost due south I had no doubt and at the end of my third night-march I knew that I could not have seen the sea: my goal had been mirage or some lake now behind me. Everywhere about me still was the same unchanging emptiness, the same endless iteration of sand and scrub. Occasionally I sighted kangaroo in the dusk; once by daylight I hurried to meet two natives who proved—so deceptive was the light—no more than two lonely magpies perched on stumps. And then at dawn on the seventh day, when my water and provisions were both exhausted, I came upon the unmistakable tracks of a white man—the imprints, too often repeated to be a trick of nature, or a booted foot just distinguishable in the loose surface of the sand. I realized that they must be fresh—a breath of wind would have obliterated them—and I hurried forward with a dreadful fear that in my weakness I could never overtake the stronger man in front. My heart leapt when I saw, not a quarter of a mile ahead, the thin smoke going up from a camp fire. I ran forward, sobbing and trying to call out from a parched throat.

The man was dead. He lay with an empty water-bottle—his sole unabandoned possession—beside him. His body, still warm, was sprawled on its face, one arm stretched out towards the smouldering fire and the hand closed round a few dry leaves. Death had taken him in the act of feeding his last desperate signal.

Something broke in me—a barrier I had built up not against the thought of imminent death or my present extremity of weakness and thirst, but against the silence of the bush. The barrier broke and I heard the silence, the hot heavy silence untouched for hours either by the dry cicada or the rustle of a breeze in the parched grass. I called out and my voice was horrible; I threw down my haversack and ran, horribly calling out, into the encompassing emptiness, away from that silent and vastly-vaulted tomb. The frenzy brought me some final access of strength and I must have stumbled forward for hours. My head was swimming and shot with piercing pains; there was a great roaring in my ears, a roaring as uninterrupted as the silence of days had been. The roaring grew to thunder. There was a moment with the quality of blinding revelation when I knew that the thunder was not within but without. Then I found myself standing on the very verge of a high cliff against which, far below, thundered the breakers of an open sea.

East and west the cliffs stretched in unbroken line, great battlements and bastions of rock glittering in the morning sun. The prospect was of a magnificence that seized me and calmed me; and with the coming of a new clarity I realized the tremendous fact of a well defined native track running eastward along the verge. I followed it painfully for some two miles to a point where the cliffs receded a little from the sea, leaving a valley of barren and sandy ground to which the path conducted by way of a narrow and precipitous gorge. I descended—with the greatest difficulty in my weakened state—and in little over an hour had found in the sandhills a couple of recent native wells. There was moreover a low scrub with a plentiful growth of red berries, and a flight of white paroquets—the first animal life I had descried for days—rose from feeding on them as I watched. I ate and had the wit to eat sparingly. After an interval I found a warm pool and bathed. My strength returned. Later and in another pool I succeeded in landing a couple of fish with my hat. Though my haversack was gone I had still the water-bottle and billy and in my pocket matches. My evening meal was a revelation of the sheer joy of taste. And that night I was lulled to sleep by a melody of waves.

For two days I travelled east along a firm beach, with sandhills and beyond them the cliffs on my left—a highway obstructed only occasionally by massive drifts of sea-weed. I had some days' supply of water and for the rest I lived on berries. My confidence had returned and I was in the constant hope of coming presently within some fringe of settlement. Land birds were becoming more plentiful, a sign of some changing character in the upland country ahead.

On the third day the cliffs narrowed to the sea and I had eventually to spend hours finding a practicable route to the top. I was again in great danger. The berry-bearing scrub was giving out; I had no means of carrying a considerable supply of the berries; moreover they could not be a satisfactory diet for many days. And—what was yet more serious—I had found no further water. Twice I awoke early and experimented with collecting the light dew on the scrub; I found that with an improvised grass sponge and severe labour I could gain between a quarter and half a pint in a morning. The effort shortened my marches and I knew that it was toil for less than a subsistence supply. My one hope was in the rapidly changing character of the country through which I struggled.

The scrub was becoming denser and ran to the very edge of the now unscalable cliffs, so that I was at times afraid lest I should be unable to make any headway at all. But in places it was diversified by considerable growths of timber and I took this as a further sign that I was approaching a more productive soil. The gum trees moreover yielded me an unexpected source of food in a species of large white grub revealed by tearing off the ragged bark. I ate these cautiously and found they brought on considerable gastric disturbance; nevertheless I believed I gained strength from them. It was in following the lure of this food that I somehow lost the sea.

A hot and leaden afternoon found me wandering in the heart of a maze of eucalyptus, my water for the second time wholly exhausted. And in the evening, abruptly, my nerve broke. Some subtle poisoning from the grubs may have been an immediate exciting cause, but it must chiefly have been a matter of accumulated strain. With some physical strength to stumble on, I had not the strength of will to rest with the closing in of night. I wandered among the great trees, possessed by the panic I had long dreaded, until I finally dropped to the ground.

For hours I must have lain semi-conscious, aware that the night was airless and oppressive beyond the ordinary. The agony of my thirst was shot through by the distinct pains of hunger and I must have groped up the tree by which I lay in the darkness in some hope of securing the familiar grubs. Suddenly my body quivered as if it had received an electric charge. The tree was ring-barked. I had come on my first trace of man.

I was unable to cry out and the night was utterly starless and obscure. I could only await the dawn, time and again reassuring myself of the reality of the bite of the axe. Dawn came, and to this day I cannot recall without bitterness and terror the irony it brought. The tree had been ringed and killed, as had half a hundred others. But the effort at clearing had been ill-judged; whoever had attempted it had long since been beaten back; the only sign of man was an empty and ruined humpy. I had resigned myself to dying on the very fringe of settlement when the storm broke above me.

Within five minutes I was sheltering in the humpy, soaked to the skin and with my billy brimming with water. Only a few minutes later the corner of the little shack remote from me was smashed by the terrifying impact of a falling tree. And I found that once more danger had brought salvation in its train. In the fallen tree—in this tree, it must have been, among thousands—the wild bees had been building. I was master of many pounds of honey.

I had come from some great solitude to the fringes of

settlement; I had only to find the sea once more and continue east to reach safety. And that night when the storm had passed I heard the murmur of the waves. I found the cliffs again no more than a mile away.

Where the great gum trees grew the soil retained no virtue for the nourishment of an undergrowth and the ground was tolerably clear. But when I left the trees behind me I found the scrub growing denser every mile; soon it presented an almost impenetrable barrier that ran to the very edge of the still stretching and unbroken cliff. Below me, between cliffs and sea, ran a narrow valley of sandhills that seemed to promise the possibility of water, and beyond this—save at high tide—there lay once more a highway of firm sand. I resolved to descend by the first practicable route, risking the chance of the cliffs again converging on the sea and forcing a tedious return journey.

I was confident and impatient; at the same time my nerve was wavering and my judgment, I suppose, beginning to fail. I took the first route that offered. It proved exceedingly hazardous; all the way down I had to fight both for foothold and against the premonition of approaching dizziness. And at length—it must have been near the bottom—I fell.

Of what happened after that I have only fragmentary memories. I remember walking without any sense of direction or of a goal along the endless beach. I remember a flock of sandpipers, rising and settling in their oblique and beautiful flight before me—perhaps leading me on when I should otherwise have fallen. I believe I had lost both billy and water-bottle: I remember finding water, retained from the storm, in a natural cistern of limestone rock. Vividly I remember a long nagging debate with myself as to whether I had heard the barking of a dog. And finally I remember lying in the dark and knowing I was in a delirium—knowing this because all round me warm night air was heavy with the scent of carnations.

• • •

The boy was bending over me. His face, golden-browned

by the sun, had the massive quality, the more than natural concreteness and weight, of a great painting. He laid down the pannikin among the carnations in the little garden won from rock and sand and called out joyfully to someone in the shack beyond: "Dad—he's come round!" Then again he lifted the pannikin to my lips. "You nearly did a perish that time, mister. But you haven't run your final yet." I must have murmured something about being lost for weeks. His eyes grew round. Then he smiled, and his smile was like a sudden sunlight on a brown Highland pool. "Yeah? Things do get a bit quiet west of Desperation Bay." I think he was ten or eleven; and his voice had all the pride of the pioneer.

Suddenly he sprang to his feet and gazed towards the sea. Then he cried out in an excitement in which I was quite forgotten: "Dad, dad—the Anson cutter's over the bar!"

2

I SHALL not here write at length of the humanity and eccentricity of Richard Anson. He took me to Port Lincoln and listened on the way to the strangely brief story I had to tell. I was a grown man—of twenty, perhaps, or twenty-one—with no history save one of a fortnight's wandering by the shore of the Great Australian Bight. I had not as much as a name; and it was as we rounded Cape Catastrophe that Anson took the whim to give me the surname of the first navigator to chart those waters. Thus, in that February of 1893, was Richard Flinders born.

I can see now that Anson believed finding to be keeping; that his plans, in the innocence of subconscious motivation, were directed to keeping me. I had been found on what was then the south-western fringe of settlement in South Australia: from Port Lincoln we sailed to Port Augusta and travelled thence to the largest of the Anson stations in a farther corner of the state; the doctors who attended me were brought—it must have been at great expense—from Sydney on the eastern verge of the continent. Had Ian Guthrie's disappearance continued a mystery I should certainly, despite my own obstinate loss of memory, have been discovered and identified. But within a few weeks, as I now know, that lonely body had been found stretched beside the ashes of its signal fire, my haversack with its few identifiable belongings lying near by. All doubt as to the fate of Ian Guthrie ceased; his only existence was at some unavailable level of Richard Flinders' brain.

In the Anson home and way of life I recognized a tradition not alien to me. The life of the land, the rambling house with its dark surfaces of old furniture, its worn and faded fine fabrics, its shadowy lines of Anson portraits watching the present fleeting generation from the walls: these were things that stirred at my mind more effectively than any psychologist's technique. Anson was a childless and unmarried man, and I saw a future opening to me that I yet had to reject. I had no wish for the life of a pastoralist; perhaps because of the experience I had been through, more probably because of hidden factors in my early years, I found the immensities of the ranges depressing and at times terrifying. I was absorbed moreover in the mystery of my own clouded mind and this gave rise to an overpowering desire to study medicine. Years later I was to publish, with certain necessary excisions and disguisements, *My Analysis of a Case of Long-term Amnesia*—a monograph that stands in odd isolation among my many attempts to further radiological science.

The generosity of Mr. Anson extended not only through my years of undergraduate study at Adelaide but through the long, lean and often fatal period that waits on the young specialist. He made Richard Flinders; and it was partly an impulse of piety, of which I cannot find it in me to be ashamed, that made me decide, when the time came, that Richard Flinders should not die.

It was my final year. I was walking one spring afternoon from the medical school to my lodgings, which lay some two miles away beyond the park lands that encircle the heart of the little city. A horse-tram drew away from in front of me and I became aware of a little crowd of people standing about a draped pedestal. They were unveiling a statue to some Scottish explorer—it may have been McDougal Stewart—and at the moment that I looked there came a skirl of bagpipes.

I walked for some yards as if in a great darkness and then I saw before me, like the tour de force of an illusionist, the figure of my brother Ranald. I saw him standing on some eminence, gazing over the endless bush. And I heard him recite, with all the dark passion of his thwarted poet's nature:

> "From the lone shieling on the misty island,
> Mountains divide us and a waste of seas;
> Yet still the blood is strong. . . ."

Voice and picture faded and I walked on with no more knowledge than before. But that night, as I looked out over the city drenched in moonlight in its lovely setting between hills and sea, I found veil after veil slipping from my mind. I knew that I was Ian Guthrie and I knew that, whatever accident had befallen, in the face of that bush fire Ranald had deserted me.

Inquiry revealed that by the death of our elder brother's children and by my own supposed death Ranald had inherited Erchany. I had always been the rudely healthy member of the family; the indecisions that mark the neurotic personality and which distinguished Ranald are unknown to me; and I remember it took me just two hours to reach my resolve. I was conscious of injury and injustice but did not think that these feelings should weigh with me. I had no desire for the life of a Scottish laird; I was already planning almost in full technical detail the steps of my medical career; I had no confidence in Ranald's honesty and I saw only vexation and distraction in the possibility of a contested claim. Australia had already given the world the Tichborne Case and I told myself ironically that in it there had been sufficient of that sort of thing for a couple of generations. In addition I had my affection for Mr. Anson, who was planning with me my career as an Australian surgeon. And I saw that it must be all or nothing; if I admitted my survival a score of embarrassments would appear and almost force me to claim the headship of my family.

So it was that I came to live out my life as Richard Flinders—mostly in my adopted country but sometimes in England and once for a long period of time in the United States. I have never been the wealthy man that the regular practice of surgery would have made me; most of my own earnings, together with a generous bequest from Richard Anson, have been devoted to the costly business of radium research. I do not know that much of the world's money is better spent. And my policy of letting no thought for my own future interfere with a possible benefit to knowledge has been amply justified. A few days ago I received notice of a great honour: I have been elected an emeritus fellow of an American foundation I had the privilege to serve years ago. I shall live in California. It is the climate for a green old age, and I want ten years for the exploration of fields that have been almost closed to me during a busy life in science. My work is over—in a sense even is rounded off in achievement—and my retirement from medicine, as from society, will be complete. In the course of my career I have had occasion to get a grip of many languages, and the literature of Europe is the right study for a man whose every second thought must be of the grave.

Only as my life's task slips from me into the hands of younger men the thought of Erchany comes back. And with the uprising of sentiment the rule of reason slackens; I am conscious again of past injustice and deprivation; I have an impulse to give Ranald a fright. If ever that impulse realizes itself I shall know my second childhood has come.

But there is the call of the place. Fives in the moat, the tower, the thrill of the parapet walk at night, the gallery where we used to enact the exploits of those ancestors who looked down on our play from the shadows. The snows on

Ben Cailie, the mists on the loch, the leaping and leaping again of the salmon at the falls . . . Still the blood is strong. Perhaps I shall see Erchany in more than dreams before I die.

Sydney, N.S.W.
St. Andrew's Day, 1936.

3

Timor Mortis conturbat me. . . . My brother has been chanting that—strangely, for it is I who am to die. I have myself very little fear.

Having pen and the liberty of my limbs I take this narrative—brought to Erchany for Ranald's information—and add to it what I can. If I hide it in some cranny of these ancient walls it may escape his vigilance and tell its story at some future time. I would have it told, dark page though it be in the long and chequered chronicle of the Guthries. All my work has been for knowledge: I believe in honest records.

I record then that my present pass is my own responsibility and fault. I have been childish and vindictive. And—what I fear irks me more—I have been a poor analyst of the mind.

In a sense vindictive, but in a sense I have cast a distorting charity over the past. I had come to feel that Ranald played me a mean trick, that he failed to play the game, and because of that I would give him a nasty jolt before going into my retirement for good and all. How childish the impulse—and how far out of the estimate of what lay between us! In running away, horses, water and all, in that crisis Ranald had betrayed himself—as a Guthrie, as a brother and as a man. And he had lived since in the eating consciousness of that betrayal, his life dominated by one shameful memory. I had fished him, a hysterical and grateful adolescent, from Fremantle harbour and a plentiful society of sharks; a few months later my blood was on his head in the bush. And the issue, to be played out in this lonely Scottish keep, is strangely tuned to the central truth of the greatest of Scottish tragedies, *Macbeth*. There is a blood-guiltiness from which there is no turning back, no way out save forward through blood. Ranald remembers not a mean trick but a betrayal and a crime. Year by year the element of deliberation in his panic desertion of me has been more evident. Year by year the dynamics of guilt have taken firmer hold of his mind, straining and finally disrupting his personality, so that in any fix he will at once envisage himself as the trapped and ruthless man. Convinced—through my own melodramatic folly, no doubt—that I was coming like some wild Guthrie of the past to execute an absolute revenge, he laid his own plans at a level of uncompromising violence—though violence tempered by some elaborateness, some intellectually satisfying subtlety, to which I feel I have by no means penetrated. My spectre has overshadowed Ranald's whole existence. Now that I have returned as if from the dead he has found some peculiar release in imposing a new perspective on my life, making the sacrifice of it no more than a move in some complicated game of which he is master. My death in the bush overwhelmed and destroyed him; my death at Erchany he will control and exploit. It is a "life line" of some interest to mental science.

I wrote to him from Australia, giving some account of myself but saying nothing of my intentions—yielding to the foolish satisfaction of concocting vague menace out of reticence. He must have had ample time to lay his plans; to isolate Erchany, to dismiss servants, to secure the help of the creature Hardcastle. Ranald is being driven by years of abnormal development and I cannot find that I very much wish for justice against him. But Hardcastle is assisting at murder for pay. I hope they will get him.

I wrote once more to Ranald and told him that Dr. Richard Flinders would arrive secretly on the night of the twenty-third of December. This will seem wanton and melodramatic enough, and its melodrama played with a nice irony into the hands of Ranald's own melodramatic fantasy. But there was some sense in it. I did not intend that Ian Guthrie should come to life again and the hour would make it easy for my brother to arrange a wholly confidential meeting. Moreover there was implicit in the choice a hint of sentiment and reconciliation. In our boyhood we had held a regular tryst at this midnight, a tryst at which we discussed what the next midnight—Christmas Eve—would bring to our stockings. This implication, clearly, Ranald was in no state to catch.

The unexpectedly heavy snows presented me with a problem. But I have long been accustomed to skis—I doubt if the world knows that there are excellent snow-fields in Australia—and skis were easy to come by at my hotel in Dunwinnie: it is a centre, crowded at present, for such winter sports as Scotland is beginning to contrive. I reached Erchany somewhat hazardously by the shores of Ben Cailie.

I was received by Hardcastle with just the caution that I expected and taken straight to this tower. And here he and Ranald between them overpowered me. That is all. It is simple, astonishing and—if only because Ranald and I are brothers—curiously horrible. This little bedroom might have been designed as a prison; may have been a prison hundreds of years ago. I have done what I can. Several of the Erchany rats, bold and sluggish creatures, I have succeeded in catching and sending out as messengers: I think it likely that they have the liberty of the whole crannied building. And I have tried as good an imitation as I can manage of the Australian *cooee*, one of the most penetrating calls in the world. But the height of this chamber, the thickness of these walls, the gale and the muffling snowfall outside make it unlikely that the sound will be heard, or if heard thought to be other than an owl or a trick of the wind. Nor have I any evidence that Erchany is not deserted except for my brother and his man.

I have been given a book: *Experimental Radiology* by Richard Flinders—I must count myself lucky that Ranald has this sort of fantastic, rather than some downright sadistic, streak. It is clear and tidy, and has pleased me as well as another book. And medicine brings me to a final record. Ranald is not mad. His thoughts and actions are logically directed to certain realizable ends—

VI

JOHN APPLEBY

1

MR. WEDDERBURN drew a long breath as I laid down the unfinished narrative. "Fratricide," he said. "And Miss Mathers was right. My interpretation of the facts came nowhere near the measure of Guthrie's ingenuity. Ian's murder by Ranald was to be read as Ranald's murder by Lindsay. He killed his brother and incriminated his niece's lover. It is madness."

I nodded. "In the face of any moral order it is madness. And yet it all abounds in logic. He was very skilfully fulfilling needs and achieving ends."

Sybil Guthrie stirred from the immobility in which she had listened to Ian Guthrie's testament. "*Why?*" she asked. "What drove him? What was his motive in such devilry?"

I considered. "There was a network of motive. You can work back in various directions, and dig down to various depths, and keep finding motives. There was what Ian saw: Ranald's life lived under the shadow of that crime in Australia; all the massive feelings of guilt that abound in the neurotic crystallized on it; a resulting fearful certainty that Ian was coming for absolute vengeance; the conviction that Ian must be outwitted and destroyed. At the same time there was some deeper symbolism at work. Ian's death in the bush had got on top of him; at Ian's second and veritable death *he* would be on top."

Noel Gylby clapped his hands like a child. "On top by several hundred feet . . . on top by the height of the tower!"

"Exactly. And a psychoanalyst would find a symbolism yet deeper. I was thinking of it earlier to-day. When a man throws himself from a height he is taking a symbolical leap from danger—the perilous *above*—to safety—the secure *below*. In hurling Ian from the tower Ranald was achieving just what he had failed to achieve in Australia. *He was rescuing Ian.* In fact his crime was a stroke of wit—of the dark irony of which we have a good deal of evidence in Ranald."

Wedderburn exclaimed. "Wit!"

"In the Freudian sense. A reconciling of violently opposed desires at a verbal or symbolical level. The desire to destroy Ian: the desire to rehabilitate himself, to prove his own manhood, by rescuing Ian."

There was a silence in which we could hear, behind the wainscoting of the gallery, the dragging movement of a poisoned rat. Wedderburn took out a handkerchief and passed it across his forehead. "I prefer," he said, "to encounter these abysses of the mind in text-books. And in medical text-books, not legal ones."

"They are bound to figure sometimes in both. But we are far from having exhausted the net-work of motive yet—nor have we all the materials. Somewhere there is a strong motive of fear, horror, hatred against Neil Lindsay, whose destruction was worked with such diabolical skill into the greatest of all the jigsaws. That we must investigate. What is clear so far is the whole picture in relation to Ian. You can think of much that fits in. The passionate shutting-up of this gallery, for instance, when Ranald inherited." I let my torch circle round the portraits on the wall. "The Guthries of Erchany! The tradition Ranald had betrayed. A wild, dark lot they may have been. But fratricide, of which Ranald had virtually been guilty in the bush, was outside the family scope."

Wedderburn nodded. "According to my friend Clanclacket they were distinguished for sticking together."

"And then the passion of impatience at the opening-up of the gallery. He had got his idea and he must see the family portraits again to assure himself of its feasibility; to reassure him that Guthries really have the strange characteristic, occasionally observable in old families, of being remarkably like each other."

Gylby broke in. "That's the point where I can't see—"

"Listen." I fished from my pocket Gylby's own journal letter and turned the pages. "It is, as you remarked, rather literary; but it gives the essence." And I read:

"Guthrie in his dust had returned to innocence; that sinister face, with the strongly marked features that speak of race, was stronger and purer, as if some artist had taken a sponge and swabbed the baser lines away. One reads of death showing such effects; to encounter them at such a violent issue was disconcertingly moving. I composed the body as I could. . . .

"*One reads of death showing such effects.* You see how nicely Ranald had calculated? Actually you were looking at a different man. But what you thought you saw was the transfiguring effect of death—a well-known and authentic thing. Death commonly does just that: makes a man look slightly different, takes away lines of pressure and anxiety so that an impression of ease or peacefulness or innocence results. Death, in fact, would turn brother Ranald into brother Ian. Conversely, Ian dead and spontaneously thought of as Ranald would certainly seem Ranald—*touched by death.* And remember that neither you nor Miss Guthrie ever saw the living Ranald in a good light. On the night of your arrival there was nothing but an ungenerous candle-light. And on the following day Guthrie took care not to appear. You see how, appearing like a bolt from the blue, you were yet fitted instantaneously into the jigsaw. The body was to be formally identified by Hardcastle who was in the know, by Mrs. Hardcastle who is half blind and by Dr. Noble who hadn't seen Ranald Guthrie for two years. The Gamleys had been sent away and Gamley's coming into the picture at all was an unforeseen mischance. But Gamley saw the body only by lantern-light and suspected nothing. Miss Mathers, the one person who would have seen at once that the dead man was not Ranald, was on her way to Canada and unlikely to be found in time for the merely formal identification which alone would be thought of. At the same time Miss Mathers' absence was part of the plan for incriminating Lindsay. And—as I say—you and Miss Guthrie, who might have been such an awkward irruption on the scheme, were brilliantly utilized to give, imperceptibly, further weight to the assumption that the dead man was Ranald. Ranald operated with superb economy, using everything that turned up, from a legend about chopped fingers to an unexpected kinswoman. Indeed he found you useful, Miss Guthrie, in more ways than one."

Sybil Guthrie looked absently into the gloom of the gallery. "I frightfully confused the issues," she said.

"No, I don't mean your story of events in the tower, we'll come to that. I mean that Ranald found your conversation useful."

Miss Guthrie opened round eyes.

"We all see, I think, what Ranald was aiming at for himself. *'Oh, my America, my new-found land.'* His early experience as an actor. His making a rapid study of general medicine. His leading you to talk of America as far back as you could remember, the America in which Richard Flinders had worked. All these things show us clearly what Ranald was intending to do—I should say what he *is* intending to do. Richard Flinders has died as Ranald Guthrie: Ranald Guthrie is going to live as Richard Flinders—a Richard Flinders who is retiring both from medical research and from the society in which he has lived for the last twenty years, who is going to live quietly in California on a pension. It is, as Ian was going to tell us when he had to break off writing, a feasible, a realizable end. And notice here again a strong appeal, a strong motive, on the symbolical level. Compare the lives of the two brothers and it is clear that Ian *won*. Ian had always been he himself tells us, 'the rudely healthy member of the family.' Ranald, on the other hand, was a 'neurotic personality.' And subsequently—"

"Ian," Wedderburn interrupted unexpectedly, "was packed off abroad because he was too successful with the young women; Ranald because he had run away to a profession that consists in hiding from oneself by dressing up as somebody else."

"A capital psychologist's point. And subsequently this position—the proposition, simply, of Ranald's inferiority—is exacerbated. Ian saves Ranald's life: Ranald betrays Ian's. Later still Ian as Richard Flinders rises to eminence in a beneficent career: Ranald's life is futile and increasingly neurotic. *But now Ranald becomes Ian!* The unsuccessful brother succeeds both in identifying himself with his successful rival and in displacing him."

Wedderburn took a turn up and down the gallery. "Mr. Appleby, it is all perfectly coherent. How strange, then, that motives of this sort are almost unknown to criminal law."

"It is because these profound motives are always—except in the case of madmen—rationalized. There is always a top-dressing, so to speak, of motive comprehensible not to the deeply passional but to the romantic or economic man. And it is with these super-imposed motives that we deal in the police courts. There is such a further motive here, in a direction we have not yet explored." In my turn I paced up and down the gallery. "And yet I don't know that this further motive is really a superficial one. Perhaps it is the master motive of all."

Noel Gylby searched his pockets for absent cigarettes; discovered instead his store of buttered biscuits. He handed them round. "Motives," he said vaguely, "to right of us, motives to—sorry: go on."

"Take another significant point in Guthrie's behaviour—and one in which we see him nearest to real madness; in which we see him at his most patently pathological point. He could impersonate Flinders. He could get up the America Flinders had known. He could get up enough medicine to protect himself in the event of an unforeseen intrusion on his privacy by medical people. But there was one big difficulty. The Californian Flinders must not display any marked character-trait which it might become known was quite alien to the Sydney Flinders. And Ranald Guthrie had such a trait—more than a trait, indeed. He had a stubborn and strange and glaring compulsion. He was a pathological miser. If he were to become Flinders he had the tremendous task of conquering that."

"Surely the impossible task?" It was Sybil Guthrie who spoke.

"Almost certainly the impossible task. But that his will would refuse to acknowledge. We know that he made efforts—and the grotesque nature of the early results give the measure of his task. He thought of his table and ordered up wine and laid in caviare. But he neglected to stop starving his dogs."

Wedderburn chuckled. "Including Doctor."

"In Ranald's miserliness, then, lay the grand impediment to his plan. But does it not also point to a motive, perhaps the grand motive? His ruling passion was miserliness; was living, little Isa Murdoch told me, on other people's threepenny bits found in the pockets of scarecrows. Which was just what he was planning to do. At last he was going to live not at his own but at other people's expense—on Flinders' pension."

Sybil Guthrie foraged for biscuit crumbs in her lap, licked a buttery finger. "Mr. Appleby, I can stand no more of this. I want action. Where is Ranald Guthrie now? For instance, is he likely to be lurking with a gun round that corner?"

"I think not. A couple of nights ago he was in Kinkeig—we must discover why—and was observed—"

Wedderburn threw up despairing hands. "The ghost!"

"Undoubtedly the ghost. And as to where Ranald is now, we can guess. He had to pick up the thread of Flinders' life as quickly as possible. And the circumstances have been perfectly designed to facilitate his doing so—the beautiful economy of the jigsaw again! Flinders had come quietly to Scotland and was staying at a big hotel in Dunwinnie, a place full to overflowing with curlers and winter-sporters generally. If Dr. Flinders went on a nocturnal expedition and came back with his hair gone slightly greyer or a wrinkle gone astray nobody was in the least likely to notice. There might be unknown elements which would make the whole thing a gamble, of course. But, that point at the hotel passed, Ranald was really in a tolerably strong position. He was Dr. Flinders *en route* for California, with Dr. Flinders' vital papers in his possession. No doubt there would be a second critical point when he took over Dr. Flinders' financial affairs, but a little forgery would more likely than not see him through. And there is no reason to suppose that up to the moment he is at all alarmed. Provided our discoveries are kept dark he will be found without difficulty."

There was a little silence, broken this time by Wedderburn taking a composed munch at a biscuit. He finished his mouthful and said: "And our next move?"

"Is to listen to Miss Guthrie. I think there was a point at which she almost upset all Ranald's plans."

2

SYBIL GUTHRIE began by turning to Wedderburn. "I'm afraid I'm chiefly worried at thinking how dense you must have thought me. When you said Lindsay had nothing to fear and that I had only to tell the truth you must have thought it strange that I didn't in the least see what was in your mind—that I could only say I found it terribly hard to believe you. But you see your case—the case that Guthrie had killed himself to incriminate Lindsay—could never occur to me for the simple reason that it was ruled out by what I knew. On the parapet walk I had seen a man sent hurtling to his death. When you proved your case before the sheriff this afternoon I knew that my continued fibbing—my second line of downright lies—had enabled you to prove what wasn't true. It was rather a creepy feeling. The evidence of the bogus telephone, of the bureau I knew Lindsay couldn't have rifled, was conclusive. That is to say, Guthrie's plot against Lindsay was conclusive. And yet I knew Ranald hadn't committed suicide. I had seen the man I thought was Ranald *killed*. And I still believed Lindsay had killed him. Of course my conscience was now clearer still. For I had to believe that Lindsay, in really losing control of himself and killing Guthrie, had merely done what Guthrie was abominably plotting to suggest he had done. That was the only way I could make sense of your case and my knowledge. And though my private morality says a Neil Lindsay oughtn't to be hanged for killing a degenerate nuisance like Ranald Guthrie under the outrageous provocation I had seen and sensed in those last moments in the tower—well, it was creepy all the same. I wondered whether perhaps Lindsay hadn't spotted Guthrie's plot and killed him in the anger of discovering it. And whether that wouldn't have been almost justifiable suicide. And whether perhaps Lindsay oughtn't to have told the truth—what I thought was the truth—and faced it." Sybil Guthrie hesitated, seemed to cast about for further words. "I mean a court of law tremendously impresses one with the abstract importance of getting the whole truth into the light. I think I was rather shy of walking up to Lindsay and shaking hands with him at the end. I believed we were both less than honest."

I don't know if I have mentioned that Sybil Guthrie had great good looks. Noel Gylby said heartily: "Well, all's well that ends well!"

I said—as the best means I could hit on for dissociating myself from this light-hearted point of view: "Miss Guthrie, previous to these improved perceptions of yours before the sheriff—you had no doubts or qualms?"

"Mr. Appleby, no. I'm not like you sworn to certain accepted canons of justice. I had only one qualm."

Gylby made a gesture as if remembering something. "The bureau."

"Yes. For a moment the rifled bureau staggered me. If it were possible that Lindsay had touched the gold he was—whatever provocation he had suffered—outside my protection. But then I realized my own certainty that he had never been near it. I think I said or hinted to Noel that the bureau merely added to the puzzle—to the mystery of what had happened. It was irrelevant to my moral problem."

Wedderburn leant forward and patted his client on the hand. "My dear, I am afraid you will one day have the practical problem of explaining your moral problem to a judge of the Supreme Court. At Ranald Guthrie's trial."

Sybil's chin tilted. "If I can see cousin Ranald in the dock I won't much worry about the figure I cut."

Quite illogical, I thought—for why protect a nervously excitable young man like Lindsay only to pursue a nervously degenerated man like old Guthrie? Was not Guthrie just the sort of hospital case that Lindsay, granted a certain pressure at one critical point in life or another, might have become? I turned away from this—the riddle that modern neurology presents to the framers of penal law—to contemplate the more concrete problem of Miss Guthrie. As my colleague Speight had decided, a nice girl. Though Speight, for that matter, might now be inclined a little to modify his verdict. It was in downright echo of Wedderburn's fatherly tones that I said: "And now we had better have in detail just what you did see."

"It won't take long. I saw just what I've said I saw: the interview, Guthrie turning on Lindsay at the end and lashing him horribly. Lindsay going out by the staircase door and Guthrie by the bedroom door—the two doors that Mr. Wedderburn discovered I just couldn't command. It's after that, and by way of omission, that the lying begins."

Gylby said briskly: "I've found a bit of chocolate." And handed it to Miss Guthrie.

Miss Guthrie took a bite. "—that the lying begins. I stood peering into the empty study for I suppose about twenty seconds, wondering if I could dash through and make my get away. And then I heard something. There was still, as you know, a terrific wind up there: what I heard was a cry or shout—and it must have been pretty loud to reach me at all from round a corner of the parapet walk. For that was where it came from—from that side of the parapet walk upon which I now know the little bedroom opens.

"I was all het up and ready for a bit of guess-work. Watching that sudden verbal attack of Guthrie's on Lindsay I felt for a moment, as you know, quite murderous; and my thought was that the two men were together again, that they had somehow got out on the battlements and were quarrelling there. The place was fearfully dangerous and I suddenly felt it was all a stupidity I wasn't going to stand for. Castle Erchany craziness: I'd had enough of it. So I groped my way along the parapet walk to tell them to drop it."

Noel Gylby swept Wedderburn and myself with a glance that plainly called upon us to admire. "Cheers," he said.

"Of course I knew I might be quite wrong. Still, I got round the corner. And there was certainly something on.

"It was a confused vision. Somebody had set up a lamp—a storm lantern—in a niche above the door from the bedroom. Below a certain line was darkness; I could see only what was above. And the first thing I saw was Ranald Guthrie's face. I had just time to see that it was wrenched awry by some violent emotion when his arm rose into the light and I realized that he was holding an axe. I called out to him to stop. I believe he heard me, though I hardly expected him to in the wind. He spun round and took a step that carried him out of the lantern's rays. I saw him for a moment as a shadow; then I think he stooped down and I could see nothing. I was aware of confused movement—I believe of a groan and then some muttered words. A moment later I saw him again—or rather I saw what I took to be him—reared up against the parapet, his head and shoulders full in the light. For a split second I saw him so and then something came between us: the mere black silhouette of a back that I took to be Lindsay's. I must have felt what was going to happen, for I shouted again and struggled forward. The shadowy back of the second man moved and Guthrie was in view again. But only for a moment. An arm shot out at him and I heard, even in that wind, the crack of a bare fist on his chin. He staggered, gave a great cry—the cry Noel heard from the staircase—and then he went sheer over the parapet." Sybil Guthrie shivered, drew her coat about her. "That's all."

I put down the notebook in which I had been scribbling. "All, Miss Guthrie? You didn't see Ranald make for his get away by the trapdoor and the winding stair?"

"I saw nothing more. What I was sure I had seen was Lindsay kill cousin Ranald, perhaps in some sort of defence against that axe. And I wasn't going to be in on it if my witness might entangle Lindsay. I turned round and retreated on an instant impulse, round the corner to the French window by which I had been standing. The beastly thing might best pass as suicide: anyway, I was going to bide my time and see."

Noel Gylby said heavily: "I would have done the same."

"And your narrative now," I said, "instead of embarrassing Lindsay actually convicts the man you thought Lindsay had killed. It is for the policeman a pleasingly complete mix-up. A mystery on classical lines with the *dénouement* quite in the right place."

Gylby made an approving and Wedderburn a disapproving noise. I had spoken, I think, with some intention of easing a tension evident on Sybil Guthrie's face. She had been under a long strain and now that the truth was told she was feeling the reaction. "Your evidence," I went on, "has acquitted cousin Ranald on one score at least."

"Acquitted him?"

"Of squeamishness. You remember that according to Mr. Wedderburn's theory Ranald failed in two particulars. He had failed to keep silent as he hurled himself to death. And his nerve had failed him too in the crux of the plan, the thing that was to incriminate Lindsay in the thought of the countryside; he had failed to take that horrible chop at his fingers in his last living moments. And when we got nearer the truth that last point remained puzzling. Had he relented at the last moment of performing the outrage on Ian—drugged, one supposes, and ready to be hurled to death by one blow? We now know he hadn't relented; he was simply interrupted by your first cry. And his action upon that interruption is our final and best evidence of the remarkable speed and economy of his mind.

"Consider just what happened. Ranald has Ian huddled helpless in the snow at his feet. The axe is raised in that particularly nasty moment of his crime when he hears a shout. Someone is on the parapet walk. A paralyzing discovery?—not a bit of it. The situation is desperate but may yet be saved. So far, only he himself can have been *seen.* He pitches the axe over the battlements, gets himself out of the light, stoops, heaves up the body of his brother into a momentarily erect position—*and into the light.* Then, himself a mere black silhouette, he hits out. The intruder, whoever he be, has no thought of an Ian Guthrie; *he sees Ranald Guthrie killed and cannot see the killer.* If Ranald can then make his get away by the winding stair, seizing and extinguishing the lamp, his plot is still in a fair way to succeed. The wind will quickly obliterate all traces of the trapdoor having been used; the intruder will not be able to swear that in the darkness the killer did not escape through the bedroom and down the main staircase—on which Lindsay, two or three seconds later, would be found according to plan. And so the case against Lindsay would be even stronger than Ranald had hoped, for of the fact of murder there could now be no doubt at all. Ranald Guthrie, in fact, is one who never says die."

"Die," said Wedderburn, "is just what he did say to two innocent men." He stood up, a handsome old man suddenly lively with passion. "But we'll get him! Ranald Guthrie has played his last trick."

From somewhere below us, shattering the silence of the deserted castle, came the harsh high reverberation of a great cracked bell.

3

It was the young lawyer Stewart back from Dunwinnie. We had quite forgotten him; and finding closed doors he had applied himself to the bell in the courtyard. With him was the minister, Dr. Jervie.

We had gone down to the door in a compact, nervous group and I think they must have read in our faces as we stood in the wavering shadows of the hall that the mystery of the place had undergone some violent revolution. But both were curiously silent and it was only when Gylby had kindled a fire in the schoolroom—a thing we might well have done long before—that Stewart said: "You have news?"

Wedderburn replied. "The strangest news. Ranald Guthrie is still alive."

Stewart was staggered. But my interest was more in Dr. Jervie. He had sat down and was staring into the first leaping flames on the hearth; and I think I have never seen a sadder face. At Wedderburn's words he looked up for a moment like one who turns from meditation to accept some fact on an indifferent plane.

"Guthrie is alive? Then I suppose I saw no ghost."

"*You* saw the ghost!"

"Yes. Perhaps your informant didn't mention me? It would be taken for granted, you know, that the ghost would appear to the minister. What else is the minister paid for, idle havering old fool that he is, than to hold in with suchlike daftness and bogle talk?" The face remained calm, but the words, parodying Scottish village talk at its least beautiful, were startling in their bitterness. Not, I thought, a chronic mood; rather the momentary product of shock. But not, it seemed, the shock of Ranald Guthrie's continued existence.

Jervie made a gesture at once of weariness and apology. "Can we have your strange story," he said, "—first?"

4

It was an hour and a half later. I had stepped through the schoolroom window and found myself on a small terrace of which I had been unaware before. Everything was very still, the air moist and oddly warm in the night thaw. The moon, almost at the full, was high in a clear heaven. To my right, through aisles of dark larches, I could see the narrow snow-covered fields of the little home farm, a serrated line of larches beyond like a line of pasteboard trees against the luminous back-drop of the sky. But to my left, down the loch, I could look far into the night, far down the long ribbon of dark ice behind an arm of which, sheer and sheerly beautiful, rose the untroubled fastnesses of Ben Mervie and Ben Cailie. I felt my heart heavy with foreboding.

Jervie came out and stood beside me, looking at the loch and the mountains in silence. Then he said softly: "How peaceful it is."

A longer silence was split from the direction of the loch by a sound like a pistol shot: the ice was cracking. The sound, sharp in that quiet, roused him. "Mr. Appleby—come in." And he turned back to the schoolroom.

Stewart had gone up to the tower; Gylby had just returned to the room with a load of wood. Jervie crossed to where he had sat, carefully folded Gylby's journal letter, laid it on a table beside Ian Guthrie's testament. Then his eye caught something at the other end of the room, he took up a candle, was presently studying the Indian bird paintings on the wall. He came back, stood before the fire and there recited—with an oddly moving effect of familiar statement:

"Sen for the deth remeid is non,
Best is that we for deth dispone
After our deth that lif may we;
Timor Mortis conturbat me."

He turned to Wedderburn. "Ranald Guthrie," he said, "has long since given himself to the Devil. And the Devil gave him the Devil's own gift in return: pride."

Uneasily Wedderburn said: "No doubt."

"Mr. Appleby, you wonder if, in all the complex of motives you have discovered, the master motive is avarice—the miserliness that is his ruling passion. I think the master motive is his other ruling passion, pride. Pride that is fiercer in him than was the avarice that sent him haunting among the scarecrows. Pride that made him take a tortuous and diabolical path to an imperative end. He forbade the marriage of Neil Lindsay and Christine Mathers. It couldn't be. But pride in turn forbade him to give the reason. Neil and Christine are brother and sister."

Sybil Guthrie gave a little cry that ebbed into silence.

"Actually, half-brother and half-sister. Christine has been supposed—if only dubiously and by implication—to be the child of Guthrie's mother's brother, who was known to have been killed with his wife in a railway accident in France. In reality, Christine is the daughter of Guthrie's own sister, Alison Guthrie.

"Alison was an eccentric and solitary woman, with a passion for birds—"

I interrupted. "Christine—"

"Quite so. She has something of the same passion. But if Alison had a passion for the creatures of the air she had too a passion, less innocent, for her own menservants. The type is known. And a certain Wat Lindsay, Neil's father, took service with her for a time when he was already a married man and shortly after Neil's birth. Christine was—"

Suddenly, as if a flood had broken, Sybil Guthrie broke into a passion of weeping. Jervie waited for a minute and went on gently. "Christine's mother died in some lonely place at the child's birth. Ranald Guthrie took the little girl but concealed her parentage with all the ingenuity of which you know him to be capable. It could, of course, have been ferreted out: Mr. Wedderburn will doubt if the estate could have been settled at Ranald's supposed death without the truth emerging. But Ranald was a driven creature and his clearsightedness had limits. He was passionately determined that the thing he morbidly regarded as shameful should never be known.

"And so it was pride, you see, and not avarice that drove him to the greatest wickedness of all. There was no need that the family history become public. An explanation to Neil and Christine as soon as he knew of their attachment, though unspeakably sad, would have stopped short of real tragedy. But it seems he couldn't do it. What the psychologists in whom Mr. Appleby is interested call the inhibition—that was absolute. He could not speak: he came to see he could not prevent the marriage unless he spoke. So here is the motive against Lindsay for which Mr. Appleby has been seeking. We can feel it, I think: the massive fear, hate, horror mounting in him. In front of these young people he saw the commission of a sin—an unwitting sin, if such a thing can be—which has always appeared peculiarly terrible to the neurotic mind. He is responsible, and he can prevent it only by speaking—or acting. And he cannot speak."

Sybil Guthrie stood up, now dry-eyed. "Where is Christine? Could I drive down—?"

Jervie shook his head. "Time enough in the morning. Christine is asleep by now in the manse—and Neil at Ewan Bell's.

"I say Guthrie couldn't speak. And that he therefore planned to act. The sense of guilt that lies heavy on his type, that had grown and grown on him with the contemplation of his treachery or cowardice in Australia, he would now tend to unload, I suppose, on Lindsay. He would project it upon Lindsay—Lindsay whose father had, in a sense, betrayed a Guthrie; who was now marching stiff-necked upon deadly sin. Nothing would save the situation, and nothing would be adequate to it, save that Lindsay should die."

In a rather husky voice Noel Gylby interrupted. "As Christine said of him, he would pit extremes only against extremes. Or what he thought extremes."

"And so," said Jervie, "we come to a new view of the

jigsaw. Mr. Appleby has seen Ranald incorporating Lindsay into his plot against his brother; I see him incorporating his brother into his plot against Lindsay." Again he made his weary gesture. "I suppose that, criminologically, it is a pretty case." He rose. "I must find strength for the duty that is laid upon me to-morrow."

Wedderburn too rose. "Jervie, you are sure? There can be no question of the truth of the facts you have told us?"

"I am afraid none. But you must know how we have come by them. We don't yet know if the child's birth—Christine's birth—was falsely registered. But whatever course Guthrie took—and we may be sure it would be clever enough—required the connivance of some other person of status in the county. He went to Sir Hector Anderson of Dunwinnie, an eccentric old man with extravagant views on blood and race. Sir Hector died fifteen years ago, so Guthrie in his present plot has had nothing to fear from him. But he has reckoned without Lady Anderson—not unreasonably, for she is now over ninety. She knew the truth, though she has never divulged it. And she still follows the local news. When she heard that Neil and Christine had been brought back from an attempted elopement she acted at once. The summons that took Stewart hurriedly away late this afternoon was from Dunwinnie Lodge. He had the whole story."

"But the recollection of so very old a lady—?"

Jervie shook his head. "There were a couple of letters preserved. Not much detail, but as to the fact—conclusive."

Sybil Guthrie said: "Dr. Jervie—nobody else knows yet? They won't be told—brutally?"

"Nobody else knows yet. And I will tell them myself."

Gylby broke in almost with violence. "Why *need* they know? It's not a *real* relationship—a buried relationship like that! It must have happened hundreds of times, and nobody the wiser or the worse."

I laid my hand on his arm. "No good, Gylby—no good at all. At Ranald's trial it must come out. Even if we concealed it—Lady Anderson and ourselves—Ranald would almost certainly divulge it in the end. It would be his only way to triumph, and almost certainly it would overcome his silence."

Sybil Guthrie jumped up and came over to me. "But, Mr. Appleby, if we left the whole thing entirely alone! At present Mr. Wedderburn's case holds the field. Ranald is off, undetected, to his retirement and his pension. Lindsay is no longer in any danger of being hanged. He and Christine are making their plans for Canada—" She broke off, turned to Dr. Jervie in sudden appeal. "Dr. Jervie, couldn't you agree?"

Jervie walked to the window and gazed out. Without turning round he said in a low voice: "No."

A futile debate. I tried to stop it. "There is no utility in discussing keeping quiet. Quite apart from ethical issues, it just wouldn't help. Ranald would keep an eye on what was happening. When he found his plot against Lindsay had failed and that the young people were off to Canada it is overwhelmingly likely he would see to it they learnt the truth."

Sybil said: "Find Ranald. Make a bargain. Silence for silence."

I shook my head. "He is an old man and he could break his bargain at his death. That the truth should come upon them after years of marriage—one couldn't take the responsibility of that. If only because it is impossible to know how they themselves would look back on our silence. There is no soft way out."

From the window Jervie said in a new voice: "There's somebody coming."

I crossed the room and we both stepped out once more on the little terrace. A car was approaching the castle; its headlamps, faint in the moonlight, were sweeping the narrow arm of loch that ran nearly to the moat. The lights caught us for a moment and circled right to follow the drive round the stretch of frozen water. Then they stopped. "The dip by the last turn of the drive," Jervie said. "It was most a slushy bog when we came; I suppose the car can't get through." A minute later two figures appeared on the further verge, scrambled down the bank and began rapidly to cross the ice.

Half way they came into the full moonlight and we recognized Neil Lindsay and Christine Mathers.

They were hand in hand, I think their spirits were high: in leaving the blocked drive to take a short cut over the ice they were doing a foolhardy thing. The ice was already cracking everywhere; they must have felt it cracking beneath them; they quickened their pace and I believe they were laughing as they ran. They were young, resilient, and they had escaped that day from the shadow of great danger. Suddenly we heard Christine's voice, clear and eager, calling out something about the night. I felt Jervie brace himself as the sound floated up to us. "It must be to-night," he said. "I will go and let them in."

From below, distinguishable now, came Christine's voice. "Impossible shoes! Lift me, Neil."

5

THEY came running down the corridor and into the schoolroom, Jervie—who had meant, I fancy, to take them to another room—out-distanced behind. I looked from one to the other. They were indeed resilient. They were happy.

"Don't anyone try to cross the ice! The next man will go in." Christine tossed off her hat and looked about her—first at her own room and then at the people in it. She ran over to Sybil Guthrie. "Miss Guthrie of Erchany! Bring peace and sanity to the castle—and fun and good plumbing too." She glanced round us again. "But where's Ewan Bell?"

Jervie said gently: "You expected him to be here?"

"Of course. He said he was going to meet us and the lawyers here for explanations—explanations that were to be kept private. I don't know—"

She had been unaware in her excitement of the atmosphere in the room; she caught it now and suddenly fell silent. And

Lindsay, who had been standing quietly by the door watching us all, spoke.

"We don't know what he meant. But it's plain there are explanations to come. There's a secret on every face in this room. What is it?"

I saw that for a moment Dr. Jervie was at a loss. What he had to say required privacy and preparation: and meantime here was young Lindsay demanding truth. As a stopgap I plunged in. "The first news is this. Ranald Guthrie is not dead. His plot against you, Mr. Lindsay, stands; only he killed not himself but his older brother, a doctor recently returned from Australia."

Barely put it must have been next to unintelligible, and I don't think Christine grasped a word. But Lindsay caught the central fact and held it. His eyes darkened. "Guthrie alive!"

Gylby from the window called out—the relief of even a moment's diversion in his voice: "Another visitor in sight. And taking the same route."

Christine spun round. "It must be Ewan Bell. He mustn't take the ice!" and she ran to the window.

We all followed. For a moment we could see only an indistinct figure scrambling down the further bank. Christine turned to Lindsay. "Neil," she said, "call to him—warn him." At the same moment the figure emerged into the full moonlight. She swayed beside me. *"Uncle Ranald!"* And Lindsay echoed: *"Guthrie!"*

Gylby leapt back into the schoolroom and plunged it in darkness. Sybil Guthrie whispered: "He must think the castle deserted. We've got him; oh, we've got him!"

But Lindsay took a great breath and shouted: "Back, man, back!" And in the same instant the ice broke.

For a fraction of a second we were all immobile, staring at the circle of dark water that spread, it seemed with the slowness of oil, in the middle of the faintly glimmering ice. Then I felt myself thrust aside by a taut arm. It was Lindsay's. And he leapt from the little terrace direct to the moat.

It looked fifteen feet but was probably less. And the drop

was to snow. Gylby and I could only follow. As I jumped I heard Christine say: "I'll get rope."

Lindsay was only seconds ahead, but he had luck or an access of strength that took him up the farther side of the moat more quickly than we could manage. When we reached the edge of the lake he was already some way out on the ice, crawling forward flat on his stomach. Without pausing he called back to us, "Not another man on the ice . . . get a rope across as quick as you can." And then he called out ahead: "Guthrie, can you hold on, man? I'm coming."

I knew he was right. If Guthrie, as seemed likely, had been stunned as he went through, our best chance of getting him out was to put as little strain as possible on the surrounding ice: an extensive break-up might make rescue impossible even on this last narrow neck of loch. For the moment we could only stand and watch, prepared to do what we could should Lindsay too come to grief. And once and again the ice cracked ominously. I kicked off my shoes and began to strip. We were likely to be diving before it was over.

Christine came running up with a coil of rope. "All there is," she said quietly. "And not good."

I glanced at the rope and then back to Lindsay: he was about half way to his goal. "Better test it," I said, "and know what we've got." Rapidly Gylby and I paid it out yard by yard, put what strain on it we could. It seemed sound but I had little trust in it: it was common wash-line stuff. And much too short to span the whole arm of ice. With luck it would reach just to where Guthrie had gone through.

We heard Lindsay's voice—confident, absorbed. "Hold on, man, and you'll be as right as rain. Do you think it's this that Loch Cailie's for on a brave winter night?"

Christine beside me gave a little gasp, stared rigidly out across the ice, "He's seen him," I said. "And there's nothing for it: I must take out the rope."

Gylby said: "I'll be lighter on the ice." But I was already crawling in the wake of Lindsay. Guthrie was apparently conscious and clinging to some sufficiently strong rim of ice;

Lindsay had almost reached him; I thought it likely I could get the rope to them. Only once did I feel the ice crack, and but for a strange intermittent tremor in it I should have had comparatively little fear. Lindsay's voice came back to me. "I've got him. Let me have the rope from as far away as you can manage." I got cautiously to my hands and knees and threw the rope. The ice cracked beneath the movement but when I got down again on my stomach it was steady under me. And again Lindsay's voice came back, "Got it. Get back and all pull gently when I say."

I got back as quickly as I could, feeling the tremor in the ice grow as I crawled. Lindsay's hail came before I had reached the shore. For a moment we pulled against a dead weight—and certainly a weight for which the rope had never been designed. Then it moved. Lindsay's voice came in triumph. "He's out! Long and steady."

I was aware that the tremor in the ice was now a faint vibration in the air, the ghost of a low moan. And just as we had got the almost inert body to safety it rose in pitch. Wind from up the loch. Lindsay's voice came, rapid and controlled: "Rope again—if you can." A second later, sharp against the murmur of that swift and treacherous wind, came the splintering repercussion of a widely breaking surface.

"Lindsay!"

There was no reply. I took one look at Christine Mathers and ran out over the now working ice.

6

THE chill of that water is still in my bones. And more, I should think, in Noel Gylby's. He was seconds behind me; he worked for an hour after he had hauled me out. But what haunts my memory with a dragging irony is the small scale of it all. Daylight showed how narrow is that last arm of the loch. It is not even very deep. And we were struggling with floating fragments of ice that a boy could pick up and pitch against a stone. Yet I do not think we failed to make every effort we could. In that sudden flaw of mountain wind the numbing water and the driving ice made a little arctic hell. And from up the loch a powerful undercurrent was pulling, threatening again and again to draw us under an unbreakable barrier. It was days before the body of Neil Lindsay was recovered.

My head was injured; and because of that joined to exhaustion I must have lain unconscious for some time. When I recovered I found Wedderburn with a brandy flask and Ewan Bell the cobbler bending over me. I struggled up and asked a question.

Wedderburn shook his head. "I am afraid there is no hope. He is drowned."

"Miss Mathers?"

"Miss Guthrie and Jervie have taken her back to the house."

I turned round and saw lying near me the body of the rescued man. It stirred as I glanced. My mind through its unconsciousness had still, I think, been working in terms of mere accident and danger. It was now flooded by the knowledge of tragedy. And my face must have shown this. For Wedderburn said: "At least, now she need not be told until some proper time."

I staggered to my feet impatiently. "Ranald Guthrie," I said; "you reckon without him still."

Bell strode over to the prostrate figure and held up a lantern. He moved an arm, a hand into the light—a hand from which a couple of fingers had been amputated long ago. "Ian Guthrie," he said. "Ranald is dead."

"Dead! You are sure?" My head still swimming, I stared at him stupidly.

The old man straightened up. "Certain. I killed him."

VII

A CONCLUSION BY EWAN BELL

1

YESTERDAY I had a letter from Christine. The postmark—*Cincinnati, Ohio*—that seemed outlandish but a year since is grown familiar now: wonderful it is how even an old man will get used to change.

Devil the change, though, could you find in the Kinkeig folk. Mistress Johnstone herself brought the letter over from the post-office and stood about for near ten minutes, right interested in other folk's old shoon. "Read your letter, Mr. Bell," she said, "and never mind me." And half an hour later in came the schoolmistress, her nose maybe a ghost of a bittock longer than the winter day she went up the glen to the great house. Would I take a ticket, she was wondering, for a right trig play the bairns were to give in the church hall, choke-a-block it would be with self-expression and child-psychology, and the whole written by the dux, a genius he was for certain, wee Geordie Gamley? And would there be any news from the world coming into Kinkeig these days?

And a week or two ago I had another letter from America, the postmark less familiar: *San Luis Obispo, Cal.* You could scarce, Mrs. Johnstone said, look for anything more heathenish than that. And would it be from a black man, now? I opened the letter and said no, it was from a schoolfellow settled in those distant parts. Which was true enough. For he well remembered, Dr. Flinders wrote, the two of us sitting under the old dominie, the time he came to the village school before being sent to Edinburgh. An unco thing for a man to write who was born in Australia when I was twenty. But Mistress Johnstone knows nothing of that.

Christine's letter yesterday I took over to the manse and Dr. Jervie and I read it together. I think he's aged, the minister, this past year; certain his hand was trembling as he laid the letter on his desk—the letter that said Sybil Guthrie had told her the truth about Neil. And for a time he bided silent, looking out over the warm garden and the glebe where the harvest, heavy and yellow, was drawing on. "And time mellows everything, Ewan Bell," he said.

I put the letter back in my pocket. "Do you think," I said, "that one day she might find a man?"

"And why not, Ewan? Maybe after Neil Lindsay Christine could never marry in the Scottish gentry. And never after Neil Lindsay another crofter lad. But now she's in a new world. And see how already she's opening to the strangeness of it, coming out of her shell to watch and puzzle and criticize. One day she'll see not the strangeness only but the beauty and then—" He stood up. "But it mayn't be in our time, old friend."

And today I've tramped up the glen. Eighteen months have passed since I first took pen to set this narrative in motion. I have a fancy to end it in the shadow of Castle Erchany.

2

JOHN APPLEBY, that clever London man, would have it that the Guthrie case defeated him. He neglected, he says, the single element that changed its whole composition at the last. There was one question, he insists, he forgot to ask. But the reader will have seen that he did ask it—and would have asked it again that night but for the speed things happened with. *Who was it slipped out of the schoolroom in front of Hardcastle and the lad Gylby when they were on their way to the tower?* You know the answer, Reader. It was Ewan Bell.

Long I'd chewed over that strange letter the daftie brought me from Christine. But, old man and slow that I am, it was

Christmas Eve before I saw that at the heart of it, unknown perhaps even to Christine herself, was an appeal. Nor perhaps did that truth of it rise clear in my own mind, for when I started up the glen in the gloaming I told myself it was only because I must bid the maid good-bye. But deep down I recognized the appeal and deeper still I must have felt the danger: I wouldn't otherwise have attempted a road that was danger and daftness itself.

I reckoned to reach the great house by about eight o'clock and trust for the night to Guthrie's hospitality or to a pallet like the schoolmistress had thought of in the loft at the farm. Only in such a reckoning I was thinking of myself as a younger man. By some freak of nature I reached Erchany alive through the storm that night, but it wanted only half an hour to midnight as I plodded up the last stretch of the drive, the storm lantern I had brought with me giving but the smallest glimmer in that yet driving snow. There was a light in the schoolroom; I climbed down to the moat and then, with some difficulty, up to the little terrace. Mr. Wedderburn was right in spying in me the ruins of an athlete; but it seems I keep a bit of muscle still.

I wonder now that I took this secret road to Christine; no doubt it shows how strong was my instinct that Guthrie was an enemy. She let me in by the window and I could see she was right glad that I had come. She had a bit suit-case—no bigger than Mistress McLaren's Sabbath hand-bag it looked—beside her, and a mackintosh over a chair. I said, "Surely you're not going to-night?"

She nodded, "It's uncle's way. And Neil says we can get fine to Mervie. He's up with uncle in the tower now and we're to go straight away when he comes down. It will be all right, don't you think, Ewan Bell?"

She was too much in love, I suppose, to allow herself more than a troubled suspicion that it must be all wrong, that there was something crazy and sinister at the core of it. I said: "I'll just be going up to see them, Christine. And when your Neil comes down away with you and write to me some day." And at that I kissed her. It was my idea, I believe, to act as a rear-guard when they were gone. My mind didn't stretch to the notion that it was their very getting away that might be fatal to them.

Christine said: "Go by the little stair and you'll more likely avoid Hardcastle." And she found me a key in case the door at the bottom was locked.

I slipped from the schoolroom—it was when Gylby and Hardcastle glimpsed me—and held for the little stair. It's something to remember that after all that trudge from Kinkeig I got up the little stair quicker than they got up the big one. And right different the story would have been had I lingered on the climb.

You must know I was familiar enough with the castle as a lad in the old laird's time, but of the tower top I had little memory. Only I knew there was an entrance from the parapet walk and when I emerged through the trapdoor it was my plan to walk boldly in and say I'd come as a friend of Lindsay's to see him safely away with his bride.

The wind was high and I stood for a moment wondering whether to turn to left or right along the open parapet walk. I chose left, which happened to be wrong. That is to say, the scene Miss Guthrie came on by holding forward from her French window I came on from the other side. The American lassie's presence I never knew of. Nor, I think, did Ranald Guthrie: she must have been wrong in thinking he heard her cry out.

I was on the scene a few seconds earlier than she; our movements can be fitted to each other accurately enough by the cry she heard—the cry that brought her away from her window. It was my cry. And I don't doubt it was loud enough. For I was going cautiously along the battlement, my lantern at my feet, when something rolled out of the darkness that almost tripped me up and sent me over the tower. I put down my lantern and stopped over it. It was a human body.

Everything was a matter of seconds after that. I saw that there was another lantern burning in a niche above a door—

the little bedroom door. And the next instant through the door came Guthrie. I straightened up from the huddled form I was stooping over—sore afraid it was Neil Lindsay's—and took a step back that overturned and put out my lantern. Guthrie became aware of me on that and his axe came up in menace—which was the moment at which Miss Guthrie got her first imperfect sight of what was forward. He advanced on me; the step took him out of the light; the next minutes were a stealthy groping. I knew I was in mortal danger—knew it as well as if Guthrie had read out a declaration of war. And on getting out of it depended not only my own life but that of the man lying helplessly at my feet. For that it was murder that the laird was about I was certain.

He was crouching somewhere in the darkness, manoeuvring for position with all the cunning of that powerful brain. And suddenly he rose up by the parapet, full in the light. He had me in silhouette—as Miss Guthrie had; he had judged that it was enough and that he would take me by surprise that way. His axe was swung back low—a rising stroke that would either gut me or cleave me from the chin up. I had to get in first and I did. So much, Reader, for the death of Ranald Guthrie.

3

I KNELT down by the figure in the snow—you'll remember that Miss Guthrie had retreated and saw nothing of this—and said softly: "Man Lindsay—are you all right?" And at that the figure stirred and turned over on its face. You may take it I was fair scunnered when I saw I was looking at a Guthrie. It was my first awful thought that in the darkness I'd killed the wrong man.

He was drugged, I think, but coming round rapidly. It was only seconds before he opened his eyes on me and whispered: "Who are you?" And at my name his eyes lit up as if he had last heard it but yesterday. He said: "I'm Ian—Ian Guthrie. Get me away—secretly."

Maybe I'd had my fair share of activity that night—enough to satisfy the Athletic Ideal of Miss Strachan herself. But there was no help for it. I pitched my own lantern over the parapet, took up the one burning in the niche, and got Ian Guthrie on my back. I've carried a calf that was right heavier often enough on my father's croft.

I got him to the trapdoor and through it, and I bolted it from below. It must have been only a couple of minutes later, I suppose, that the Gylby lad was out on the deserted battlements looking about him. With a little help Ian staggered down that long winding stair and along the corridor to near the schoolroom. I looked in; Christine had gone. I got him in and he rested a bit, warming himself before the little fire. Presently he said: "Ranald?"

"I killed him—knocked him over the parapet."

His face was paper-pale, but now it drained yet paler. "Poor crazy chap!" He was silent for a moment. "He was just going to kill me, Mr. Bell—after a little operation." And he spread out his right hand. "Hence the axe."

It was to be a long time before I fully understood that.

You'll remember Mr. Appleby saying that the California Flinders must display no marked character-trait which might become known as quite alien to the Sydney Flinders, and how because of that Ranald had to attempt to get the better of his miserliness. That was true enough. But there was something else about the Sydney Flinders that Appleby didn't know—and that Ranald, thanks to what Ian had written him, did. In the early days of his radiology Flinders had lost two fingers—as you can easily do, it seems, with that unchancy stuff. Well, Ranald could arrive in California without two fingers readily enough: a little surgical reading, a period of seclusion, rather more than common fortitude—these were all that was necessary. But the body that was to be found in the moat and taken to be Ranald Guthrie's presented a more difficult problem. Clearly it must not display two fingers man whose attitude to the Erchany estate was his own affair. And silence for a time on the full and final story, while it was but indulgence to him, was mercy to Christine Mathers.

4

AND so the Guthries have gone from these lands and Castle Erchany is to let. What gear was left in the place unrotted has been dispersed; the family portraits and all the schoolroom stuff were shipped away to Sybil and Christine and then there was a grand sale. The great Flemish table where they sat and had their caviare that night was bought by Dr. Jervie for the kirk session. The globes that wee Isa Murdoch hid behind in the gallery were bought by Mistress Roberts of the Arms; she sits in the private now with her teapot on one side and the terrestrial globe on the other, ready to show you what port her bairns wrote from last. Fairbairn of Glenlippet—him that licences his motor ever by the quarter—bought a great granite louping-stone from the court; folk were sore puzzled to know what use he would make of it but Will Saunders says it will bear a brave inscription to Mistress Fairbairn one day. And all the mouldering theology in the gallery I bought myself: right solid stuff to chew on it has proved and a grand stand-by in the discussions I whiles hold with the minister.

To-day I have wandered through the great house perhaps for the last time. The winds that ever eddy about Erchany are sighing through the broken windows; warm and scented from the braes though they are they scarcely bring to the castle a suggestion of summer or of the sun. Utterly the place has slipped into the past: I doubt that its only tenants hereafter will be the rats—they have already forgotten the dottled Hardcastle wife—and the martins that know their season. Stone will fall from stone and this high tower to which I have climbed be as forgotten as the Lindsays' tower in Mervie—the Guthries of Erchany, that have so passionately lived in the life of Scotland, like their rivals remembered only in footnotes to history.

But the Gamleys are back at the home farm. One of Gamley's lads has taken a wife, a Speyside lass, and now I hear her singing in the field—some crude ephemeral tune such as has nigh killed the true minstrelsy of Scotland. And yet—because it rises joyous and full-throated from the earth—I hear it as an enduring song.

THE PERENNIAL LIBRARY MYSTERY SERIES

Ted Allbeury

THE OTHER SIDE OF SILENCE P 669, $2.84
"In the best le Carré tradition . . . an ingenious and readable book."
—*New York Times Book Review*

PALOMINO BLONDE P 670, $2.84
"Fast-moving, splendidly technocratic intercontinental espionage tale . . . you'll love it." —*The Times* (London)

SNOWBALL P 671, $2.84
"A novel of byzantine intrigue. . . ."—*New York Times Book Review*

Delano Ames

CORPSE DIPLOMATIQUE P 637, $2.84
"Sprightly and intelligent."
—*New York Herald Tribune Book Review*

FOR OLD CRIME'S SAKE P 629, $2.84

MURDER, MAESTRO, PLEASE P 630, $2.84
"If there is a more engaging couple in modern fiction than Jane and Dagobert Brown, we have not met them." —*Scotsman*

SHE SHALL HAVE MURDER P 638, $2.84
"Combines the merit of both the English and American schools in the new mystery. It's as breezy as the best of the American ones, and has the sophistication and wit of any top-notch Britisher."
—*New York Herald Tribune Book Review*

E. C. Bentley

TRENT'S LAST CASE P 440, $2.50
"One of the three best detective stories ever written."
—Agatha Christie

TRENT'S OWN CASE P 516, $2.25
"I won't waste time saying that the plot is sound and the detection satisfying. Trent has not altered a scrap and reappears with all his old humor and charm." —Dorothy L. Sayers

Andrew Bergman

THE BIG KISS-OFF OF 1944 P 673, $2.84
"It is without doubt the nearest thing to genuine Chandler I've ever come across. . . . Tough, witty—very witty—and a beautiful eye for period detail. . . ." —Jack Higgins

HOLLYWOOD AND LEVINE P 674, $2.84
"Fast-paced private-eye fiction." —*San Francisco Chronicle*

Gavin Black

A DRAGON FOR CHRISTMAS P 473, $1.95
"Potent excitement!" —*New York Herald Tribune*

THE EYES AROUND ME P 485, $1.95
"I stayed up until all hours last night reading *The Eyes Around Me*, which is something I do not do very often, but I was so intrigued by the ingeniousness of Mr. Black's plotting and the witty way in which he spins his mystery. I can only say that I enjoyed the book enormously."
—F. van Wyck Mason

YOU WANT TO DIE, JOHNNY? P 472, $1.95
"Gavin Black doesn't just develop a pressure plot in suspense, he adds uninfected wit, character, charm, and sharp knowledge of the Far East to make rereading as keen as the first race-through." —*Book Week*

Nicholas Blake

THE CORPSE IN THE SNOWMAN P 427, $1.95
"If there is a distinction between the novel and the detective story (which we do not admit), then this book deserves a high place in both categories." —*New York Times*

END OF CHAPTER P 397, $1.95
". . . admirably solid . . . an adroit formal detective puzzle backed up by firm characterization and a knowing picture of London publishing."
—*New York Times*

HEAD OF A TRAVELER P 398, $2.25
"Another grade A detective story of the right old jigsaw persuasion."
—*New York Herald Tribune Book Review*

MINUTE FOR MURDER P 419, $1.95
"An outstanding mystery novel. Mr. Blake's writing is a delight in itself." —*New York Times*

THE MORNING AFTER DEATH P 520, $1.95
"One of Blake's best." —Rex Warner

Nicholas Blake (cont'd)

A PENKNIFE IN MY HEART P 521, $2.25
"Style brilliant . . . and suspenseful." —*San Francisco Chronicle*

THE PRIVATE WOUND P 531, $2.25
"[Blake's] best novel in a dozen years . . . . An intensely penetrating study of sexual passion. . . . A powerful story of murder and its aftermath."
—Anthony Boucher, *New York Times*

A QUESTION OF PROOF P 494, $1.95
"The characters in this story are unusually well drawn, and the suspense is well sustained." —*New York Times*

THE SAD VARIETY P 495, $2.25
"It is a stunner. I read it instead of eating, instead of sleeping."
—Dorothy Salisbury Davis

THERE'S TROUBLE BREWING P 569, $3.37
"Nigel Strangeways is a puzzling mixture of simplicity and penetration, but all the more real for that."
—*The Times* (London) *Literary Supplement*

THOU SHELL OF DEATH P 428, $1.95
"It has all the virtues of culture, intelligence and sensibility that the most exacting connoisseur could ask of detective fiction."
—*The Times* (London) *Literary Supplement*

THE WIDOW'S CRUISE P 399, $2.25
"A stirring suspense. . . . The thrilling tale leaves nothing to be desired."
—*Springfield Republican*

Oliver Bleeck

THE BRASS GO-BETWEEN P 645, $2.84
"Fiction with a flair, well above the norm for thrillers."
—*Associated Press*

THE PROCANE CHRONICLE P 647, $2.84
"Without peer in American suspense." —*Los Angeles Times*

PROTOCOL FOR A KIDNAPPING P 646, $2.84
"The zigzags of plot are electric; the characters sharp; but it is the wit and irony and touches of plain fun which make the whole a standout."
—*Los Angeles Times*

John & Emery Bonett

A BANNER FOR PEGASUS P 554, $2.40
"A gem! Beautifully plotted and set. . . . Not only is the murder adroit and deserved, and the detection competent, but the love story is charming." —Jacques Barzun and Wendell Hertig Taylor

DEAD LION P 563, $2.40
"A clever plot, authentic background and interesting characters highly recommended this one." —*New Republic*

THE SOUND OF MURDER P 642, $2.84
The suspects are many, the clues few, but the gentle Inspector ferrets out the truth and pursues the case to its bitter and shocking end.

Christianna Brand

GREEN FOR DANGER P 551, $2.50
"You have to reach for the greatest of Great Names (Christie, Carr, Queen . . .) to find Brand's rivals in the devious subtleties of the trade." —Anthony Boucher

TOUR DE FORCE P 572, $2.40
"Complete with traps for the over-ingenious, a double-reverse surprise ending and a key clue planted so fairly and obviously that you completely overlook it. If that's your idea of perfect entertainment, then seize at once upon *Tour de Force.*" —Anthony Boucher, *New York Times*

James Byrom

OR BE HE DEAD P 585, $2.84
"A very original tale . . . Well written and steadily entertaining."
—Jacques Barzun and Wendell Hertig Taylor, *A Catalogue of Crime*

Henry Calvin

IT'S DIFFERENT ABROAD P 640, $2.84
"What is remarkable and delightful, Mr. Calvin imparts a flavor of satire to what he renovates and compels us to take straight."
—Jacques Barzun

Marjorie Carleton

VANISHED P 559, $2.40
"Exceptional . . . a minor triumph."
—Jacques Barzun and Wendell Hertig Taylor, *A Catalogue of Crime*

George Harmon Coxe

MURDER WITH PICTURES P 527, $2.25
"[Coxe] has hit the bull's-eye with his first shot."
—*New York Times*

Edmund Crispin

BURIED FOR PLEASURE P 506, $2.50
"Absolute and unalloyed delight."
—Anthony Boucher, *New York Times*

Lionel Davidson

THE MENORAH MEN P 592, $2.84
"Of his fellow thriller writers, only John Le Carré shows the same instinct for the viscera." —*Chicago Tribune*

NIGHT OF WENCESLAS P 595, $2.84
"A most ingenious thriller, so enriched with style, wit, and a sense of serious comedy that it all but transcends its kind."
—*The New Yorker*

THE ROSE OF TIBET P 593, $2.84
"I hadn't realized how much I missed the genuine Adventure story . . . until I read *The Rose of Tibet*." —Graham Greene

D. M. Devine

MY BROTHER'S KILLER P 558, $2.40
"A most enjoyable crime story which I enjoyed reading down to the last moment." —Agatha Christie

Kenneth Fearing

THE BIG CLOCK P 500, $1.95
"It will be some time before chill-hungry clients meet again so rare a compound of irony, satire, and icy-fingered narrative. *The Big Clock* is . . . a psychothriller you won't put down." —*Weekly Book Review*

Andrew Garve

THE ASHES OF LODA P 430, $1.50
"Garve . . . embellishes a fine fast adventure story with a more credible picture of the U.S.S.R. than is offered in most thrillers."
—*New York Times Book Review*

THE CUCKOO LINE AFFAIR P 451, $1.95
". . . an agreeable and ingenious piece of work." —*The New Yorker*

A HERO FOR LEANDA P 429, $1.50
"One can trust Mr. Garve to put a fresh twist to any situation, and the ending is really a lovely surprise." —*Manchester Guardian*

MURDER THROUGH THE LOOKING GLASS P 449, $1.95
". . . refreshingly out-of-the-way and enjoyable . . . highly recommended to all comers." —*Saturday Review*

NO TEARS FOR HILDA P 441, $1.95
"It starts fine and finishes finer. I got behind on breathing watching Max get not only his man but his woman, too." —Rex Stout

THE RIDDLE OF SAMSON P 450, $1.95
"The story is an excellent one, the people are quite likable, and the writing is superior." —*Springfield Republican*

Michael Gilbert

BLOOD AND JUDGMENT P 446, $1.95
"Gilbert readers need scarcely be told that the characters all come alive at first sight, and that his surpassing talent for narration enhances any plot. . . . Don't miss." —*San Francisco Chronicle*

THE BODY OF A GIRL P 459, $1.95
"Does what a good mystery should do: open up into all kinds of ramifications, with untold menace behind the action. At the end, there is a bang-up climax, and it is a pleasure to see how skilfully Gilbert wraps everything up." —*New York Times Book Review*

FEAR TO TREAD P 458, $1.95
"Merits serious consideration as a work of art." —*New York Times*

Joe Gores

HAMMETT P 631, $2.84
"Joe Gores at his very best. Terse, powerful writing—with the master, Dashiell Hammett, as the protagonist in a novel I think he would have been proud to call his own." —Robert Ludlum

C. W. Grafton

BEYOND A REASONABLE DOUBT P 519, $1.95
"A very ingenious tale of murder . . . a brilliant and gripping narrative."
—Jacques Barzun and Wendell Hertig Taylor

C. W. Grafton (cont'd)

THE RAT BEGAN TO GNAW THE ROPE P 639, $2.84
"Fast, humorous story with flashes of brilliance."
—*The New Yorker*

Edward Grierson

THE SECOND MAN P 528, $2.25
"One of the best trial-testimony books to have come along in quite a while." —*The New Yorker*

Bruce Hamilton

TOO MUCH OF WATER P 635, $2.84
"A superb sea mystery. . . . The prose is excellent."
—Jacques Barzun and Wendell Hertig Taylor, *A Catalogue of Crime*

Cyril Hare

DEATH IS NO SPORTSMAN P 555, $2.40
"You will be thrilled because it succeeds in placing an ingenious story in a new and refreshing setting. . . . The identity of the murderer is really a surprise." —*Daily Mirror*

DEATH WALKS THE WOODS P 556, $2.40
"Here is a fine formal detective story, with a technically brilliant solution demanding the attention of all connoisseurs of construction."
—Anthony Boucher, *New York Times Book Review*

AN ENGLISH MURDER P 455, $2.50
"By a long shot, the best crime story I have read for a long time. Everything is traditional, but originality does not suffer. The setting is perfect. Full marks to Mr. Hare." —*Irish Press*

SUICIDE EXCEPTED P 636, $2.84
"Adroit in its manipulation . . . and distinguished by a plot-twister which I'll wager Christie wishes she'd thought of." —*New York Times*

TENANT FOR DEATH P 570, $2.84
"The way in which an air of probability is combined both with clear, terse narrative and with a good deal of subtle suburban atmosphere, proves the extreme skill of the writer." —*The Spectator*

TRAGEDY AT LAW P 522, $2.25
"An extremely urbane and well-written detective story."
—*New York Times*

Cyril Hare (cont'd)

UNTIMELY DEATH P 514, $2.25

"The English detective story at its quiet best, meticulously underplayed, rich in perceivings of the droll human animal and ready at the last with a neat surprise which has been there all the while had we but wits to see it." —*New York Herald Tribune Book Review*

THE WIND BLOWS DEATH P 589, $2.84

"A plot compounded of musical knowledge, a Dickens allusion, and a subtle point in law is related with delightfully unobtrusive wit, warmth, and style." —*New York Times*

WITH A BARE BODKIN P 523, $2.25

"One of the best detective stories published for a long time." —*The Spectator*

Robert Harling

THE ENORMOUS SHADOW P 545, $2.50

"In some ways the best spy story of the modern period. . . . The writing is terse and vivid . . . the ending full of action . . . altogether first-rate." —Jacques Barzun and Wendell Hertig Taylor, *A Catalogue of Crime*

Matthew Head

THE CABINDA AFFAIR P 541, $2.25

"An absorbing whodunit and a distinguished novel of atmosphere." —Anthony Boucher, *New York Times*

THE CONGO VENUS P 597, $2.84

"Terrific. The dialogue is just plain wonderful." —*Boston Globe*

MURDER AT THE FLEA CLUB P 542, $2.50

"The true delight is in Head's style, its limpid ease combined with humor and an awesome precision of phrase." —*San Francisco Chronicle*

M. V. Heberden

ENGAGED TO MURDER P 533, $2.25

"Smooth plotting." —*New York Times*

James Hilton

WAS IT MURDER? P 501, $1.95

"The story is well planned and well written." —*New York Times*

S. B. Hough

DEAR DAUGHTER DEAD P 661, $2.84

"A highly intelligent and sophisticated story of police detection . . . not to be missed on any account." —Francis Iles, *The Guardian*

SWEET SISTER SEDUCED P 662, $2.84

In the course of a nightlong conversation between the Inspector and the suspect, the complex emotions of a very strange marriage are revealed.

P. M. Hubbard

HIGH TIDE P 571, $2.40

"A smooth elaboration of mounting horror and danger."

—*Library Journal*

Elspeth Huxley

THE AFRICAN POISON MURDERS P 540, $2.25

"Obscure venom, manical mutilations, deadly bush fire, thrilling climax compose major opus.... Top-flight."

—*Saturday Review of Literature*

MURDER ON SAFARI P 587, $2.84

"Right now we'd call Mrs. Huxley a dangerous rival to Agatha Christie." —*Books*

Francis Iles

BEFORE THE FACT P 517, $2.50

"Not many 'serious' novelists have produced character studies to compare with Iles's internally terrifying portrait of the murderer in *Before the Fact,* his masterpiece and a work truly deserving the appellation of unique and beyond price." —Howard Haycraft

MALICE AFORETHOUGHT P 532, $1.95

"It is a long time since I have read anything so good as *Malice Aforethought,* with its cynical humour, acute criminology, plausible detail and rapid movement. It makes you hug yourself with pleasure."

—H. C. Harwood, *Saturday Review*

Michael Innes

APPLEBY ON ARARAT P 648, $2.84

"Superbly plotted and humorously written." —*The New Yorker*

APPLEBY'S END P 649, $2.84

"Most amusing." —*Boston Globe*

Michael Innes (cont'd)

THE CASE OF THE JOURNEYING BOY P 632, $3.12
"I could see no faults in it. There is no one to compare with him."
—*Illustrated London News*

DEATH ON A QUIET DAY P 677, $2.84
"Delightfully witty." —*Chicago Sunday Tribune*

DEATH BY WATER P 574, $2.40
"The amount of ironic social criticism and deft characterization of scenes and people would serve another author for six books."
—Jacques Barzun and Wendell Hertig Taylor

HARE SITTING UP P 590, $2.84
"There is hardly anyone (in mysteries or mainstream) more exquisitely literate, allusive and Jamesian—and hardly anyone with a firmer sense of melodramatic plot or a more vigorous gift of storytelling."
—Anthony Boucher, *New York Times*

THE LONG FAREWELL P 575, $2.40
"A model of the deft, classic detective story, told in the most wittily diverting prose." —*New York Times*

THE MAN FROM THE SEA P 591, $2.84
"The pace is brisk, the adventures exciting and excitingly told, and above all he keeps to the very end the interesting ambiguity of the man from the sea." —*New Statesman*

ONE MAN SHOW P 672, $2.84
"Exciting, amusingly written . . . very good enjoyment it is."
—*The Spectator*

THE SECRET VANGUARD P 584, $2.84
"Innes . . . has mastered the art of swift, exciting and well-organized narrative." —*New York Times*

THE WEIGHT OF THE EVIDENCE P 633, $2.84
"First-class puzzle, deftly solved. University background interesting and amusing." —*Saturday Review of Literature*

Mary Kelly

THE SPOILT KILL P 565, $2.40
"Mary Kelly is a new Dorothy Sayers. . . . [An] exciting new novel."
—*Evening News*

Lange Lewis

THE BIRTHDAY MURDER P 518, $1.95
"Almost perfect in its playlike purity and delightful prose."
—Jacques Barzun and Wendell Hertig Taylor

Allan MacKinnon

HOUSE OF DARKNESS P 582, $2.84
"His best . . . a perfect compendium."
—Jacques Barzun and Wendell Hertig Taylor, *A Catalogue of Crime*

Frank Parrish

FIRE IN THE BARLEY P 651, $2.84
"A remarkable and brilliant first novel. . . . entrancing."
—*The Spectator*

SNARE IN THE DARK P 650, $2.84
The wily English poacher Dan Mallett is framed for murder and has to confront unknown enemies to clear himself.

STING OF THE HONEYBEE P 652, $2.84
"Terrorism and murder visit a sleepy English village in this witty, offbeat thriller." —*Chicago Sun-Times*

Austin Ripley

MINUTE MYSTERIES P 387, $2.50
More than one hundred of the world's shortest detective stories. Only one possible solution to each case!

Thomas Sterling

THE EVIL OF THE DAY P 529, $2.50
"Prose as witty and subtle as it is sharp and clear. . .characters unconventionally conceived and richly bodied forth . . . . In short, a novel to be treasured." —Anthony Boucher, *New York Times*

Julian Symons

THE BELTING INHERITANCE P 468, $1.95
"A superb whodunit in the best tradition of the detective story."
—August Derleth, *Madison Capital Times*

BOGUE'S FORTUNE P 481, $1.95
"There's a touch of the old sardonic humour, and more than a touch of style." —*The Spectator*

THE COLOR OF MURDER P 461, $1.95
"A singularly unostentatious and memorably brilliant detective story."
—*New York Herald Tribune Book Review*

Dorothy Stockbridge Tillet
(John Stephen Strange)

THE MAN WHO KILLED FORTESCUE P 536, $2.25
"Better than average." —*Saturday Review of Literature*

Simon Troy

THE ROAD TO RHUINE P 583, $2.84
"Unusual and agreeably told." —*San Francisco Chronicle*

SWIFT TO ITS CLOSE P 546, $2.40
"A nicely literate British mystery . . . the atmosphere and the plot are exceptionally well wrought, the dialogue excellent." —*Best Sellers*

Henry Wade

THE DUKE OF YORK'S STEPS P 588, $2.84
"A classic of the golden age."
—Jacques Barzun and Wendell Hertig Taylor, *A Catalogue of Crime*

A DYING FALL P 543, $2.50
"One of those expert British suspense jobs . . . it crackles with undercurrents of blackmail, violent passion and murder. Topnotch in its class."
—*Time*

THE HANGING CAPTAIN P 548, $2.50
"This is a detective story for connoisseurs, for those who value clear thinking and good writing above mere ingenuity and easy thrills."
—*The Times* (London) *Literary Supplement*

Hillary Waugh

LAST SEEN WEARING . . . P 552, $2.40
"A brilliant tour de force." —Julian Symons

THE MISSING MAN P 553, $2.40
"The quiet detailed police work of Chief Fred C. Fellows, Stockford, Conn., is at its best in *The Missing Man* . . . one of the Chief's toughest cases and one of the best handled."
—Anthony Boucher, *New York Times Book Review*

Henry Kitchell Webster

WHO IS THE NEXT? P 539, $2.25

"A double murder, private-plane piloting, a neat impersonation, and a delicate courtship are adroitly combined by a writer who knows how to use the language." —Jacques Barzun and Wendell Hertig Taylor

John Welcome

GO FOR BROKE P 663, $2.84

A rich financier chases Richard Graham half 'round Europe in a desperate attempt to prevent the truth getting out.

RUN FOR COVER P 664, $2.84

"I can think of few writers in the international intrigue game with such a gift for fast and vivid storytelling."

—*New York Times Book Review*

STOP AT NOTHING P 665, $2.84

"Mr. Welcome is lively, vivid and highly readable."

—*New York Times Book Review*

Anna Mary Wells

MURDERER'S CHOICE P 534, $2.50

"Good writing, ample action, and excellent character work."

—*Saturday Review of Literature*

A TALENT FOR MURDER P 535, $2.25

"The discovery of the villain is a decided shock." —*Books*

Charles Williams

DEAD CALM P 655, $2.84

"A brilliant tour de force of inventive plotting, fine manipulation of a small cast and breathtaking sequences of spectacular navigation."

—*New York Times Book Review*

THE SAILCLOTH SHROUD P 654, $2.84

"A fine novel of excitement, spirited, fresh and satisfying."

—*New York Times*

THE WRONG VENUS P 656, $2.84

Swindler Lawrence Colby and the lovely Martine create a story of romance, larceny, and very blunt homicide.